THE
BIG
REWIND

WILLIAM MORROW

An Imprint of HarperCollinsPublishers

THE
BIG
REWIND

LIBBY CUDMORE

THE BIG REWIND. Copyright © 2016 by Libby Cudmore. All rights reserved. Printed in the United States of America. No part of this book may be used or reproduced in any manner whatsoever without written permission except in the case of brief quotations embodied in critical articles and reviews. For information address HarperCollins Publishers, 195 Broadway, New York, NY 10007.

HarperCollins books may be purchased for educational, business, or sales promotional use. For information please e-mail the Special Markets Department at SPsales@harpercollins.com.

FIRST EDITION

Designed by Diahann Sturge
Title page art © by Apashabo/Shutterstock, Inc.

Library of Congress Cataloging-in-Publication Data has been applied for.

ISBN 978-0-06-240353-7

16 17 18 19 20 OV/RRD 10 9 8 7 6 5 4 3 2 1

To my mom and my dad,
and to everyone who's ever made me a mix

I've been searching high and low for you
Trying to track you down

—Warren Zevon, "Searching for a Heart"

THE
BIG
REWIND

Chapter 1

BROOKLYN (OWES THE CHARMER UNDER ME)

Nothing good ever comes in the mail. After my lack of cash forced me to let my *Mojo* subscription lapse, the only time I ever saw the name Jett Bennett was on cell phone bills and student loan payments. Six months ago a Swiss Colony Christmas catalog had arrived on the first chilly breath of fall, and I devoured it with the intensity of a teenage boy on his first porn site. I kept the battered pages hidden under my mattress long past Christmas and into spring, telling myself that this would be the year I splurged and ordered those beautiful petit fours. I told myself the same thing every year.

That day's mail brought two bills, a flyer for a new dry cleaner, and a small package wrapped in a magazine ad with a bunch of cartoon frogs and too much tape. I've got a smartphone, but I'm not too young to remember the exact weight and feel of a Maxell mix tape. They're just slightly heavier than a regular cassette, weighed down with love and angst, track lists thick with rubber cement and collage.

But this tape wasn't for me. It had a Binghamton postmark and was addressed to my downstairs neighbor, KitKat. She was a party on a purple ten-speed, a neat-banged brunette who baked red velvet cupcakes and pot brownies, read tarot, and had both an

NES and a Sega Genesis. For five hundred bucks a night, she'd pedal to your place and kick your party into stoned, sugared-up, future-knowing, eight-bit overdrive. Of course someone was sending her mix tapes. I was just surprised it wasn't packaged in a vintage suitcase or a mason jar filled with glitter.

I'd arrived in New York just over a year ago, with a master's in music journalism and big dreams of backstage passes and bustling newsrooms. But instead of following Toto on their first U.S. tour in nearly a decade or snagging an exclusive interview with Daft Punk, like my grandmother assured me I would do the moment I arrived in her city, I wound up with a third-shift temp gig proof-reading for a private investigating firm. It was not as glamorous as Humphrey Bogart or Jim Rockford made it seem, but it beat waiting tables—at the very least, it involved less small talk.

But what my grandmother did give me was a sublet of her rent-controlled apartment in the Barter Street district of Brooklyn, just east of Williamsburg and, judging by how people dressed, slightly beyond Thunderdome. She was traveling on a transcontinental honeymoon with her new husband, Royale, and I had been on the verge of getting kicked out of the eleven-person, four-bedroom artist loft I had been living in over in Williamsburg. For $350 a month, I'd gotten an inflatable twin mattress between two curtains, two milk crates for storage, one shelf in our room's mini fridge, a five-minute shower at 10:25 P.M., and a half hour of television every Tuesday and Saturday. I'd once woken up to my left-side neighbor filming me for one of the random-image films he made us watch during his Monday night TV time, while my right-side neighbor snorted a lot of coke and screamed at her canvases because she said the fear in her paint made for bolder colors. One of the girls at MetroReaders, the temp agency that kept me in Trader Joe's and Netflix, had known the apartment had an opening, and I'd conned my way in by telling them I was a performance artist. But just before my grandmother left, I suspected they were catching on to the fact that my "performance" consisted of eating pesto and watching movies on my laptop. I managed to get out before they called one of their "artist meetings," where they all talked shit about someone under the guise of intervention. I saw it coming and had moved into my grandmother's place before they woke up the next afternoon.

KitKat was the first person I'd met when I moved in; she showed up at my door with a basket of muffins and lightbulbs, a list of takeout places, and the offer to show me around the neighborhood when I got settled. In the six months I'd been there, we'd only hung out a few times, but I liked her in a big-sister kinda way.

I loved the place, with its enormous claw-foot bathtub and tiny kitchen, and there was a part of me that hoped my grandmother would move into Royale's penthouse on Ninetieth and Central Park West, allowing me to stay there forever. I could easily afford the $700 a month she'd paid since 1975, when Barter Street was a working-class neighborhood made up of beat cops and public school teachers instead of a hipster paradise of art-house baristas and record store clerks.

My grandmother was, by far, the oldest person in her four-story building, a rent-controlled holdout who made tea when the other, younger tenants came by to borrow her chairs for their parties. When I first moved in, every person I met told me how cool they thought my grandmother was—they loved her antique china set, her huge collection of art books, her stories of what the neighborhood was like when she'd first signed the lease. In a way, I suppose, my grandmother was the original Barter Street hipster, which probably explains why she stayed on the block as long as she did. She was even in on the Barter Street system, helping the neighbors' kids or siblings with math homework in exchange for help fixing her computer or setting up her TV.

But she had been single for nearly forty years after my dad's father died, and, in exchange for borrowing her vintage lace tablecloths for a photo shoot, one of her neighbors had helped her set up a dating profile on a site for mature singles. Almost immediately, she met Royale, and they were married a year after their first date. He, a former Manhattan law partner, had whisked her away to visit all the sights that she, a modest-living CUNY math professor, had only ever seen on the Travel Channel, leaving me to sublet.

I took my mail upstairs and left it in a single pile on the kitchen table. I would sort it later, but the afternoon was getting late, and that meant KitKat was probably baking. Dropping by with a piece of her mail would surely land me a cupcake, a cup of tea, and a chance to chat at the table she'd decoupaged with pictures of food. All I could hope was that she wasn't baking vegan, gluten-free bricks for Perk Up!, the coffeehouse at the end of our block, where all the too-hip mommies drank soy lattes and tried to out-mommy each other. KitKat insisted Perk Up! used to be a cool place, filled with straight-edge types writing screenplays, but all the ex-hipsters who'd wed in handfasting ceremonies, where the guests dressed like Coachella rejects, needed someplace to blog about the organic bamboo nappies Artisan and Corindolyn were wearing. Better there than Egg School, where the rest of us brunched.

If she were any other neighbor, I would have just left the package on the table next to the mailboxes, but KitKat had established, early on, that she didn't want her mail left out. But she did it in her quirky KitKat way, bringing me an envelope of mine that had gotten put in her box by mistake, along with a tiny bottle of sparkling lemonade. She explained that if I got a piece of her mail, I should bring it right to her, and it made enough sense that I didn't question it.

But just in case she had left to make a delivery, I took her extra key. Whenever she went away, she left me in charge of feeding her fat old cat, Baldrick, paying me with a pancake breakfast and a week's worth of Nintendo rentals, which still wasn't enough time for me to beat *Legend of Zelda II*. But that's how things were done around here—cash was seen as a vulgar necessity, something strangers exchanged because they didn't trust you to come through with the offer to fix their laptop or babysit on their anniversary. Even Egg School, where a table on Sunday had more trade value than a vintage British bicycle, seemed reluctant to take actual, real payment, and every so often held pledge drives where food was traded for services at a later date. The system had taken a little getting used to, but now there were times I had to remind myself that the subway's MetroCard machine didn't take album reviews as payment for goods rendered.

Outside her apartment, I could hear Baldrick yowling through the door and I panicked, wondering if she'd gone away and I had forgotten to feed him. For a while, it had seemed like she was going out of town every weekend, but she hadn't asked me to watch him in a few weeks. Or had she? How long had he been down here alone?

"KitKat?" I called, knocking. "KitKat, I've got some of your mail."

When she didn't answer, I unlocked the door. Baldrick got out of my way and ran into the kitchen. I followed him, and there was KitKat, sprawled out on the linoleum, blood splattered across her cabinets and pink oven like gory spin art. She was still wearing the David Bowie T-shirt apron I'd traded to her for baking a red velvet birthday cake for my friend Sid, but someone had done a hard job on her face. Her marble rolling pin was sticking up in the sink, the water stained pink with her blood. I choked back sick, shuddering hard. This couldn't be real. This had to be a dream brought on by a cop show marathon with Sid, too much red wine, and work anxiety all jumbled into one terrible nightmare I was going to wake up from any second. . . .

But the acrid smoke billowing out of the oven told me it was anything but a bad dream. She'd long ago disabled her smoke detector; it could have been days—or a fire—before anyone found her down here. If I was going to turn it off, I was going to have to step over her.

"Sorry, KitKat," I muttered. "I'll call the cops soon, I promise."

I took two deep breaths, counted to five, and made my way to the stove. I turned off the heat and opened the door, coughing.

Waving the smoke away, I saw a burned pan of brownies. Whoever had come for KitKat had left without her stash.

I put on an oven mitt and gathered up the pan like I was collecting a dish after a potluck. Baldrick was howling from the living room in a way that broke my heart. I couldn't just leave him there, crying next to the body of his cat-momma, possibly to step all over her crime scene more than he already had. I took him up under my other arm, cooing as best I could to comfort him. I carried the cat and the pan upstairs, Baldrick howling, the halls filling with the pungent scent of weed and scorched chocolate. Inside my apartment, I set Baldrick down and double-bolted the door. I took the pan to the window and tossed the brownies into the alley.

Then I ran to the bathroom and threw up everything I'd eaten possibly ever.

Baldrick wandered in and perched on the edge of the bathtub to watch me retch.

"Next time, hold back my hair," I gasped, slamming the lid closed and flushing. "What the hell happened to her?"

Baldrick told me everything, but unfortunately, I didn't speak Cat. I finally managed to stand on shaking legs, wobbled around until I found my phone, and called the police. It wasn't until after I hung up that I realized I still had her tape in the back pocket of my skinny black jeans.

Chapter 2

THE TOUGHEST GIRL IN THE WORLD

When the cops swarmed the building to take statements, Linda in 2B got the cute, spiky-haired blond in the sharply pressed uniform. I got interviewed by a thick, balding detective with a doughnut gut and a bad tie knotted so tightly his neck had a muffin top. He asked about the body. I told him how I'd found her. He asked about her visitors. I hadn't seen any since her boyfriend, Bronco, left this morning. He asked about the oven. I wove him a tale of flaming cupcakes I bravely doused in the sink and threw out the window so as not to endanger the other residents. He asked about the smell of weed. I told him I knew nothing.

A woman from Animal Control checked Baldrick for injuries and wiped blood from his paws. Detective Muffin Top took my fingerprints for crime scene elimination. "Did you hear anything that sounded like a struggle?" he asked.

"I just got home from work," I said. "I didn't hear anything."

"Where do you work?" He tried to make it sound like a casual conversation, but I knew better.

Still, I wasn't going to dick around. "I'm a temp with Metro-Readers," I said. "I can give you their number, if you want."

That answer seemed to satisfy him. "Any idea who might have done this?" he tried. "Did she have any ex-boyfriends, bad neighbors . . . ?"

I shook my head. "Everyone loved KitKat," I said. The sad truth was that I didn't know that for sure. She had lots of friends, plenty on Facebook, a thousand or so Twitter followers, but we'd never exchanged anything beyond neighborly laughs and the occasional cup of tea. For all I knew, she had a stalker or a customer who felt screwed, deep gambling debts, or a side business selling goods a lot harder than grass and gluten.

He flipped his notebook closed and flattened his lips in something between concern and an attempt at comfort. "You got someplace safe to stay tonight?"

"I've got some people I can call," I said. "You need that phone number?"

He nodded and I wrote it down on a piece of paper. I hoped he wouldn't call. The last thing I needed was to lose this job because the dispatcher at MetroReaders got skittish. He gave me his card and put on his coat and was gone.

But I didn't call anyone. I wasn't ready to explain what I'd seen. I didn't want to be the one to set off the chain of information: *KitKat's dead. OMG, KitKat was murdered. Did you hear about KitKat?*

I took a walk down to the Key Food and bought cat food and some litter. I bought a foil turkey pan to use as a cat box. I bought some Doritos because, fuck, I deserved them. I started to buy chocolate cupcakes, but just that word on the package reminded me of her bloody face. I put them back on the rack. My hands were shaking as I counted out the bills at the register, and as I approached my building, I had to force myself to go inside. I wanted to cry, but I couldn't. Crying required breath, and I couldn't get enough air in my lungs.

At home I set up Baldrick and put *Warren Zevon* on my suitcase record player. Normally, the opening notes of "Frank and Jesse

James" were narcotic enough to send me into a blissful music coma, but today I couldn't sit still long enough to let Zevon's deceptively simple piano tranquilize me. I let the record play out the A-side and paced around the apartment in spinning silence, trying to sort out my head.

What are the stages of grief when you hardly knew a person? KitKat and I were friends enough to chat, sure, but the most intimate moment we'd shared was one she hadn't been alive to experience. I had the honor and the horror of finding her body. Not the cleaning lady or the cops, just a neighbor with a mistaken piece of mail. Maybe I'd spared Bronco or KitKat's sister, Hillary, from seeing her like that, but in sparing them, I was assured that I'd never forget what I saw.

I finally called Sid. I didn't tell him anything, just asked if we could meet. He suggested a burger at the Happy Days Diner in Brooklyn Heights. I agreed even though I didn't feel like eating. The Doritos still sat, unopened, on my kitchen table.

By the time I got to the subway, word of KitKat's death had already gotten out. Girls in floral-print dresses and Laura Ingalls boots were sobbing over her Tumblr, and guys in bright cardigans were faking their grief to try to get laid. I dug my fingers into the plastic seat, choking back a scream. In the fashion show that was the L train, I was wearing my laundry-day T-shirt from the "Save Our Bluths"–themed run last fall for Habitat for Humanity, meaning that I was completely invisible in a surging tide of seafoam Toms and ModCloth skirts.

A blonde with femme fatale lipstick and a librarian blouse tapped me on the shoulder. "Can I have your seat?" she asked, holding up a picture of KitKat on her iPhone. "My best friend just died and I really need to sit down."

I glared up at her. If there are vampires anywhere in the world, they're in this end of Brooklyn, sympathy-sucking leeches living every day like it's their own private reality show, latching on to anything that might get them a moment of attention, a warm body, a subway seat on a ten-minute ride. "This is my seat," I growled. "Because I'm the one who found her body."

The train screeched into the station. Everyone stared at me as I stood and parted like the Red Sea to let me off. Fuck them all. I'd walk the rest of the way.

Chapter 3

HEAVEN KNOWS I'M MISERABLE NOW

id was already waiting in a booth when I arrived, still wearing his gray vest from work, his tie slightly loosened, tobacco-colored hair soft on his widow's peak. Like the southern gentleman he was, he stood when I came in.

"You're shaking," he said, holding my shoulders in a way that made my knees go weak. "Darlin', what's wrong?"

Darlin'. Finally, someone who felt sorry for me instead of just for themselves. I didn't get to wallow in public angst, hoping strangers would pat my shoulder, follow me on Twitter, or fuck me all better. The regret I carried was something deeper, like a bullet lodged in bone. I fell apart in his arms, sobbing in a way that made the other patrons look up from their cheeseburgers and crossword puzzles to stare at me. I just didn't give a fuck anymore.

"Jett, Jett, easy, sweetheart, easy," he cooed, easing me into the booth. "What happened?"

I blubbered everything—KitKat and Baldrick, the cops, the hipsters on the subway—while I wiped my tears and blew my nose on napkins that disintegrated at my touch. I even told him about getting sick. He held my hands between his, blowing warm breaths onto my frigid fingers until two coffees I hadn't heard him order arrived. He shook his head when I took a deep shaking breath and a sip that burned my tongue. "That's awful," he murmured. "Just awful."

All I could do was agree. And just as suddenly as it had all come on, I didn't want to talk about it anymore. "Change the subject," I said. "Talk about something else. I'm sick of thinking about it."

"Let's order first," he said. "Sounds like you could do with something solid in your stomach."

I cringed. Work at MetroReaders had been slow these last few weeks, and my paycheck was about as skinny as a teenage fashion model. A cup of coffee and a Danish at Egg School on Sunday was the only splurge I could afford, and having dinner with him today meant that I'd have to make an excuse not to brunch this week.

"Get surf and turf if you want," he said, not looking at me as he glanced at the menu. "It's my turn to buy and my rent's already paid."

My stomach grumbled. Much as I wanted to take him up on the offer, my body was not equipped to handle that much grease and fat and protein. When the waitress came back around, I got a refill on my coffee and ordered a bowl of chicken noodle soup. Sid, tantalized by his own suggestion, got a T-bone. He winked. "Your turn next time."

He always said that but Sid only let me pay if we were going out for something cheap: hard cider and frites, bubble tea, candy on movie night. He made a lot more than I did and had quick hands to seize a check. *I don't have a girlfriend,* he once told me. *So I might as well spoil you.* It wasn't like he didn't have offers—girls adored Sid; I don't know whether it was his electric white smile or his bouncy little ass or his peach-pie accent, but no matter where we were, I caught them staring, sneaking pictures, and whispering. If he noticed, he never took them up on the implied offers. He hadn't dated anyone since he moved here.

In the five months I'd known Sid, he'd become my favorite person in the world. We met at one of Natalie's art parties; his roommate, Terry, had dragged him along by way of introducing him to the neighborhood, and we'd talked in the corner for most of the night. When everyone else was loud, sloppy, and drunk in that inevitable aftermath of privileged boozing, we slipped off the scene like criminals and holed up at a twenty-four-hour diner that closed about two weeks later. We had pie and coffee at eleven thirty P.M., and I sopped up every trace of his accent. He had a passion for New Wave unrivaled by any hipster in a Wang Chung T-shirt from Rags-A-Gogo, and it was almost hysterical to hear him talk about Devo in a drawl usually reserved for singing off-key to Toby Keith.

Like me, he was a transplant trying to make his way among natives, and it bonded us as fast friends. He traveled light, arriving with a tablet and a new phone, a few vests and ties for work, a pair of weekend jeans, and an electric razor. I reintroduced him to the physical pleasures of vinyl one night over Trader Joe's brie in puff pastry, and as he began to build his collection of XTC and Duran Duran, I let him keep his platters at my place. It assured us at least one date a week, like visitation rights to records I had primary custody of. For the first month we were friends, I hoarded those nights like pirate treasure, living in this constant fear that he would find someone cooler to hang out with. What was a bottle of wine and some old vinyl compared to the city's vast array of nightclubs and wild, willing girls? I'd already lost the last guy I loved, Catch, to such a world, and I kept waiting for it to seduce Sid into its neon arms. But he kept coming by, week after week, with a new record in hand and that same Christmas-light smile, and my fears began to settle.

"Maybe this will make you feel better," he said, unwinding his earbuds and handing me the right one. "Tenpole Tudor, 'What You Doing in Bombay.' I just discovered them and I'm kind of obsessed with this song. The bass line is almost identical to REM's 'Can't Get There from Here,' but don't let that deter you."

He queued up a cheerful post-punk track, just under three minutes of solitude, away from the other diners, away from the death I could still feel on my back. I could think of a lot of things

I could do in Bombay—Mumbai now, if I remembered anything from high school geography—chief among them not being here in Brooklyn.

I handed him back his headphones when our meal arrived and felt a little better with a new tune in my head. "So I guess that means you probably don't want to continue with our scheduled viewing of *Homicide*," he said. "We're about to get to the Vince D'Onofrio episode and it's pretty rough."

In addition to eighties music, Sid was obsessed with old cop shows. "*The Shield* is great, don't get me wrong," he'd told me once, "but it completely changed the genre, and now everything's trying to be gritty. You can't just have a detective solving a crime anymore—he has to be a morally ambiguous antihero with a violent streak, and it just bores me. Vic Mackey bored me. I was always Team Dutch, myself."

"Maybe not *Homicide*," I agreed, blowing on a spoonful of soup too hot to swallow. "Is there any Stephen J. Cannell ground we haven't covered? I liked *The Rockford Files*."

He gave it some serious thought and two bites of steak before he answered. "It's not my man Stephen, but *Cagney and Lacey* might not be a bad call," he said. "Or *CHiPs*. There's no problem so terrible that Pocherello can't fix it."

"As long as it's not *Miami Vice* and as long as you don't show up wearing an unstructured jacket and sockless loafers," I joked, my sense of humor coming back with my appetite. "What about this weekend?"

He rolled his eyes. "This weekend's no good." He groaned. "I told Terry I'd go out with him. He's been bugging me for weeks, keeps saying he has the perfect place to take a 'southern gentleman' like me. It will probably be boring as hell and possibly suicidal, given what his idea of southern is, but the only way to get him to stop bugging me to go out with him is to actually go out with him. I figure this should buy me at least a month of ignoring him."

"What, like duck hunting? Cooking meth?" I joked. "I did

pretty well in chemistry, can I come along too? Heaven knows I could use the cash."

"Darlin', I could not live with myself if I forced you to spend an evening with him, especially after what you've been through." He reached across the table for my hand and kissed it. "But I'll probably be texting you throughout the whole ordeal, so it will be like you're right there with me."

I got a giddy feeling in my stomach that was normally reserved for waking up from a dream about Stephen Colbert. "And when you do come over, you can cook me a delicious barbecued squirrel," I said, trying to mask my sudden bliss.

Sid took a bite of his T-bone and chewed for a moment. "I'm pretty sure that's what this steak is," he said.

For one perfect moment, I forgot about KitKat. For a moment, everything was normal again, just dinner with my best friend, talking about music, mocking his idiot roommate. I thought about suggesting we slumber-party in a motel for the night, watch pay-per-view with bags of microwave popcorn and minibar booze, but I didn't have the money for dinner, let alone a night in a Manhattan high-rise.

We finished our dinners. Sid dropped me off at my subway station with a long hug and a kiss on the cheek and left me with nowhere to go but home to my crime scene.

Chapter 4

THE BATTLE OF WHO COULD CARE LESS

Within a week, KitKat's crime scene was cleaned up and the papers had a new headline, a new corpse, a new scandal. Her body had been shipped home to New Hampshire to be buried. All that was left to do was pack up her stuff so the landlord could rent out her apartment. The super swore us all to secrecy about what had happened there.

Hillary was charged with cleaning the place out and put an invite on Facebook saying that everyone was welcome to come take what they wanted on Friday night, bring booze, bring food. Her family had held a private memorial service, so this was the time for all of us to say the good-byes we couldn't post on Twitter.

I knew I wasn't going to be able to go down there alone. It was going to take everything I had to walk through that door again, to get a drink from that same kitchen where, just a week ago, her blood had been spilled. Sid agreed to go with me in lieu of our planned *CHiPs* marathon, and even as we stood at her doorway, my hand shook in his. He'd only met KitKat once or twice; he'd told her that her red velvet cake was better than his grandmother's, and she'd posted it as her favorite review on her website. By the time we got there someone with a blue sticker had already claimed her recipe binder.

Crying tattooed girls leafed through her record collection, and boys in oversized glasses and sweater vests hung around her decoupage kitchen table, where the liquor and chips were stocked. I didn't know most of her friends, but I recognized Natalie and Mac over by the bookcase, who gestured to me with the traditional hipster greeting of a chin toss and a glance away, pretending to be in the middle of something so important that it couldn't be disturbed for a proper hello. KitKat had introduced me to Natalie at one of her Stitch 'n' Bitch nights, and Natalie, in turn, introduced me to Mac, whom she had, at the time, been dating. In addition to managing the Brenner Gallery, Natalie also maintained a blog about her dating adventures titled *The Village Bicycle*. Although she and Mac had broken up, if Natalie stopped hanging out with all the people she'd slept with, she'd probably have to leave Brooklyn.

"This is the weirdest memorial I have ever been to," Sid said under his breath.

Weird, twee, and oddly appropriate. KitKat would have been totally into this scene if it had been for anyone else. Even in death, she embodied the heart of Barter Street. For a moment, I forgot my part in her passing and just enjoyed the high of interconnectivity we were all sharing.

That all vanished when I saw Hillary, perched on the kitchen windowsill, smoking, ignoring everyone. She looked twice as old as when I'd last seen her, at KitKat's thirtieth birthday party: the blue streaks faded out of her blond hair, left-arm tattoo sleeve covered by a chunky gray sweater, no jewelry but the twisted-rope metal of the wedding ring her ska-band-trombonist husband had given her. She was the first person I'd felt genuine sorrow for other than myself, but I couldn't find the words to express any of it.

"H-hey, Hillary," I stammered. "How're you holding up?"

She flicked her cigarette butt out the window and shrugged. "I just want this all over with." She sighed. "God, all these people are so fucking annoying. Frauds, all of them. I should have just dumped this shit off at the Salvation Army."

Two shrieks erupted from the bedroom, and Hillary huffed herself off the windowsill to investigate. I followed, taking the glass of red wine Sid held out to me like he was in the water line at a marathon. Jylle, with her blond bangs and cowboy boots, was crumpled in a heap on the bed, clutching the sleeve of a red vintage dress, while Brandi, with sob-streaked mascara, held the rest.

"This . . . is . . . my . . . favorite," Jylle sobbed in staccato. "KitKat would *want* me to have it!"

"You're too fat for it!" Brandi said with a snarl through her own black tears.

"For fuck's sake." Hillary rolled her eyes. She snatched the pieces of the dress out of both their hands and shoved it onto me. "It's yours, Jett. Enjoy. You two, get out."

They stared at her. Hillary threw shade that would have made a drag queen shiver. I looked at the whole scene and then at the dress in my hands. The girls gathered themselves up and left without another outburst. I shoved the sleeve into my pocket and tossed the dress over my shoulder, following Hillary until I got back to Sid.

"What was that all about?" he whispered.

I shook my head. Hillary returned with a Whole Foods bag and a sheet of green garage-sale labels with two already missing. "Just stick these on whatever you want," she said. "And you can keep Baldrick. I went ahead and claimed his food and water bowls for you. Our aunt Jenny made them; they should stay with him. I've got his cat carrier too, if you want it."

"Sure," I said, holding up my labels. "I'll . . . uh . . . go claim it."

Sid refilled the bourbon in his glass and dropped two octopus ice cubes in with a barely audible clink. I put a sticker on the ice cube trays. I didn't need or want them, but I felt like I had to take something, like accepting a homemade cookie even though you couldn't stand raisins.

I took my wine and my date over to where Mac was thumbing

through KitKat's DVDs. "I always wondered where she got the name Baldrick from," he said, holding up *Blackadder Goes Forth*.

"She always said that Monty Python got overquoted," said Natalie, taking a seat on the ottoman and adjusting one of the lion-mane scarves she wore effortlessly draped around her neck. "She said once you heard a douchebag in a fedora recite 'Dead Parrot' for the hundredth time, you had to start exploring other areas of British comedy."

"He's just sleeping!" yelled some drunk, fedora-sporting douchebag from the other room.

Natalie rolled her eyes. "And that one's with me," she muttered.

"Here," Mac said, passing the DVDs to me. "You got the cat, you should get the source of his name too."

That was when I teared up. I felt like a thief. Everyone in this room had adored her, and here I was, sharing their same grief. Was I no better than the girl who'd tried to take my seat on the subway? I hadn't even told anyone but Sid about finding her body.

"We'll all miss her," Mac said, giving me a side-hug. "She was a real bright spot on this block."

I let him hug me. It made me feel less like an outsider. I took a deep breath and Natalie squeezed my hand. I took a drink and looked around. It was okay to mourn. It was okay to be sad in this place. No one was taking a survey of who was really her friend and who was a faker. Well, no one except Hillary, but she seemed to like me. And for the first time since I had arrived on Barter Street, I felt like I belonged to the neighborhood.

"Oh man, remember that time she and Bronco hosted the *Nick Arcade* party when his annual Fourth of July Calvinball game got rained out?" Natalie asked.

"I still have the T-shirt where she wrote our high scores on the back!" Mac exclaimed. "I haven't gotten that far in *Golden Axe* since, and I have it on my fucking phone."

Bronco. All of her other friends were present, but her boyfriend was nowhere to be seen. "Why isn't Bronco here?" I asked.

"No one's heard from him since we all found out," Natalie said. "I bet he's pretty beat-up about it."

"Hillary said he was at the funeral," Mac said. "But he isn't answering his phone, hasn't posted to Facebook, nothing."

"I'm worried about him," Natalie said. "I'm going to drop by tomorrow and bring my vegan lasagna."

Group visits were a huge part of Barter Street life, complete with cookies and semi-ironic casseroles. When I first moved in, I joined a Facebook group dedicated to posting photos of ugly casserole dishes in an ongoing game of who could find the most hideous. I wondered who had gotten KitKat's yellow and white paisley dish, which had taken prizes for both ugliness outside and delicious chicken-and-bacon goodness inside. Whoever had the pink tag had already laid claim to it.

Natalie pulled a panda alarm clock out of her bag and checked the time. "Which means I'd better get to the store now if I'm going to get some soy cheese." She pointed to me, then withdrew her hand. "I was going to ask if you were up for going to Axis for Homework on Saturday, but I guess it doesn't seem right to go without KitKit."

Homework was a weekly dark-eighties dance party that Natalie, KitKat, and I had dropped by occasionally. I thought about the tape still sitting on my dining room table and briefly toyed with the idea of contacting DJ MissTaken and asking her to play it in tribute to KitKat. But I didn't even know what was on it, and chances were, MissTaken wasn't lugging a boombox around with her mixing board.

"Maybe we'll just get coffee," I said. "Give me a call."

It was hugs and call-mes all around, and then Natalie left, dragging her drunken date out with her. Mac wandered off into the kitchen to intrude on a conversation about Faith No More, leaving Sid and me sitting awkwardly next to the now-empty bookcase. I had a torn dress, some DVDs, an ice cube tray, and her cat. I didn't really need anything else.

Chapter 5

BOYS ON THE RADIO

Saturday night found me halfheartedly watching a rerun of *30 Rock* when I heard a knock on the door. It was Hillary, holding a big pink Betsey Johnson box and a binder. "Here," she said, passing them to me. "I don't know what to do with these—they're her old mix tapes. Doesn't seem right to just throw them out, but no one took them."

I muttered a thanks and tried not to show my hesitation. She might as well have given me a bag of KitKat's mismatched socks or her high school yearbooks. I didn't have a tape player, and even if I did, the tapes would have meant nothing more to me than a brief nostalgic trip with Ace of Base or something new to download. Hillary would have been more likely to know the people who'd made the tapes and might have even made a few herself. It didn't seem right that they should be handed over to a stranger.

"You want to come in for a drink?" I asked, not knowing what else to say and hoping I had an extra bottle of wine in case she agreed.

"Nah," she replied. "I'm catching the late train back to Boston. I kinda can't stand it here." Baldrick hopped off the couch and rubbed against her legs. She crouched down and scratched his face. "Take good care of him," she said. "He was KitKat's baby. She found him behind our house when he was just a kitten and took him with her everywhere for the first month she had him. She wouldn't go anyplace he couldn't go too—he used to sit on her lap at the movies. One time she accidentally ate one of his cat treats in the dark, thinking it was a Raisinette."

KitKat had never told me that story. There were a lot of stories that she never got to tell me. I'd always liked her but never made enough of an effort to go downstairs and ask her out for coffee, dinner, a movie night. I told myself it was because we were both busy, but the truth was, even with only two years' age difference between us, she was the cool senior to my awkward freshman. I hadn't wanted her to think I was some needy dork trying to hang with the queen bee, so I'd avoided any situation where I might look desperate.

Add that to the pile of regrets.

Hillary stood up and gave me a grim little smile. "KitKat really liked you," she said. "She may have been way too into this whole stupid scene, but she thought you were genuinely cool. Not like the rest of those pretentious fucks." She put a cigarette in her mouth, but didn't light it.

I opened the door a little wider. "You can smoke out the living room window," I offered. "One for the road, right?"

She came in and sat on the low bookcase, opened the window, and flicked open a silver Zippo. Baldrick jumped into her lap and she petted him with her free hand. There was a momentary flicker of happiness across her face. "A cat and a cigarette," she said. "What more could any girl want?"

"Maybe a cupcake?"

"Why, you got one?"

I didn't.

"Figures," she said. "And some Brony covered in shitty tattoos took her recipe book. He's in for a surprise. You know what her secret was?"

Once again, I didn't know the answer. I shook my head and she continued. "Cake mix," she said. "Just ordinary cake mix. She added stuff, yeah, but it wasn't even the good shit from

Whole Foods—it was the kind of dollar-store cake mix that's so cheap the company can't even afford a box, just the pouch." She laughed, but I could see there were little fringes of tears on her thick black lashes.

"When we were in Girl Scouts, she was so awful at baking that our troop leader, Mrs. C, finally just gave her the badge out of pity. She didn't improve when she got here; she made these cupcakes from scratch and they all tasted like variations on concrete. She must have tried a dozen different recipes before going to cake mix. Did you ever have the ones she made with the rose petals and custard? They were amazing." She sighed and wiped her eyes, taking plenty of her mascara off with the back of her hand. "I'm going to really miss her."

"We all will," I said. "Have you had a chance to talk to Bronco?"

"Not since the funeral," she replied. "I like that guy, I really do, but he was acting, sort of, you know, weird." She exhaled like it exhausted her. "And not weird like the rest of her friends—present company excluded, of course—just, jumpy. Distant. I can't really explain it."

She took a last drag and looked around for an ashtray. I got her the plate I'd used for the leftover pizza I'd eaten for dinner. She snuffed out her cigarette and slid off the bookcase. "Look," she said. "I didn't just come here for a smoke and to give you KitKat's shit. I need a favor."

"Anything," I said, hoping she'd ask for something I could actually deliver. I'd already failed her on the cupcake front.

"Natalie said you do some private investigator work," she said.

"I work for a PI, yeah, but it's all insurance fraud, and all I do is proofread—"

She cut me off like she wasn't even listening. "I know she's just another dead body in a city full of them, but she was my sister. I need all the help I can get on this. I need to know who murdered my sister, Jett, and I need to know they'll be punished."

"I'm sure the cops have a handle on it—"

"Half of the murders in this city go unsolved every year," she said insistently. "I don't want KitKat to be in the unsolved half. They have no motive, no suspects, and one fingerprint. One lousy fingerprint. The chances of it matching anybody are astronomical. Please, Jett, whatever connections you have will help."

How was I supposed to say no to that plea? "I-I'll see what I can do," I offered. "But I can't make any promises."

That seemed to satisfy her. She gave Baldrick a last stroke and gave me a hug. "Whatever you can do," she said. "Just let me know."

Chapter 6

WHAT HAVE I DONE TO DESERVE THIS?

Mix tapes are like diaries. Each corresponds to a very specific place and feeling, and to go pawing through someone else's collection is a huge breach of trust. It's musical espionage, emotional voyeurism, and just plain rude.

But KitKat was dead, and curiosity quickly got the better of me.

I opened the binder with a thick plastic crack. Preserved in plastic sheeting was a lifetime of track lists, each with a photograph of the tape's compilation artist.

The first was a track list handwritten in pencil on torn-out composition paper, titled *Hi Katie from Luke*. I'd never thought about her name being anything but KitKat. It was a tape that could have been played at any middle school dance in the country: John Michael Montgomery's "I Swear"; Bryan Adams, "(Everything I Do) I Do It for You"; Celine Dion, "Falling into You." I didn't know boys were *allowed* to put Celine Dion on a mix tape.

I dug the tape out of the box. It was the only one without a case, the label lay slightly crooked, the title written in ballpoint pen. The matching Polaroid showed Luke as a blond boy with a jade-green T-shirt from Freehold Middle School—I recognized the T-shirt as one KitKat had worn as a tube top—posing with a preteen KitKat in front of a panther diorama at a museum. KitKat had her eyes closed; Luke was grinning with the sad dirty face of a kid just a few years away from his first beer, his first smoke, the last of his innocence wasted on the lies of becoming a man. He reminded me of my second-grade boyfriend, Josh, who'd pushed me on the swings at recess until third grade, when we got put in different classes. He'd started coming to class drunk in sixth grade, dropped out in ninth, and would routinely show up in the *Loring Free Press* police blotter.

Calvin, creator of the next mix tape, *Let's Get the Hell Out of This Place,* was photographed in the moment he'd heaved his graduation cap off the edge of the Grand Canyon, sandy, soft hair blowing in the wind, flannel shirt wrapped around his waist. He had decorated his case with a road map and mislabeled "Baba O'Riley" as "Teenage Wasteland." Thom, of *You & Me @ the End of the World,* was a beautiful geek, all angles and glasses and open-lipped pout, posed with his telescope in a concrete-walled dorm room. His track list, comprised mostly of Weezer and Radiohead and Mazzy Star, was typed on the back of one of KitKat's college astronomy tests. She'd gotten a 90. Good for her.

Baldrick hunkered down in the space left in the box by the cassettes I'd pulled out. There were tapes for parties, tapes from summer camp, mixes of dance music, and Broadway show tunes. On page after page of her musical scrapbook were photos of KitKat and her friends from Girl Scouts to college, track lists covered with stickers and magazine cutouts, songs I knew by heart, bands I'd never heard of. There were boys who loved her, friends I'd never met, stories I'd never heard her tell. I was beginning to feel like I'd never known KitKat at all.

But for the last three track lists at the back of the binder, there was no photograph of GPL.

GPL, whoever he was, had compiled three tapes—*How Fucking Romantic, Songs for a Girl Genius,* and *Without Words.* He wrote his titles in small, evenly spaced handwriting, centered on the label, and his track lists were all neatly typed with the faded ink of an old typewriter.

Though there had been no name on the return address of the tape I'd received the day she was killed, the handwriting in the upper left matched the print on these three tapes. Paying no attention to the care that had gone into wrapping it, I tore the paper open.

There was no typewritten track list. No letter. I even checked the back of the paper I had just shredded. Nothing except a cassette labeled *Cure Kit* in that same meticulous handwriting. I flipped back to the first track list for *How Fucking Romantic*. Whoever GPL was, he had been crazy about KitKat. All three track lists read like a hipster love song compilation off late-night TV—Stevie Wonder's "Knocks Me Off My Feet"; the Magnetic Fields, "Nothing Matters When We're Dancing"; Marshall Crenshaw, "Whenever You're on My Mind," each with a little note about why he'd chosen that particular song. Next to Sara Hickman's "Simply," he'd typed, *How better can I say it? I've fallen for you.*

But if some other man was sending her love songs, what did that say about Bronco?

My stomach had a long crawl back to where it had dropped from. I might have been holding in my hand what cop shows called *a motive*. Maybe that's why Bronco was acting weird at her funeral, why he hadn't shown up at the memorial. My throat went dry, and although I got up and got a drink of water, it didn't help. If Bronco had killed her in a jealous rage, he had a pretty good reason to play it normal at the funeral and lie low afterward. The last time I had seen him was the day she died, in the foyer as he was leaving KitKat's and I was headed to work. He'd been all smiles, and we made a few minutes of small talk before he got on his bike and rode away.

I picked up the card Detective Muffin Top had given me from where I'd left it on my side table and started to dial. But I hung up before I finished. Something in my gut didn't feel right, and it wasn't the two-day-old pizza I'd had for dinner. I wanted to do a little more digging before I turned Bronco over to the hard boys. I just couldn't believe, for myself, that he would kill her like that.

I tried to entertain another notion. Maybe it was a romantic game for them, a chance to pretend like they were fifteen again. Then I remembered that Bronco was a tech junkie, the kind who waited in lines for a new phone or the latest tablet. He rolled his eyes whenever anyone talked about vinyl. If it was a choice between eating meat and making a mix tape, he'd probably order the bacon double cheeseburger.

I called Bronco's number. I got his voice mail. He still hadn't updated his Facebook or his Twitter. It wasn't like him at all to be so disconnected, and I hoped he was all right.

Frustrated, I put the box of tapes away and flipped on the TV to a *Law & Order* marathon, but it was Chris Noth, and I hate Chris Noth, so I turned it off. I'd check back when it was Jerry Orbach.

That left me in the silence of the clues at hand. Baldrick hopped up on the couch beside me and nestled against my leg. I once watched a show that claimed that if a case wasn't solved in a week, it was never solved and wound up stuffed in the file cabinet of some overworked civil servant. I may not have known her as well as I should have, but KitKat was my friend, and with her one-week-old case already collecting dust, I owed it to her to help put her spirit to rest. It was the least I could do.

The problem was, I didn't even know where to begin. I couldn't take DNA samples or bag up evidence, didn't have a hot light to interrogate our friends under. Hell, I didn't even know where she'd gotten the supplies for her pot brownies. Maybe her dealer killed her because she owed him money. No, that didn't make any sense; it was a couple of dime bags, not a brick of China White. *Shit, what do I do?*

I pulled up KitKat's Facebook page. Even a week later, memorial posts and old photos were still coming in strong. The most recent was from Thom, the same one who'd made her *You and Me @ the End of the World*. *I've been playing "High and Dry" over and over since I got the news,* he wrote. *I miss you every day, KK.* He was married now, expecting a child, doing postdoc work at the University of Kansas.

I scrolled through a week of posts but found no one with a name starting with G, let alone the whole set of initials. A scan of her friends came up empty too. I checked her Twitter and her Tumblr for followers, but for as much as his track lists proclaimed his love, GPL was a digital ghost.

I closed my laptop and tried to walk back through the crime scene in my head, ignoring the sick feeling in my stomach as I played the scene out over and over. *I stood in the hallway. I put my hand on the doorknob. I put the key in the lock. . . .*

The door.

The door had been locked when I got there. All the doors in the building locked from the inside automatically, which meant that KitKat had probably known her killer enough to open the door and invite him—or her—inside. The killer would have closed the door on his—or her—way out, and it would have locked automatically after. This wasn't some lunatic on bath salts coming up the back staircase. This was someone she knew.

But that didn't narrow down the list of suspects, and it certainly didn't rule out Bronco. In addition to her friends, KitKat had a lot of clients and had lived here long enough that it was fair to assume she felt safe inviting strangers in. That's what people did on Barter Street, whether it was a friend of a friend at a house party or to exchange a teapot from Freecycle. We opened doors. We invited people in.

And I got up to double-check that mine was double bolted.

Chapter 7

WATCHING THE DETECTIVES

I was still mentally walking around KitKat's crime scene when my work ringtone, Loverboy's "Working for the Weekend," interrupted me from where I had left my phone on the table. "You want to go to the Hartford Firm on the third shift?" Susan, the MetroReaders dispatcher, asked when I answered. "They want you to come in at ten tonight."

I didn't normally like third shift, but I wasn't exactly ready to go to sleep. Maybe working among the investigative reports and the legal jargon would spur me on, help me with this case. Of all the places MetroReaders sent me to proofread, Hartford was my favorite. The law offices were stuffy and the financial sector attracted the late-hour crazies, but Hartford kept a small enough roster that I knew someone on call no matter what shift I was working. "Sure," I said. "Tell them I'll be there."

I RAN INTO Birdie, one of the other Hartford regulars at Metro-Readers, on her way out of the temp lounge. "I'm making a coffee run, you want anything?" she asked. I started to shake my head, but she quickly added, "Hartford's footing the bill—"

"I'll take a cherry Danish and a vanilla latte."

She grinned. "I knew you'd listen to reason," she said. "And hey, make sure to grab one of my postcards—I got a show coming up with a guy that was in *Kill Bill,* says Tarantino's going to be there opening night."

Temp work was a better look into New York's art, music, and theater culture than any review in the *Village Voice.* All the temps at MetroReaders were actors, musicians, filmmakers, and other wonderful weirdos. Unlike the trust-fund dopes I used to live with, they were genuine artists who needed the freedom and space only temp work could provide. There would be months where someone wouldn't show up for work, only to return with stories of six months spent driving to dirty nightclubs and summer festivals in a van with no AC, a film shoot with an A-lister who'd complimented them on the way they delivered their three lines, or backstage whispers of the Broadway diva they'd danced chorus for. It was the center of enjoyable narcissism, and no work night was complete without someone slipping you a flyer for their upcoming show or the link to their latest YouTube short film. More than once I'd been hit up for an album review, and more often than not, I gave it. It was a way of getting my name out there, a portfolio I could show around to *Rolling Stone* and Spin.com and finally get my journalism career off the ground.

I picked up Birdie's card and stuffed it into my backpack. Now it was just a matter of time before Lauren, the third-shift secretary, arrived with an envelope full of investigative reports to proofread. It was easy enough work, and late at night, there was never much to do. Most nights, I could even catch a nap.

Lauren came in, but her arms were empty of the manila folders that told us it was time to get off the couch. "Mr. Hartford would like to see you," she said.

None of us temps ever interacted directly with the investigators; most of them were gone by the time the third shift arrived, and we were told never to speak to them directly unless spoken to first—which, as far as I could tell, had never happened. Birdie had told me of one legal office she'd worked at where the lawyers had used the temp lounge like a private brothel. My stomach dropped back to the first floor as the elevator doors opened.

By the time Lauren announced my presence, I was sure I was going to black out from anxiety. Maybe I should be flattered, I thought, that someone thinks me pretty, easy, and enough of a corporate climber to be willing to sleep with me. Or maybe, more likely, I would simply do.

Philip Hartford was that kind of clean-shaven, middle-aged handsome that *Mad Men* tries to convince us is common when in reality, most middle-aged office guys look more like a sitcom dad. He wore black suspenders and a blue shirt, a mute-patterned tie and a serious, quiet expression.

"Thank you, Lauren," he said in a voice that betrayed no familiarity or comfort. I swallowed so hard I'm sure he must have heard the saliva hit my stomach.

"Jett Bennett," he said, as though reading an imaginary file on all my comings and goings. He gestured for me to sit in a leather office chair waiting at the front of his desk. "How long have you been working here?"

"Six months," I answered, my mouth dry.

"You like it here?"

"Yes, sir."

"You're good," he said. "Lauren says you're always on time, your work is clean, and you get along with the others. That's important in this line of work."

Was I being fired? Promoted? Propositioned? My palms were starting to sweat, leaving rings of gross on his nice chair.

"I need to know that what I tell you—regardless of whether or not you decide to accept my offer—will stay between us. Can I count on your confidentiality?"

Oh God, it was a proposition. But he *was* handsome, and it had been a while since I'd gotten laid. I imagined myself sauntering into the Hartford lobby in a trench coat with a red lace negligee underneath, stiletto heels clicking on the marble tile, the envious stares of Birdie and Lauren. It wasn't my hottest fantasy—that was the one about eating barbecue naked with Jack McBrayer—but it would work. There were worse guys to bone on my way up the corporate ladder. Helen Gurley Brown was smiling down on me from heaven.

When I nodded, he smiled. "Good to hear." He reached into his wallet and pulled out a Victoria's Secret charge card, placing it on the desk between us. A good sign. At least he would be paying for my red lace negligee.

"I wear a large, an extra-large in camisoles, and I prefer bikinis, not the string kind," he said. "I like blues and greens, no reds."

I couldn't believe what I was hearing. Surely, this had to be a joke. I looked for any traces of jest, a visible panty line, a hint that if I said yes, I might be fired for being a pervert, a weirdo, or just plain dense.

Mistaking my curiosity for interest, he continued, strolling behind me at a pace that almost made me squirm. "You'll be required to pick up and launder the dirty ones, replacing them with a fresh set. I'll leave you some of my laundry soap; it's a nice lavender-basil scent, you're welcome to try a little out on your own delicates. But you cannot say a word to anyone, do you understand?"

"Of course," I murmured.

He stopped and turned to me, smiling placidly. "When Susan calls, she'll tell you to bring in the documents," he explained. "You switch out the laundered ones with the dirty ones and I'll leave a check in the envelope, plus three hours on your time card to avoid suspicion at the agency. No proofreading, just in and out and you get paid, guaranteed at least twice a week. How does that sound?"

I couldn't bring myself to say no. I'd rather have risked humiliating myself than insulting him. I could deal with everyone laughing, but offending him would surely end up with me looking for another job. I couldn't deal with a murdered neighbor and getting fired from an enviable temp gig in the span of two weeks.

He leaned down, reaching over the arm of my chair to pull

the card across the desk toward us. "Go on, take it," he said. "And when you go out, pick yourself up something nice. A matching set, a nightie, whatever you want. Don't worry, I won't ask to see."

I picked up the card, still waiting for him to burst out laughing, tell me he was joking, and send me back downstairs. Instead, he handed me an office key on a black leather fob and put on his overcoat. "Retrieve the documents before you leave tonight," he said. "Come on, I'll walk you back downstairs."

He escorted me back to the temp lounge, where my latte and Danish were waiting. I was alone and someone had left the TV tuned to *The Big Bang Theory*. I watched him leave out the front door and clicked off the TV. There wasn't any work to do, so I stretched out on the couch with my headphones on, pondering the strangeness of what had just happened. The first lesson we got at MetroReaders was to never seek out the higher-ups at any agency we worked at. I wondered what Susan would say if she knew I was not only interacting with Philip but picking out his lingerie.

It was too much to comprehend at midnight. Between this and KitKat's murder, my life was quickly turning surreal, and I turned instead to something that made sense: music. I dug out my headphones and hit shuffle.

I played a little game with myself whenever I put my songs on random, trusting the chance and math of the shuffle feature to dictate the mood of the room. I would follow the path as if it were a tarot deck, predicting my future and peering deep into my soul. It wasn't always accurate, but it was always kind of fun.

But tonight, perhaps inspired by KitKat's box of tapes, every song reminded me of some great lost love—driving with William under the endless autumn sky to the mournful wail of October Project's "Bury My Lovely"; New Year's Eve hanging around Mikey's Pizza in Loring with Jay as he filled a hundred drunken orders and gave me a quick, shy midnight kiss to the Smashing Pumpkins' "Tonight, Tonight," like we were ringing in 1996 instead of 2006. It had been a long time since I'd let a new song remind me of anyone, but like KitKat, I still had an archive of every tape and CD all my boyfriends had made me.

But the aching nostalgia really kicked in with July for Kings' "Champagne" and all of a sudden I was back in college, sprawled out on the floor with my vintage red cocktail dress pushed up around my waist and Catch's arms around me, tie abandoned, jacket thrown over my chair, shirt unbuttoned. It was so real I could almost taste the stolen champagne on his lips as he leaned in close, half-proposing marriage in between breathy kisses. We'd swiped the bottle from the department reception for our senior recital. We'd been performing together for about a year by then, and we had arranged a jazz version of Warren Zevon's "Searching for a Heart," his trumpet muted and mournful, my vocals smoky and deliberate. It was the hit of the show, and when we'd reached the peak of giddy adulation at the after-party we'd grabbed the champagne and retreated to his dorm room. It was not the first time we'd made out on his floor, but whether it was the champagne or the high of performance, kisses had quickly turned to eager hands, and soon we couldn't get each other's clothes off fast enough.

My phone buzzed, jolting me out of my daydream. *Have I got a story to tell you,* Sid wrote. I loved that he typed out his text messages in full, no stray *2* or *u* like Prince. *Brunch tomorrow?*

Can't wait to hear it, I wrote back. *11?*

See you then. Good night, darlin'.

I played the song again, trying to will myself back into the beautiful memory, but nothing came except for the reminder that Catch, like his own apparition, was long gone.

Chapter 8

THE BOYFRIEND BOX

Baldrick was asleep on my bed when I got home just after three A.M. For the first time since I'd gone off to college, I felt guilty coming in late. I flicked on the light, and he ran to his bowl and sat there waiting even though he had plenty of food. I poured in a little more just to appease him and went into my room. I'd do Philip's laundry tomorrow.

Back in college, I made friends with Reese, a genuine Jersey boy with black hair and thick lips and bottomless eyes who now lived in Portland and reviewed video games for a living. But back then, he lived in the corner suite on my dorm floor, and it was in that room, watching *Sealab 2021,* that I started to get over my freshman-year breakup with William, who had dumped me by getting engaged to someone else when he transferred to Dartmouth. Reese was many things—brutally funny, an early adopter of low-fi indie music, and always in the mood to order a pizza— but he wasn't good at dealing with a crying girl he'd met just over a month ago. In an effort to cheer me up, he put the Mr. T Experience's "The Boyfriend Box" on a mix he made me, titled *Hardcore Pining,* possibly in hopes that it would help me get over William. Instead, it had prompted me to compile every token of lost love—all the letters, stuffed animals, bad poetry, and mix CDs—in one place. They weren't organized with any nostalgia, as KitKat's mix tapes and track lists were; everything was shoved in there like cursed pirate treasure. The box had traveled, unopened, with me every time I moved. As long as it was there, I didn't have to think about it—like it was the Dorian Gray picture of my heart.

I put on the Blondie T-shirt and checkered flannel lounge pants that served as my pajamas and wrestled the box out of the closet. Seeing all of KitKat's old tapes had awoken my own anxieties about my romantic past, the boys I'd left behind, the ones who'd broken my heart.

Taking a deep breath, I pulled off the lid. *Just one item,* I told myself. *Just one thing to satisfy your curiosity.*

I pulled out a CD from Jeremy, titled *Bright Lights, Little City,* the track-list collage like a soccer mom's scrapbook page—red sequins along the outer edge of the paper, torn-up scraps of sheet music, all surrounding a backstage picture of us in too much makeup with overexuberant grins and demon-red eyes reflecting the shoddy flash of a disposable camera. The curtain must have just come down. There is no moment so happy as the end of the opening-night show, the relief that, despite hell week and sore throats, tongue-twister lines and terrifying solos, it had all come together in two glorious hours of song and dance.

Jeremy and I had dated very briefly in our freshman year of high school, during that strange vortex of stage time when you're spending every minute together and it develops somehow into love. The show was *Annie;* he was Rooster and I was Lily St. Regis. I should have been Miss Hannigan and he should have been Daddy Warbucks, but those roles—surprise, surprise—both went to upperclassmen. On opening night, during "Easy Street," he'd slapped me on the ass just after my solo and kissed me for the first time during intermission.

He made me this CD just after the show ended and three weeks before our monthlong love affair ended. He didn't date anyone else for a while, so we'd stayed friendly until the divergences of class schedules and new social groups drifted us apart.

He went on to play Billy Crocker in our sophomore production of *Anything Goes* while I was stuck as one of the Angels; then he was Curly in *Oklahoma!* while I was Ado Annie Carnes. Senior year, he played Danny Zuko in *Grease.* I skipped out because I'd always thought the eponymous line in "You're the One That I Want," which the director added in over the curtain call, was the musical equivalent of cockroaches skittering up your arm. After graduation, Jeremy was accepted into the musical-theater program at Carnegie Mellon and, as far as I knew, had never returned to Loring.

It was the first mix CD anyone had ever made me. His dad was a lawyer and made good enough money that he had a stereo system with tape-to-tape transfer and a CD burner built in that, more often than not, would tack on the last song three or four times before the CD ran out of space. Jeremy started a CD-burning business for our classmates, which, at ten dollars a pop, paid for more than one date at the one-screen movie theater two blocks from his house.

I opened the case and took out the track list. It was almost all show tunes: "If Ever I Would Leave You" from *Camelot;* "I've Never Been in Love Before" from *Guys and Dolls;* Jeremy singing "All Through the Night" from *Anything Goes,* his soulful, beautiful tenor distant and obscured by poor recording equipment. But he'd thrown a handful of pop songs on there, too, because it was the late nineties: the gag-worthy "Truly Madly Deeply," by Savage Garden; Faith Hill's dippy "This Kiss"; the 10,000 Maniacs version of "Because the Night"; and "2 Become 1" because he'd had an irrational love for all things Spice Girls. Once, I spent all night by the phone, trying to be caller ninety-seven at Sweet 97.7 to win us tickets to see the *Spiceworld* tour at Madison Square Garden. I never got the tickets, and anyway, we'd broken up by their July tour date.

Of all the musical-theater nerds in the J. C. Kevlin High School drama club, Jeremy was the most likely to have really made it onstage. I hoped he had. I slid the CD into my laptop and hummed along as I searched for him online. And sure enough, there he was, starring as Amos Hart in *Chicago.* He was there, in my city, doing what he loved. He'd made it. And maybe, I thought as I yawned and closed my laptop, he might even want to see an old friend.

Chapter 9

EVERYDAY IS LIKE SUNDAY

was still drying my hair with a Batman beach towel when I answered the door to a starry-eyed Sid, one earbud dangling loose.

"Listen," he said, pressing it to my ear. "Doesn't that just sound like love? Right there, that jangly guitar right before the first verse, *that's* what it sounds like when you're walking back from a party and you've just met the love of your life; you've got a few drinks on your brain and her number on your phone and it's just the happiest goddamn feeling in the whole world. Bernard Sumner captured that feeling and distilled it down to six minutes and fifty-nine seconds of pure magic."

I loved the narratives Sid created for his music. It was never just, "I like this song"; he always had an elaborate scene to describe how it made him feel.

"What is it?" I asked. I wasn't as up on my eighties music as I probably should have been, especially for being friends with Sid.

"New Order, 'Temptation,'" he said, putting one arm around my waist and waltzing me in a circle. "Just hearing it makes my heart swell—I've listened to it twice since I got off the subway."

I wished I shared his early-morning musical enthusiasm. I hadn't gotten much sleep after Facebook-stalking Jeremy; Baldrick had woken me up by ramming his hard fluffy head into mine around nine, and it hadn't seemed worth it to go back to sleep if we were going to Egg School at eleven. I had barely put together a decent brunch outfit—a black pleated cheerleader skirt, vintage plaid double-breasted jacket, fourteen-eyelet Doc Martens with rose-print knee socks poking out like I was an extra from *Clueless*—while Sid had on an effortless ensemble of dark blue jeans with the cuffs turned up and a tucked-in flannel shirt in purple and gray check. Anyone else trying to pull it off would have looked like a hipster lumberjack, but Sid carried it off with a cool, straight-backed elegance. He only wore his black-rimmed glasses on Sunday. Natalie had once remarked to me that he looked like a cowboy Morrissey. If she had been thinking of making him the next entry on her blog, she'd never actually made the move.

"You look cute," he said, wrapping his headphones around his phone. "Like Winona Ryder in *Heathers*."

"Thanks," I said. "So what's this story you've got to tell me?"

He flopped down on the couch. "Jett, you're not even going to believe me if I tell you," he said, grinning.

"Try me," I said. "It'll keep me entertained while I do my hair."

"All right, so Terry takes me to this strip club, called Fairy Tales," he began. Already I wasn't interested, but I still had most of my head to braid. "It's insanely tacky, all these women dressed in these skimpy princess costumes, like the damn village on Halloween, only you have to slip them a twenty instead of an eight-dollar shot. Terry's got the hots for this one girl, Tinker Bell, but they got in some kind of row and he ended up getting kicked out of the club while I was in the Rose Room getting a lap dance from Cinderella."

"You went into the Rose Room?"

"Terry made me," he said, getting a little red in the cheeks. "But that's not even the best part—so here I am, all alone at this club I've never been to, in a part of town I didn't even know existed, with this girl, Cinderella, and we get talking. Turns out she's a misplaced southerner too, a Georgia girl, goes to church with her grandmother on Sundays. And before I know it, it's two A.M. When I leave, she follows me out to the parking lot and gives me this little kiss on the cheek." He gestured to the spot on his face like it was sacred.

"Sid," I said, trying to twist my frown into some semblance of an ironic smile. "She probably does that to all the guys—it's her job."

"I know that, but this was different," he said insistently. "I saw how she acted with all the other guys, and I know this was something else. Think I might go back to see her later tonight."

Out of nowhere, I pictured Amanda, the girl Catch left me for, in that little Cinderella costume. Jealousy bubbled up inside me like a poisoned well, and I tried to fight it back. *This isn't Amanda, this is just some stranger,* I told myself. *She's not trying to steal your man because Sid isn't yours to steal.* That made me feel worse, and before I could stop myself, I spit out, "You think she's going to remember your lap over the hundred other guys she's serviced this week?"

All the blush drained from his face. "Forget it," he said, standing up.

"Sid . . ." There was an apology tacked in there somewhere, but I couldn't wrangle it out of my throat.

"No, you're probably right." He wouldn't look at me, just fiddled with his phone. "Come on—we've got to motor if we don't want them to give our table away."

BRONCO WASN'T AT Egg School, but his name was. The cops had picked him up the night before for KitKat's murder and every tabloid had the headline. They'd gotten a partial fingerprint from the rolling pin, and another neighbor had seen him entering the apartment just hours before she was killed. As everyone waded through the story, I tried not to think about the tape on my table, the motive in my head. I wanted to believe he was innocent, I wanted to believe that someone I knew wasn't capable of this kind of brutality. But I knew Bronco even less than I knew KitKat, and these days, you just don't know. After brunch, I told myself. After brunch I would call the cops and turn over the tape.

Today Egg School wasn't turning anyone away. Those who didn't have tables by lottery or connections hunched over friends, reading the spread over their shoulders. The room was thick with the smell of coffee and cigarettes and last night's perfume. Mac and Natalie waved us over to their table, and we squeezed into the last free corner of the bench next to three people we didn't know. I subtly leaned into Sid, hoping I wouldn't faint or throw up from my own overwhelming anxiety.

"He didn't do this," Mac said. "R-rated movies make him squeamish. He couldn't have."

Natalie adjusted her cat-eye glasses and picked up one of the papers that everyone had already read. "'A jealous, reefer-fueled rage'?" She read the headline in a voice dripping with disgust like grease off diner bacon. "What is this, 1936?"

A skinny kid in a Dr. Who shirt started to say something, but the burly guy he was with shushed him. I didn't recognize either of them from previous brunches, but they seemed ready enough to defend Bronco that they couldn't have just been walk-by traffic. GPL, perhaps?

"Who's that?" I asked Natalie.

"That's Bronco's friend Bryce," she said. "He's a bartender at the Inconvenience Lounge. The guy with him is the owner, Wally. They do drag nights. We should go."

"Yeah," I said, even though the last thing I was interested in right now was making plans to go barhopping. I went back to reading the paper over Mac's shoulder, hoping it might give me some clues as to what the hell was going on in my world.

"This is just the pigs picking on another black man," Mac chimed in. "I guess we should be grateful they didn't shoot him on sight."

"He was a vegan, for fuck's sake," Natalie added. "He couldn't eat cheese, but he could bash his girlfriend's head in with a marble rolling pin? No fucking way."

Sid piped up. "You never know. Back in Oklahoma City, the scout leader of my cousin Sally's troop just up and one day shot her husband. People snap."

I elbowed him in the ribs.

"Fuck you, you fucking redneck faggot!" a porkpie-sporting neckbeard shouted from the back of the room.

"Guys, chill!" Lovelle, the barista, hollered. She unwound the scrunchie from her dirty-blond dreadlocks before pulling them back again nervously. "Randy and I have already started up his defense fund and bail. We've got a jar on the counter, and if you're on our Facebook or Twitter, we'll let you know about upcoming events."

"We've got a jar at the record store!" Mac added.

The guy next to Mac, in a Beastie Boys T-shirt, piped up. "And our band Chicken Puppet's doing a benefit show—"

"—at my gallery!" Natalie finished.

"What's important right now is letting him know we support him," said Randy. "Lovelle's got some sign-up sheets to visit him in jail; if you can, either sign up for a visit, send a letter, or donate to a care package."

I signed my name when the clipboard came to me and passed it on before picking up my menu. "Does anybody know anyone with the initials GPL?" I asked, trying to act casual.

Natalie barely looked up from her menu. "No," she said. "Why?"

Well, that did me a whole lot of no good. "I got a package for her from someone with the initials GPL. A mix tape. There were a couple more tapes from the same person in a box her sister gave me. Does that sound like anything?"

Natalie laughed and rolled her eyes. "God, KitKat and her mix tapes. She probably ordered it off Etsy. If KitKat had the space in her apartment, she would have kept all her VHS tapes too." To the lumbersexual to her left, she said, "Order me the eggs Benedict with turkey bacon. Wheat toast. I need a smoke."

It wasn't an Etsy find. No one wrote *I listen to this song when I ache for you* next to the Lightning Seeds' "Pure" for a customer, even a repeat one. But no one else at the table offered up any other suggestion as to who GPL might be, leaving me right back where I started—nowhere.

"I didn't mean to offend anyone," Sid murmured from behind his menu.

"No worries," I said. "You didn't know." If that's the reaction Sid got with a theory, I sure as hell wasn't going to offer up the evidence I had without vetting who I asked and in what order. If word of that tape got out and it fell into police hands, it might convict Bronco merely by what it implied, making me a pariah in the process. There had to be more to this story than a jealous boyfriend. That much, I had to believe, if for no other reason than to preserve my own illusion of security.

GPL's MYSTERY TAPE was still waiting for me when I got back around one. I checked Natalie's Etsy theory just to be sure. There were a handful of mix tapes for sale, all customizable, none shipping from anywhere remotely close to Binghamton. So much for that.

The detective's card was still on my fridge. I looked at the tape on my table. I thought about Bronco and the headlines, the few things I knew and all that I didn't. I wanted to believe in law and order, that good cops always caught the bad guys, but this was ugly math, wrongs making more wrongs. Sure he was there the day of the crime. Sure they had a fingerprint on what they declared to be the murder weapon. But my gut was telling me the cops had the wrong guy. If they were going to find him guilty, they didn't need my help.

I tore up the detective's card and scattered the fragments across the junk mail and cereal boxes in my recycling. Bronco was a friend, and he needed me to prove his innocence. If he was guilty, I could face that later, but right now, I had to test out my intuition that GPL and his tapes were somehow linked into this—for good or for ill.

But with no tape deck, I wasn't going to find out what he was trying to say and whether or not that held any clues about Kit-Kat's death. Maybe he'd been stalking her and the tape would be nothing but his breathing hard and jerking off. Maybe he was in a terrible garage band and he was sending her a demo in hopes she'd pass it along to some cool indie producer.

I wouldn't know—and Bronco might stay in jail—unless I found that answer. And unless I had a time machine to take me back to a RadioShack in the nineties to purchase a boombox, I was going to have to make some Luddite friends.

A few weeks ago while we were both on the second shift at Hartford, my friend Marty gave me a flyer for his Sunday afternoon Tom Waits show at Bosco's Lounge on Purcell Street. I liked Marty; whenever we were on the same shift, we would talk about music in the spare moments between documents. We swapped playlists I wasn't sure either of us ever really listened to—I know I didn't—boasted of our vinyl finds, and played for each other whatever song we were obsessed with at the moment. The last time I saw him, he'd just finished restoring a reel-to-reel player he'd found in a pile of curbside junk on the Upper West Side.

If anyone would have a tape player, it would be Marty.

Chapter 10

SUCKER FOR MYSTERY

Bosco's was one of those bars that tried too hard to look like a dive and charged nine bucks for a beer because hipsters in vests and faux-vintage concert tees would pay it. Marty was performing *Blue Valentine,* cigarettes he didn't smoke rolled up in his T-shirt, cabbie cap pulled low over his eyes. He was growling "Red Shoes by the Drugstore" with all the record cracks and hisses in his voice. I had no idea how he did that.

He met me at the bar when he'd finished the A-side. He got a drink and I gestured for two. The bartender rolled her eyes and slid me the glass so hard it soaked my coaster. I took a sip. Plain Coke. I stuffed two bucks in her tip jar and smiled ruefully. She didn't smile back.

"I can't drink when I do these shows," Marty said, clinking his plastic cup against mine. "Relaxes me too much. Have to get into that space, you know?"

I nodded even though I hadn't come here to hear his vocal diet. "Weird question, but I was wondering, do you have a tape deck?"

He leaned back against the bar, took a drink, and shook his head. "My last one busted a couple of weeks ago, and I haven't had a chance to fix it," he said. "But Josie, she's got one. I used it to make her copies of *Heart Attack and Vine* and *Foreign Affairs;*

she needed to learn the words to "I Never Talk to Strangers" for a show we're doing next month. She said she learns music best when she's driving from one catering venue to the other." He pulled out his phone. "Want me to ask?"

"Sure," I said. I knew Josie peripherally—she ran a catering company that specialized in art openings and small-plate affairs like the ones Natalie had at her gallery—but if she had a tape deck, we were about to become really close friends.

He massaged his screen without looking. "What do you need a tape deck for?" he asked. "Got some never-reissued rarity you're trying to transfer?"

"A mix tape, actually," I answered. "I can't remember what's on it. Just curious, you know?" I didn't feel like explaining my whole investigative process; I didn't want anyone knowing what I was doing in case none of us liked the outcome.

"She's still got the setup." He held up the brightly lit screen. "Here's her number; give her a call and set up a time." He took one last swig and clapped me on the back. "I've got to get back up there," he said. "Good luck with your tape."

ONCE OUT OF Bosco's, I called Josie and left a message. In the meantime, I had another mission to complete, this one with a charge card and a veil of secrecy. I hopped on the F train with a straight-arrow path to the Victoria's Secret in Herald Square.

With the Talking Heads playing "The Book I Read" in my ear, I watched a college-age couple in art school fashion snuggle in the seat diagonal from mine. He had his arm around her and she had her head on his shoulder, happiness radiating off them, filling the car with an effervescent light. It was the kind of love baby boomers told us we were too immature and slutty to feel. It was the kind of love I wanted to feel for someone, anyone, the kind of love that doesn't hurt or ache or feel like you're dying when he's not there. The giddy kind of love David Byrne was singing about at that very moment, my only frame of reference for what that might feel like.

They gathered themselves for some kind of lover's adventure at Twenty-Eighth Street, and I was sad to see them go. That sadness stayed with me even when they were out of my line of sight.

I was sick over what I'd said to Sid before brunch. I wasn't his girlfriend; I had no right to dictate who he fell in love with. Besides, I had a *This Is What a Feminist Looks Like* pin on my bag; I knew better than to slut-shame his stripper sweetheart. But when I tried to text Sid, I couldn't write *I'm sorry* in any language that felt sincere. I put my phone back in my bag. Maybe the words would come later.

My self-pity psych-up was interrupted by the unmistakable sound of a dudebro on the prowl. I'd learned to block out the sound of catcallers, but this one was loud enough to hear even through my earbuds. "Where are you going?" he asked a girl in a thick wool peacoat, hat pulled down low over her heavy curls. " 'Cause wherever it is, I can help you get off."

I rolled my eyes. A normal guy would have taken her disinterest as a sign to move on to other targets, but not the wild dudebro. He was on the hunt, and he wasn't going home without his prey. "What, you think you're too good to talk to me?" he snarled. "You're a fucking lardass, you ugly skank. You should kill yourself, you fat bitch."

No other passenger looked up from their phones or their newspapers. He kept railing, and she made subtle shifts around the pole, like a stripper in slow motion, turning redder with each move. "Moo, you fat cow," he continued. "Next stop, I'm going to push you in front of the fucking train, you dumb bitch."

Something in me snapped. All my anger at myself, at Sid, at Bronco's headline and the porkpie hat at Egg School, came boiling to the surface. He wasn't going to quit until either she gave him a fake number or his stop came up, and no one else seemed interested in looking up from Tinder or Grindr or *Fruit Ninja* to help. I stood and advanced toward him with a Terminator walk, as though the car wasn't buckling or rocking beneath my feet. "Leave the innocent alone," I said. "I am an angel of true justice, and I can see the evil in your heart. Leave her alone."

The girl looked freaked out, but not as freaked out as the dudebro. "What the fuck is your problem?" he asked.

I shoved him just hard enough to rattle him. "The devil's in your soul and you need to cast him out. I will bring hellfire and char the flesh from your bones. You will not take her innocence away. She is magical, but you are wicked."

Still, no one was paying attention but the girl and dudebro, who was trying hard to keep his cool. I was kind of having fun.

"You bitches are crazy," he said as the car lurched to a stop. He hustled off and ducked into the next car to try his Prince Charming routine again. I smiled at her, but for a moment, she didn't look convinced I wasn't going to turn on her.

"I didn't mean any of that," I said.

She let out a sigh of relief. "Thanks," she said. "But what the hell were you doing?"

I'd seen Natalie chase off a catcaller using the same routine, but with more screaming. Normally Natalie loved being hit on, but we'd been in Central Park one day and this acne-cratered broseph would not stop bugging us, so she'd launched into this tirade worthy of the craziest street-corner prophet. "New York crazy," she'd explained. "No one will bother you if they think you're crazier than they are."

"I'll remember that," my new pal said when I recounted this to her. "Back in Maine, the cold shoulder always did the trick, but I guess not here, huh?"

"New York dudebro is a whole different species," I said. The car slowed and I smiled at her. "Good luck," I said.

"Thanks again."

I felt a little better when I got aboveground. Maybe my good deed would karmically cancel out the bad ones. But the instant

I stepped inside Victoria's Secret, I was lightning-struck with paranoia that the other customers and clerks could sense what I was doing, that I was shopping for someone else because I was a lonely loser. A woman with too-pointy heels and caked-on eyeliner wafted over in a cloud of Very Sexy perfume and Virginia Slims. "Oh, honey," she said, looking at my ass and the pair of blue satin bikinis I was checking the tag on. "Those will be *way* too big for you."

"They're for a friend," I said. "For her birthday."

"Then, honey, she's not going to want *plain* panties," she said insistently, putting her electric-green manicure between my shoulder blades and guiding me over to a selection of push-up bras with thick padded cups larger than my head. "Our Very Sexy is more in line with gift-giving." She held up a black lace vagina noose with a rhinestone detail. "I bet she'd love these."

"It's for my aunt," I blurted. "For her fiftieth birthday."

"But you just said—"

"I'll let you know if I need anything," I said. "Thanks."

She eyed me as I labored to pick out the requisite sizes and colors, likely making sure I didn't stuff a floral-print thong or a mini Angel perfume into my jacket pockets. I'd almost forgotten that Philip said I could pick something out, but then a pair of polka-dot boxer pajamas caught my eye, and onto the pile they went. I even had them gift wrapped: pink box, black bow. Later, perhaps, I would pretend that my imaginary boyfriend, Adam Scott on *Parks and Recreation,* had sent them for our anniversary. *Wow,* I realized as I took my bag from the salesgirl. *I am a dork.*

It was nearing four by the time I was done with my shopping. I put on my headphones and started for the subway. I hit shuffle and the first song to come up was "Say You'll Be There." For a moment I forgot how and why I'd even put the Spice Girls on my playlist. A wrongly labeled MP3 file? A goofy fit of nostalgia brought on by a Buzzfeed listicle?

No. It was the block party KitKat had organized just after I'd arrived on Barter Street. There was a nineties theme, and afterward, she'd given everyone the playlist as a digital keepsake. I'd never listened to it in full, but occasionally, the songs would find their way onto shuffle.

I hesitated on the corner. I wasn't far from Forty-Ninth Street and the Ambassador Theater, where Jeremy had surely just finished belting out "Mr. Cellophane" to an awestruck crowd. I quickened my pace. I just hoped that he would be able to recognize me, a decade later, through the throng of backstage admirers.

Chapter 11

SAY YOU'LL BE THERE

Ah, sweet little musical-theater nerds. Overdressed teenage girls clutching *Playbills* and phones ready for a blurry picture they'd post on Instagram no matter how weird a face they were making. Their chaperones and most of the boys hung by the edge of the alley outside the theater, some scowling as they watched their girlfriends swoon over a song-and-dance man almost twice their age.

Through the throng, Jeremy gave me a twice-over before recognition split a smile on his face. He wove through the group and swept me up in a big bear hug. A handful of girls glared at me like I'd just crashed their prom. He kissed me on the cheek.

"Jett, Jett, how *are* you! I didn't know you were down here!"

"I would have looked you up sooner if I had known you were here too," I said. "I'm really glad to see you make it like this."

"Isn't it a *trip*?" he gushed. "When they called me up and told me I had the part, it took me three days to realize that it wasn't just a dream. I all but walked into Times Square traffic trying to prove to myself it was real." He quickly turned and smiled for a camera shoved in his face. "Let me just sign a few more and we'll go get dinner."

I hadn't been expecting that. "I really just stopped by to say hi," I said. "If you've got other plans."

"Oh my God, no," he said. "You do *not* just come by after

ten years and stay for ten minutes. Besides, I am *starving*. Only so many carrot sticks you can eat in the greenroom, right?"

"What, Cindy Smithson's mom doesn't bring brownies anymore?" I joked. Rumor had it that Cindy had gotten the lead in every show because her mother made these incredible brownies with a secret recipe she wouldn't even give Cindy. For all we knew, the white powder she dusted them with was pure cocaine, but they were so insanely delicious even McGruff the Crime Dog would have taken one taste and said, *Eh, it's worth it.*

Jeremy made an exaggerated orgasm face and let out a dreamy sigh. "Don't tease me with memories of postshow chocolate," he said. "I would kill—literally, murder my director and his whole family—for one of those brownies. I swear to God I still *dream* about them."

If the waiting fangirls overheard his plot, it didn't deter them from continuing to push pens and "Ermahgerd, you're *sooo* great!" in his direction. I beamed as I watched him sign autographs and pose for pictures with his radioactive smile.

"Are you his girlfriend?" one plump girl in a short, sequined tulle skirt and a souvenir T-shirt asked.

"Just an old friend," I replied. "We used to do musicals in high school together."

"You are *so* lucky," she said. "I wish some of the boys in my school had talent like his. He is totes amazing."

A sharp whistle blast ricocheted off the brick alley walls and the girls all shuffled toward their chaperones, some beaming as they posted their photos for all to see, others glum that they'd been ushered away before they could brush up against Jeremy's fame, as though it might rub off on them as they headed for their own college auditions.

"Do you want my autograph too?" he said to me when the last one had turned the corner out of the alley.

"I have an original cast recording, *Bright Lights, Little City,* from before you were a star," I said. "Maybe I'll put it on eBay, let all your fangirls clamor for it."

His eyes got wide. "Ohmigod, you are *so* cute," he said. "I can't believe you still have that. Didn't I put 'Spice Up Your Life' on there?"

"'2 Become 1,' but close," I said.

"A few years ago, I was in London doing *Guys and Dolls*—I was Benny Southstreet—and Geri Halliwell brought Bluebell to see the show. When she got backstage and told me how much she loved me singing 'Guys and Dolls,' I *just. About. Died.* So, dinner? I have to get changed first, but come on, come backstage, I'll make some introductions." He pulled out his phone and hit a number. I could hear ringing. "You really have to come see the show sometime," he said while he waited for the other line to pick up.

"Hi, Jim, look, I'm going to be back late, you won't believe who I ran into—Jett!" He smiled at me. "No, you remember, she was a girl I did theater with in high school. Oh stop, you've seen pictures of her. No, that was Cindy, Jett was Lily. Anyways, she's in NYC and we're going out to dinner, you want me to bring you something? Okay, then I'll see you at home. No, I won't be too late. Love you. Bye."

I asked a question I already knew the answer to, just to be polite. "Who was that?"

"My fiancé, Jim," he said. "He's the best. Too often you date these theater guys who mince and prance and will stab you in the back the *minute* you are up for a part they want. Not Jim. I had to *drag* him to opening night; show tunes are just not his thing and it is *such* a relief."

I wasn't as surprised as I thought I should have been. Not because he was in musical theater, not because he loved the Spice Girls, not because he'd never tried to take off my bra. He hadn't set off a gaydar or flailed about like a token character in a cheap sitcom. There'd just been something otherworldly about him that I'd always chalked up to having a big personality in a too-small town. Now it all made sense, and I was happy that he was able to make sense of it himself, to construct his psyche into something beautiful.

Chapter 12

THIS CHARMING MAN

Jeremy and I got dinner at TGI Fridays, for old times' sake, making dinner out of appetizers and ordering our daiquiris virgin.

"Jim would *never* let me get away with this," he said, catching stray mozzarella-stick cheese on his index finger before popping it into his mouth. "Ugh, last year he went through a *vegan* phase; we almost had to break up. Even now if I order bacon at breakfast, it's like I'm cheating on him." He took out his phone and held it up, pulling me in close. "Let's taunt him with our love affair," he said, picking up a potato skin and passing it to me.

We both made ironic duck faces and I held the potato skin up to his mouth, tilting it so Jim could see all the bacon piled on top. The flash went off and he quickly texted it. A few minutes later the phone buzzed with a photo of Jim, spooning a piece of cake into his gaping maw. He had a neatly trimmed goatee and clever eyes, a striped polo shirt and a leather cuff bracelet. "He went out and got an Entenmann's lemon cake," Jeremy explained. "He knows I love them, and now he's threatening to eat the whole thing before I get home. What a jerk!" A second message rang in and he smiled. "Jim says you're very pretty," he read. "He can't wait to meet you."

My own phone buzzed with a message from Sid, his picture

flashing up on the screen. "Who's that?" Jeremy said, snatching my phone out of my hand. "He's cute. Jett, please tell me he's your boyfriend."

"Just a friend," I said, surprised at how sour the words tasted on my tongue. I took a bite of brownie sundae to wash out the taste. "Wants to know if we're still on for TV Tuesday night." I texted him back a *yes* as I talked. "We've been doing these cop-show marathons." I still hadn't come up with an apology, but if he was trying to set up dinner plans, maybe that was his way of letting it all go. Chalk it up to a lack of sleep and pretend it never happened.

"That is too darling," he said. "Jim is addicted to *Cold Case*—the two of them could talk about that while we sing show tunes on the Wii in the den."

I laughed. "That sounds like the best double date imaginable."

"Then let's make it happen. I'm going on tour with *Jesus Christ Superstar*—I'm playing Herod, obviously, duh—in two weeks, but when I get back, we'll make a plan."

He paid the check and held my hand as we walked to the subway. "I'm so sorry I didn't keep in better touch," he lamented. "It wasn't personal; it wasn't even gotta-get-out-of-this-small-town angst. I'd think about you and plan to look you up and then I'd just . . . forget. You know how it goes."

"It was just time," I said in agreement. "I could have looked you up too, but life gets busy."

There was a warm glow of pride in my heart. He had made it. Where everyone else in our small-town class—including me—seemed so doomed for dead ends and middle management, he'd clawed his way to the top of his dream. If it had been anyone else, I might have been envious, but I loved Jeremy with the soft, sweet kind of love that stays long after you've set a man free to fulfill his destiny. It couldn't have happened to a more deserving person.

He took both my hands and kissed me on the cheek. "It's really great to see you," he said. "Of all the girls I tried to date, you were always my favorite."

I drifted all the way home on that compliment. The idiot rom-com part of my brain wanted to be a little sad, to feel cheated that the two of us would never be together even though he was so perfect. I saved his number in my phone. His CD didn't go back in the Boyfriend Box. Instead, I put it on the shelf with the rest of my musicals. It deserved no less of an honor.

There was a postcard from my grandmother in my mailbox. Greetings from Paris, love from her and Royale. I fed Baldrick and added Jeremy on Facebook. I sent a friend request to his fiancé too.

Okay, so maybe I couldn't date Jeremy—but I was starting to feel confident that I could reclaim my past, make right the wrongs that had taken love from me in the first place.

Chapter 13

NOT ABOUT LOVE

Even after work on Tuesday, Sid was carrying a fresh cup of coffee. It had only been a few days since I'd seen him, but he looked exhausted and jittery, like a junkie informant on prime time. He hadn't shaved since brunch and his wrinkled blue dress shirt only made his eyes look more bloodshot. "Rough couple of nights?" I asked.

I wasn't expecting him to smile and I sure as hell wasn't expecting him to reply, "Best nights of my life."

"Yeah?" I asked. "Care to share?"

Instead of answering, he produced a corkscrew from his jacket pocket and wrestled with a bottle of pinot noir while I lit the candles. "One of these days I'll buy you a damn corkscrew," he teased.

"But then you won't have an excuse to come over anymore."

"I'm sure I could find one," he said, handing me a glass of wine. "After all, we haven't even started on *Magnum, PI.*"

Normally Sid and I just ate frozen stuff from my Trader Joe's pilgrimages. My kitchen was a joke; while all my peers were starting food blogs and writing recipes for making gluten-free vegan lasagna in the microwave, a real fancy night for me might involve putting bacon, eggs, and toast all on the same plate. But tonight I'd planned ahead and bought a chuck roast to braise in my grandmother's Crock-Pot. My mother had e-mailed me her secret barbecue sauce recipe, given to her by a North Carolina cousin who swore all three of her husbands had proposed after the first bite. I'd burned myself browning it and almost dropped it on the floor, but all that was forgotten as the whole apartment filled with the smell of late summer.

I wasn't expecting Sid to propose, but I felt bad about the last few times we'd gotten together—KitKat's memorial, the incident at Egg School, all my snark about his stripper love interest—and if there was any way to a man's heart, my mother's cousin told me, it was through meat.

"Everything smells delicious," he said. "You couldn't buy this scent at Whole Foods or Fairway."

"I slaved over the Crock-Pot all day," I joked, holding up my glass for a toast. "Cheers, Sid."

"Cheers, Jett."

I took a drink and *mmm*'d in approval. I'd gone through a brief wine snob phase—like everyone did—when *Sideways* came out; Catch, Reese, and I would go for tastings because it was the cheapest way to get a drink, buy ten-dollar cabs and pinots and imagine we could taste notes of grass and strawberries. But now, thankfully, I just drank it like a normal person.

Sid put on Duran Duran's *Rio* while I plated our meals. "What's this?" he asked, picking up KitKat's tape from where I'd left it sitting on the end of the table, next to mail for my grandmother. "A mix tape?" He examined it like Indiana Jones. "Wow, I can't even remember the last time I held one of these."

Panic. I hadn't meant to leave it out, but I'd been caught, and if I was going to fess up to anyone, it would be Sid. After all, he was the only one who knew I'd found her body. "It was for KitKat," I said, putting down our plates and taking my seat. "It ended up in my mailbox by mistake. . . . When I took it downstairs . . ." I took a long drink of wine, as though that could wash my memory clean.

He squeezed my hand under the table. "Who made it for her?"

"That's what I've been trying to figure out," I said after swallowing. "Call me crazy, but I cannot get over this weird feeling that something on that tape is linked to her murder."

"What, you mean like a full confession?" he asked. "How convenient would that be, Joe Friday?"

"I don't think it's that," I said. "It's just this feeling I've got. Call it a hunch if you want to get technical."

"The best detectives listen to their guts," he said. "What do you have so far?"

"Nothing," I said. "Just a set of initials—GPL, a mystery in itself. Her sister gave me a box of tapes and there were three others from the same person, but no picture, no one with those initials on her Facebook or Twitter, nothing to say who he—or she—is. The secrecy alone is enough to make me suspect."

"So you think maybe she had something going on the side," he said, finishing my thought. "That doesn't make Bronco look too good."

"I know, and that's why I want to figure this all out," I said. "Bronco's my friend too; I saw him the morning she was killed. I don't want to believe that he could do this, but if he did, I want to be able to hand over the most damning piece of evidence." I took a bite and chewed for a minute before continuing. "My friend Marty suggested I call Josie; heard she had a tape player. Maybe once I know what's on it, I'll get a better sense of its connection. Unless there isn't one, of course. Then it's back to one—or worse, zero."

Sid leaned back in his chair and grinned. "I'm impressed," he said. "I probably wouldn't have put those pieces together."

"What else could I do?" I asked. "She was my friend, and with Bronco on the ropes for her murder, I don't see any other choice."

He wiped barbecue sauce off the corner of his mouth and stood up. "And that, Miss Bennett, is why you're Sherlock. I'll be your Watson, if you'll have me."

I loved when he called me Miss Bennett. Coming from anyone without a southern accent, it might have sounded corny, but the lilt in his voice sent shivers down my spine. I held out my hand and he escorted me to standing. "I welcome your assistance, Mr. McNeill."

"Guess this means our weekly viewings have turned into training," he said. "Maybe we should be taking notes."

"Sid, it's bad enough no one invites me to record parties anymore, not after I derided Mumford and Sons as being 'like Flogging Molly if all the punk rhythms and talent was removed,'" I said. "Can you please let me just watch TV for the sake of watching TV?"

"Fair enough," he said. He picked up the tape again and held it between two fingers. "I can't even remember the last time someone made me a mix CD, let alone a tape. But when you hear that first song and your heart soars and you *know* . . ." He sighed. "It's the best feeling in the whole fucking world."

Chapter 14

THE IMPRESSION THAT I GET

It was two days later when Josie called me back. "Sorry, I was doing a wedding out on Shelter Island," she said. "Huge affair, but they let me use their kitchen. It was bigger than my apartment, I swear. But I'm free this evening and I have a *ton* of leftovers."

"Can I bring anything?" I asked.

"Just a bottle of wine," she said. "White, dry, don't pay more than fifteen bucks. Call when you get here and I'll buzz you up."

I put Sid's copy of *Go West* on the turntable and spent fifteen minutes trying to figure out how to put together an outfit that conveyed casual carelessness with deliberate intent. I settled on a silkscreened squirrel shirt I got at the last Irony Auction, a gray dad cardigan, and leggings with ankle boots. The only thing separating my ensemble from straight-up pajamas was the red pashmina I'd picked up on St. Mark's. But a pashmina, I realized as I walked out the door, is really just a security blanket adults can wear.

At Bouquet Liquors I picked out an eleven-dollar Riesling with a funky label. That was how Catch and I had always picked out wine. I hadn't had a Riesling since we'd broken up, and it seemed so long ago, I couldn't remember if it was a deliberate act of casting him off or just changing taste. It left me with two bucks cash and less than a hundred in my checking with student loan payment due soon. I was going to have to get work—real, full days of work, not just three-hour washerwoman duties—soon.

Josie lived in a studio apartment in Brooklyn Heights above one of those boutiques that carries only four items, none of which are in your size. She'd painted each wall a different color: green around the kitchenette, blue behind the futon—which had striped sheets on it—bright red behind the record cabinet and bookshelves, and purple in the bathroom.

"I like your scarf," she said after hugging me at the door. Today, hers was blue, worn over an untucked black blouse so sheer it looked like it was made of spiderwebs and dreams.

She already had our two plates waiting on the table, plated effortlessly with frilly-toothpick meatballs, caprese salad, and tiny egg rolls. "These were just the prewedding appetizers," she said, pouring the wine into *Pokémon* juice glasses. I got Meowth; she had Togepi. "I must have made twenty different tapas plates, and bridezilla had the nerve to bitch that my quiche cups didn't look *exactly* like the ones on her Pinterest board. By the end, I wanted to dump a tray of chicken satay on her head. But eat up, there's plenty more. I know I'm supposed to get rid of it after the event, but that just seems so wasteful for such good food."

"I won't sue if I get food poisoning," I joked. I hadn't eaten since the scrambled eggs and toast I made for breakfast, and I was so hungry it was taking everything I had not to just dump the entire plate into my face, frilly toothpicks and all.

She held up her glass for a toast. "To KitKat," she said.

"To KitKat," I repeated, clinking my cup against hers. I tasted Catch in the first sip. His hands, his eyes, his laugh all washed over my palate. Memory linked this bottle with the last one we'd shared, watching *Pacific Heights* on VHS while the entire city was shut down with snow, his arms around me, wine-fragrant breath warm on my cheek. But now I wanted to spit him out, wash him away with Listerine, bleach him out of my brain and blood and heart forever. Instead, I crammed a meatball into my mouth and tried not to cry.

"So let's get to this tape," Josie said, taking a sip of her own drink. "I'm excited—when was the last time you got a real physical mix someone actually made?"

"I can't even remember," I said, handing her the cassette. That was a lie. I remembered the moment perfectly, the same way I remembered every moment with Catch. He had come to pick me up for a movie, and while I fretted with my earrings, he'd reached into the pocket of his leather jacket and produced *She Doesn't Think My Tractor's Sexy Anymore:* Live's "All Over You"; Garbage's "The World Is Not Enough"; Bryan Adams and Sting and Rod Stewart, "All for Love," because at his core, Catch was an utter cornball. I'd kissed him quick and played that CD until it skipped on Nightwish's "She Is My Sin."

"I'd be lying if I said I didn't miss those days," Josie said. "Finding that tape in your locker, playing it over and over, trying to figure out what he was trying to say. Tapping a playlist off some guy's iPhone just isn't the same, you know? How the hell else are we supposed to know what love is, from a Facebook update? Give me a Sony any day. Where did you even find this?"

I hoped the mozzarella in my mouth would disguise my lie. "I found it while, uh, Dumpster diving. I thought I'd give it a listen." I may have told Sid my intentions, but that didn't mean everyone else had to know.

She examined the tape with a jeweler's eye. "*Cure Kit*—sounds romantic." She turned it over and cracked the case. "No track listing, no artwork, what is this, amateur hour? Who is this GPL? Someone needs to have a word with him about proper mix tape etiquette."

She took it over to the elaborate stereo setup and popped it in. The tape opened with Squeeze's "Tempted," and already, I felt a silent tension hook reverberating in my chest. Track two—the Smiths' "I Want the One I Can't Have"—didn't do anything to make me feel better.

"Aww, this guy is pining," Josie cooed. "But seriously, the Smiths? The eighties are over; find a new band. Or at least a new Morrissey song. Heaven knows he's written plenty."

I wished I could listen with the same sarcastic nostalgia as Josie. *I want the one I can't have and it's driving me mad,* Morrissey wailed. But GPL already had KitKat. Clearly Bronco wasn't standing in the way; the three track lists already in KitKat's binder implied that the two of them were in agreement about their love. So far, this was more suitable as a confession of wine-drenched abandon, and all I could think of was the first time Catch had said he loved me, parked in his '89 Camry while we waited for Reese to get out of work so we could all go to the drive-in. We were eating Red Vines and drinking Dr. Pepper, and he'd just blurted it out like it had been swelling inside him for days. I was so surprised that all I could do was cram another Red Vine into my face because love was too fucking common for people who felt things as deeply as we felt things. I couldn't let myself believe him because if I had, that might have meant I was penetrable, defenseless, vulnerable. And that night, after he dropped me off at my shitty little grad apartment without even trying to steal a kiss, I went inside and played his CDs over and over, trying to decipher if maybe he really did love me through U2's "All I Want Is You" and the Cult's "She Sells Sanctuary" and Feeder's "Just the Way I'm Feeling." Could you ever really know what a man was thinking in someone else's words?

"I don't know this next one," said Josie as the song changed over to a pretty piano and a delicate woman's voice. She tapped her iPad and pulled up the lyrics to the Innocence Mission, "My Waltzing Days Are Over." She took another sip of wine and sat back on the couch. "This is so beautiful," she said. "I'm downloading it right now."

At my age, I'm content to watch . . . so go on, go on . . .

"Shit," I breathed. "He was breaking up with her."

"No way," Josie said. She cocked her head and listened a bit. "No. Nobody makes a breakup mix. She must have already dumped him, but he's still in love with her. He's trying to win her back."

"Hey Nineteen" by Steely Dan was next, followed by Billy Bragg's "A Lover Sings." The mix was coming together almost too perfectly, a soundtrack for mutually broken hearts.

"He's saying he's too old for her," I said. "That they don't have anything in common." I was starting to get a picture of an aging punk, hair weak from years of dye and Elmer's glue, selling his band shirts at a garage sale, dumping his black jeans off at the Salvation Army. In a way, I was glad KitKat had never received it and instead died believing that GPL still loved her.

"Dumped via Billy Bragg? That's rough," Josie said, draining her glass. "But that doesn't explain the first two songs. If he's so tempted, if she's the one he can't have, then why is he going to such lengths to break up with her?"

The Magnetic Fields' delicate, sorrowful "Smoke and Mirrors" ended side one, and she got up to flip the tape. I helped myself to a few more chicken satay skewers.

"Is this some kind of 'You can't friend-zone me, I'm dumping you' bullshit?" She poured a little more wine into our glasses and I didn't protest. "If so, fuck this guy."

"I don't think that's it," I said. "I think he's trying to say that although he wants her, he knows they can't be together. It's complicated."

"I guess," Josie said as she tapped her iPad over the unmistakably nineties sound of a chick rocker. "Syd Straw, 'CBGB's,'" she said, ID'ing the song. "But if he puts 'Hands to Heaven' on here, I'm going to smash my stereo and make you buy me a new one."

"Fair enough," I admitted. It was even more haunting, now that CBGB was as gone as their love affair. *And I don't know why we never met again . . . but I still think about you sometimes, every now and then.* When was the last time they saw each other—weeks, months, years? Was this tape unexpected, one last gem forged in the middle of the night when longing fought off sleep, or the last spoken line in a long good-bye? And why the hell did love always have to be so fucking coded? I vowed the next time I fell in love I was just going to come out and say it instead of relying on Joe Jackson to do it for me.

The next song was not "Hands to Heaven." It was Concrete Blonde's "Someday." "He's pretty heavy on the chick rockers," Josie said. "Maybe he was gay and that's why they couldn't be together—she wouldn't drive him to Lilith Fair or help him pick up guys at the Inconvenience Lounge."

The wine soured in my mouth. This tape was so much deeper than that, and she was brushing the whole thing off like it was a joke. Some people just don't understand real love, the kind that hurts somewhere deep inside, in a place you didn't even know you had. GPL understood that. I could only wonder if KitKat had or if he'd been just another fanciful curiosity, a cupcake, a *Paperboy* cartridge, a party guest who existed solely to be quirky and cute and adore her. I wondered if any of us had been anything more than that—KitKat and I had never had a deep conversation or a cry together, even if I had considered her a pal. But she had a lot of friends, and maybe I was just one more retro toy on an already-overstuffed shelf.

There were a few more songs on the B-side—Smashing Pumpkins' "Perfect," the Rolling Stones' "Ruby Tuesday," and the Sundays' "Here's Where the Story Ends"—but neither of us recognized the last song. *I wither without you,* a woman cooed, her voice distant behind a scratchy, faded recording. *I crumble before you.* Josie typed the lyrics into her search, but nothing came up. She tried the second verse, *Stars fall flash and slash my heart.* Still nothing. She held up the phone to the speaker, but Shazam came back empty.

"Rewind it," I demanded.

"I can't," she said. "The rewind doesn't work—we'd have to listen to the whole thing again."

I grabbed my phone and scrambled to make note of the lyrics as they slipped into the nothingness. It struck something inside me, twisted my guts into sick knots of love and longing. I couldn't remember the last time a song had made me ache so beautifully, and I never wanted it to end.

But it did end, and there was nothing left to do but finish the wine and say good night. I hummed it all the way home, not caring if I got dirty stares on the subway, knowing that the only important thing was to preserve this lost song like a piece of evidence, a fossil, a fly caught in amber. And when I couldn't sleep, I stayed up typing the lyrics out on my grandmother's old typewriter. At the very least, it kept Catch's ghost at bay.

Chapter 15

RUNNING ON ICE

Mac worked at Ol' Vinylsides, the kind of record store where guys in horn-rimmed glasses and ringer tees hung around waiting for someone to buy a Huey Lewis album so they could mock them with quotes from *American Psycho*. But Mac was a walking zine, a *Rolling Stone* commemorative coffee table book of B-sides and bass players. If anyone would be able to hunt down this unnamed song off KitKat's tape, it would be him.

One of his fellow record nerds had cut out an elaborate construction-paper banner spelling out WILLIAM JOEL APPRECIATION DAY behind the counter and "She's Always a Woman" was playing loud enough to rattle my guts.

"Have you come to peruse our fine selection of William Joel records?" Mac asked, gesturing to the three stolen white Crowley milk crates packed with tattered vinyl. "We have many, many, *many* copies, and they're all on sale—or free, if you spend twenty-five dollars on music that doesn't totally suck."

"I think I'll pass on that generous offer, thank you," I said. "But I'm hoping you can provide me with your expertise in music outside of Planet Joel." I slid my typewritten lyrics sheet across the counter.

"What, is this some new single you're trying to get recorded?"

He unfolded it and read through. "It's pretty good. I mean, it's not 'Movin' Out' good, but we can't all possess the songwriting genius of Mr. William Joel."

Brad, his coworker, who hadn't gotten the hairstyle memo that the nineties were over, snatched the lyrics out of his hands. "Do you need any session musicians? My brother Steve is a great keyboard player, and I could play drums . . ."

"It's already been recorded, but I want to know by who," I said. "I heard it someplace, but can't find any information on it. I titled it 'Wither without You,' but that might not be the real title. Google and Shazam both failed me at every try."

"Shit, that's the worst," Mac said, taking the paper back. "I'll see what I can find, but on one condition."

I had to have that song and I would do anything to get it. I couldn't remember the last tune that had struck me as hard in the heart as this unknown track. It sounded like love. It sounded like loss. It sounded like something I'd forgotten how to feel, and all I wanted to do was feel it forever. I would give Brad's next album a hundred stars on Amazon. I would sing "The Wreck of the Edmund Fitzgerald" at karaoke.

"Name it," I said.

He reached under the counter and handed me a copy of *The Bridge*. "You have to buy this."

I WAS OUT five bucks for the record, but I trusted that Mac could find the history of my mysterious song. And if he didn't, I was going to make a bowl out of the record, fill it with candy, and give it to him to enjoy before he discovered that Billy Joel had invaded his home like bedbugs.

Back at the apartment, I took a quick inventory of the case. I had a tape I couldn't play again and a track list full of anguish. I had a set of initials and what looked like a motive. But I still didn't have the connection between KitKat, Bronco, and GPL.

I did, however, have another postcard, this one from Spain.

My grandmother hoped I was enjoying spring in Brooklyn. I wished I had a way to write to her, to ask her advice, to hear her wisdom in her airy trill. *Dear, you're a smart girl. You'll figure this out,* she'd say, pouring me another cup of tea. Just those words, said over the phone before a big test or over lunch on my first day here, would be enough to propel me through, if only I could hear her say them.

I put on Sid's copy of Cocteau Twins' dream-laden *Heaven or Las Vegas* and left Baldrick watching the record spin with eager eyes while I washed Philip's laundry in the bathtub. He wasn't kidding. His laundry soap smelled amazing.

I heard Hartford's ringtone and answered, expecting Susan.

"It's Philip," he said. "I'll be in your neighborhood this evening; if everything's done, I can pick it up."

"I could have it done, yeah," I answered. Maybe Philip would be willing to give me a little advice on how to go about solving a case. I had the track list—most of it—and was on my way to solving that final mystery. But all I had was a theory I couldn't prove and a name I had no idea where to find. I was at a dead end, and it couldn't hurt to ask someone who knew better than me. Especially while holding a packet of his freshly washed secret underpants.

I WASN'T USED to seeing Philip in jeans and a sweater, but even so he had a coolness about him that completely betrayed the fact he was wearing ladies' underwear underneath it all. I found myself wondering what color he was wearing today and if he liked the ones I had picked out.

"You're too kind," he said, accepting a cup of coffee and taking a sip. "Good coffee. If my own secretary ever leaves, I'll hire you on in a heartbeat."

"I use a French press," I said. "Mind if I ask you something?"

"That explains it—the office just uses a drip machine. They tried to get a Keurig, but I told Lauren I'd fire her if one of those coffee robots showed up in my office. Sure, ask away. I can't stay too long, but now that I have a cup of coffee, I might as well sit."

I took a seat at the table and he took the chair across from mine. "How do you solve a case?" I ventured to ask. "I mean, how do you go about getting all the information? What kind of questions do you ask?"

"It's easier than you think," he said. "You just keep asking what you want to know until you start hearing the same thing over and over again."

I had already been doing that. I had asked Marty to find me a tape player, Josie to help me decode, Mac to find the song. But I was still at a dead end unless GPL appeared in a wisp of vapor. "How do you know who to ask?"

"You ask everybody," he answered. "Landlords, neighbors, coworkers, grocery store clerks. No one keeps a secret to themselves for long, and someone always knows something."

I stared at the gold ring on his finger, wondering who else knew *his* secrets.

"Why do you ask?" he said. "Are you writing a screenplay?"

"No," I said. "A friend of mine got accused of a crime, and I want to help prove that he's innocent."

He had the coffee cup halfway to his mouth, but he set it down and got very serious. "Jett," he said. "This is not Nancy Drew. Detective work is not something you can just play around with. There are laws in place, there are protocols. You could get yourself—and your friend—in real trouble."

"But what about him?" I asked. "What if they don't believe he's innocent?"

Philip sighed. "I wish I could give you more hope that the justice system would work," he said, "but you and I both know that's not always the case. If you want, I can recommend a good lawyer, but, Jett, I want you to listen to me when I say you need to stay out of it." He took a last sip of his coffee and stood up, collecting his package under his arm. "If you really are interested in becoming a PI, I can set you up to take a certification course online. And if you want to come work for Hartford, they'll pay for it. But I'm warning you: it's not all bourbon in your desk drawer and leggy dames and fedoras."

"So why did you become a detective?" I asked.

"I like puzzles," he said. "I like fitting everything together. But I didn't have the stomach to deal with the kind of crimes cops deal with—murders and rapes and kidnappings—so the private sector was more for me. Sometimes I wish it was a little more exciting, like on TV, but the upside is that I've never had to look at a dead body that wasn't already laid out in an expensive casket."

"I'll think about it," I said. "Thanks for the chat."

"Thanks for the laundry," he said. "I'll schedule you for Friday evening, if that's convenient."

"I'll put it on my calendar," I said.

"Make it seven o'clock," he said. "And I'll see you then."

I thought about what he said after he left. Up until now, I hadn't asked anyone about GPL because I hadn't wanted to tip my hand, reveal to anyone that I was doing anything behind the scenes in case I failed. But I also knew I wasn't going to walk away from finding out who really killed KitKat, even if Bronco was the guilty one. And now I knew I had to ask someone, and better still, someone who would know better than anyone.

Chapter 16

YOUR PHONE'S OFF THE HOOK, BUT YOU'RE NOT

After Philip left, I put in a call to Hillary. If anyone might know the identity of the mysterious GPL, it would be Kit-Kat's sister. I dialed her number and rinsed out the French press while I waited.

There was loud music when she picked up. "Hey, Jett," she said. "You're going to have to speak up; I'm helping Vern do a sound test before his show tonight. What's up? You in town?"

"I wish," I said. Baldrick hopped up on the counter and batted at the faucet. "I've been going over those tapes you gave me and I wanted to know if you were in touch with any of the creators—thought maybe they might want them back as a memento."

"Not really," she said. "I mean, we saw her first boyfriend, Luke, at the gas station when we were home for Christmas, but her Facebook page would be the place to ask around—it's kind of become a makeshift memorial."

I was going to have to be a little more direct. "There's one here that's just initials, GPL—does that sound like anyone she talked about?"

"Could be Greg Larkin, he was her friend Jennifer's brother," she said. "But I don't think he ever made her a tape. They were just friends."

I got out the binder and flipped through the track lists. There were two mixes from Jennifer but none from Greg. "I don't think so—can you think of anyone else?"

Someone yelled something in the background. "I gotta go, they're having a problem with the drums. I'll dig through her phone and see what I can find."

She hung up before I got a good-bye in, but a few minutes later, a text came from KitKat's old number. At first, it didn't feel right to open it, a ghost, a message from beyond the grave. And when I did open it, there wasn't a phone number—instead, Hillary had sent me a photo of KitKat holding hands with a man at least ten years her senior. He was wearing a yellow shirt and a Red Sox cap; she had on a Binghamton University sweatshirt and a red polka-dot skirt. I vaguely remembered KitKat telling me she'd done her undergrad work at Binghamton. Anthropology, I think, probably because they didn't have a degree in being quirky.

This pic was labeled GBU in her photos, Hillary wrote. *No clue who he is. Never seen him before, but I hope it helps.*

I stared at her picture with tears in my eyes. She was smiling in the photo, happy enough to look almost alive beyond the pixels. I only had a few photos of her and none of them were of the two of us—group shots from the Save Our Bluths run, brunch Instagrams, party candids. For two weeks, I'd carried around the abstract knowledge that she was gone, the day-to-day understanding that I wouldn't see her in the foyer or at a party. But looking at her picture with her cat by my side, the hard reality of her death hit me square in the chest. It wasn't fair. It never is, but seeing her so vibrant in this small digital scrap only reinforced the fact that she was taken from us too young, too violently, and seemingly without sense. And my task—whether Philip agreed or not—was to put all the pieces together.

I sat down on the couch with my laptop. Baldrick knocked into my shin with his head, and I reached down to scratch him behind the ears. BU for Binghamton University, like her sweat-shirt. I pulled up the college website and plugged in all the G names I could think of. Greg L, two hits. Gerald L, none. George L, fourteen names came up.

But only one of them was George Parker Lennox.

Chapter 17

ANGELS OF THE SILENCES

rofessor George Parker Lennox taught music theory, the History of Rock, Intro to New Wave, Punk Theory, and Yacht Rock Senior Seminar. That explained Steely Dan and Billy Bragg. He'd authored an intro-to-music textbook and written the foreword to a book on the Talking Heads. The headshot on his bio matched the man in KitKat's photograph, Red Sox cap and all. He had a blog. He had a Twitter feed.

And he had a wife.

The tape was starting to make sense now. He was the unavailable one and that's why he was ending it. It wasn't a breakup, it was a farewell. He probably assumed that she hadn't contacted him because she understood the tape. And now I wondered if my interception made me responsible for telling him what really happened. Bronco had no reason to be jealous—it was over between the two of them, it might have even been over before the tape was made. There was too much heartbreak in those lyrics for it to be a fond farewell *and* a fuck-you.

But it also meant that GPL's wife could be a suspect. Binghamton was only a few hours away, and it wouldn't be the first time in history that a wife took care of her husband's mistress. If I was trying to prove Bronco's innocence, she was making a pretty strong case for herself without even knowing it.

I scanned KitKat's cupcake blog, her Facebook, her Twitter for any conversations that might have tipped the wife off. If they were having an affair, they'd kept it very quiet. He'd never left a comment, wasn't listed as a follower or a friend. But he was going to have to find out she was dead someday, and I was probably going to have to be the one to tell him.

I was shaking. I closed the laptop. Baldrick yowled and I poured out the last of the cat crunchies into his dish. He ate while I put on my coat and walked down to the grocery store for distraction, silently begging, *Please don't let me run into anyone, please don't let me . . .*

"Hi, Jett." I was surprised to see Randy by the vegetable corner. Key Food seemed too pedestrian for him and Lovelle; I always assumed they got all the supplies for Egg School and their own kitchens at a more free-range grocery store. "Picking up some goodies for Bronco's care package?"

Bronco. I had completely forgotten that I was supposed to visit him tomorrow.

Randy had a full basket of organic and gluten-free offerings. All I had in my basket was the cheapest, smallest bag of cat food that would get Baldrick through until the direct deposit fairy magically planted money in my checking account. Right now, my washerwoman duties were the only thing keeping me in MetroCards and Trader Joe's.

"That and a few other things," I lied, hoping it would explain the cat food.

Randy nodded. "Lovelle and I have a box of things other customers have dropped off—some puzzle books, snacks, stuff like that. But if you could pick up some soy cheese and a couple of those egg-free, casein-free cookies they have over at Hotte Lotte, I know he would appreciate it."

"Can't you guys just send some egg-free cookies?" I asked. "Those ones that you get are pretty good." *For being dry and disgusting,* I thought. I had accidentally ordered one a few months ago when I'd been too hungry to make an informed decision and had regretted it the whole time it was crumbling in my mouth.

Randy looked at me like I'd asked him to burn down his store and use the insurance money for bail. "This is about community support, Jett," he said. "We need to show Bronco that we're all rallying behind him."

"I just know he really likes the cookies you guys have—"

He cut me off. "You'll be riding with Bryce; he'll pick you up. Just remember, no raisins in anything. Prisoners can use them to make booze."

"They could start a distillery and sell it to hipsters in Williamsburg," I joked. "I bet guys in seventies running shorts and cop-show mustaches would line up to drink Raisin Jack."

Randy didn't find that funny. Truth is, I didn't either. I was feeling bitter and mean about everything. He muttered some kind of good-bye and went back to buying kale. I looked at the cat food in my basket and decided that was all I was going to buy. I liked Bronco, but this week, there was only enough cash to feed one man in my life, and it was going to have to be the fluffy one.

Chapter 18

A GIRL IN TROUBLE (IS A TEMPORARY THING)

My ride to Rikers was the skinny kid from brunch with the Dr. Who T-shirt, only this time he was wearing a sweater vest over a short-sleeved plaid button-down. He drove a blue Honda Accord that was more rust than metal and had a radio receiver plugged into a Discman. There wasn't even a clock.

"I'm Bryce," he said, handing me a cup of coffee. "You'll have to hold it in your lap—no cup holders."

"Here," I said, handing him *The Bridge*. "To thank you for giving me a ride."

He looked at it like I was handing him a dead roach. "Keep it," he said. Guess I couldn't blame him for that reaction.

I got in the front seat and wondered if the car would hold together on the ride. We sat in the heavy morning traffic in silence until he cleared his throat and asked how I knew Bronco. I told him about living upstairs from KitKat, that I knew them both from parties, that I didn't believe he was capable of this.

"So . . . ," he drawled. "Are you the bitch that said Bronco was seen leaving the apartment?"

"No!" I said insistently. "No. I'm the one that found her body." I don't know why I told him that as though it would clear my name; all it probably did was give me more motive to narc. "I saw him leave that morning, but that wasn't unusual."

"Yeah, he was over there, but someone got the times mixed up, told the cops he was seen leaving that afternoon. That's not possible."

I drank my coffee. "What, are you his alibi?"

Bryce sighed and looked at me hard. "Look," he said. "You can't tell anyone I told you this, but I know he didn't do this."

"So why can't I tell anyone?" I replied. "You know, like his lawyer?"

"Because he doesn't want it getting out . . . that he was with me. He was doing a muscle show at the Inconvenience Lounge, same as every other Wednesday, and he spent all afternoon getting ready."

"What's a muscle show?" I asked, and immediately felt like a Pollyanna.

Bryce rolled his eyes and took a sip of his coffee. "It's exactly what it sounds like," he said. "Afterward, we went back to my place—hope I don't have to spell that out for you too."

This was a revelation, to say the least. "But what about KitKat? Wasn't she his . . ."

"His bestie and his beard," Bryce said. "He said she was his girlfriend when his family visited. They're those kind of snotty born-again types who think gay sex should stay between Dad of the Year and the kid he's diddling down the street. I didn't like it, thought he should be honest with them, but he just wasn't ready. Some people never are."

If I thought about Bronco hard enough, I was more surprised that he pretended to be straight than that he wasn't. "But in Bushwick, seriously? Why stay closeted here, of all places?"

"Because you can't just be gay in one place," said Bryce. "Admitting he was dating me meant broadcasting back to everyone in Armpit, Arizona, that he was out and proud. And being black, gay, and dating a white boy? He said he just wasn't ready to face his family with all that."

"So how do I know you didn't kill her to force him to come out?"

"Bitch, please," he said. "You watch too much *SVU*. I adored KitKat. She was going to bake our wedding cake . . ." He sighed and stared somewhere beyond the traffic. ". . . when he finally told his family about us."

I'D NEVER EVEN been to the principal's office, let alone a prison visiting room. I was immediately seized with the fear that they'd somehow find contraband in my purse: a pocketknife I'd thrown in for a picnic because I needed the bottle opener; a strip of condoms forgotten from a long-ago hookup; a chocolate bar that could, in theory, be a brick of cocaine. I had visions of being slammed against a wall and strip-searched, forced to don an orange uniform and bunk with some murderous junkie named Sherrie. She'd tattoo me with a Bic pen; Sid and my parents would have to visit by phone through panes of Plexiglas. . . .

But instead, the guards nodded at the contents of our care package and waved both Bryce and me through to the sterile room. The yellow walls had just the opposite effect than was probably intended. There was no way anyone could feel happy or relaxed when an armed guard was glaring at your every move, as though each embrace was a secret transaction of drugs, weapons, cash, or contraband Snickers.

Bronco didn't look out of place here. He was a big guy, covered in tattoos, though his Mohawk was now wet down and plastered to his head. The only difference was that his eyes were sweet and sad and soft. They didn't have the hard look that the eyes of the man two tables down being visited by his mother had.

"We're going to get you out of here," Bryce said, reaching across the table.

Bronco pulled away. "Not here," he hissed. "I don't want any trouble."

Bryce shrank back like he'd been slapped.

"How are you holding up?" I squeaked out.

"Well, I think I've had more visitors in the last two weeks then I've had since I was ten, when I had my appendix removed in the fifth grade."

"Next time I'll bring you a coloring book," I joked, opening up the care package. "I think there's some crosswords in here to pass the time until then."

Bronco smiled for the first time since we arrived. Bryce didn't like my stealing his thunder and quickly added, "There won't be a next time—we're going to get you out of here. We're holding a benefit and Lovelle says that we should raise enough money to secure your bail."

"That's a relief," he said. "It's not so bad in here; quiet mostly. But the food is going to kill me—all that animal fat, ugh. I feel so sick and sluggish all the time."

"We'll get you a juice detox when you get out," Bryce promised. "I would have brought some tea, but they don't allow anything labeled 'herbal remedies' in here. Just work out as much as you can, sweat and drink lots of water. It won't be much longer."

I let the silence settle for a minute before I spoke again. "We missed you at KitKat's memorial," I said, cringing at my clumsiness and hoping he didn't notice. So much for my L.A. gumshoe routine.

He either didn't know it was an interrogation or didn't care. "I just couldn't go," he said. "I got as far as the door and I just started bawling. There wasn't anything I could take from her place that would preserve her memory better than I could in my heart." He paused to wipe tears from his eyes. A weird little storm settled over Bryce. I was sorry I'd said anything—at least in front of his boyfriend.

He took a deep breath, wiped his eyes with the sugar-skull tattoo on the back of his hand and continued. "And I didn't want everyone there treating me like a widow. It wouldn't have been fair to Bryce or to anyone else." And when no one was looking, he reached under the table and squeezed his boyfriend's hand.

I wanted to ask Bronco about George Parker Lennox, but I felt weird asking in front of Bryce. I squirmed a little, and Bronco seemed to pick up on the vibe. "Babe, you think you could get me a soda?" he asked. "They won't let us carry cash."

"I don't think they carry fruit spritzers in that machine," he said.

"At this point, I don't even care," he said. "A Dr. Pepper would taste so good."

Bryce rolled his eyes and got up, muttering about high-fructose corn syrup.

"Something you want to say, Jett?" Bronco said in a low voice.

"Did KitKat ever mention anyone else she was dating? Someone you were her cover for?"

He drew back his hand and went quiet for a minute. He glanced over to make sure Bryce was still wrestling with the vending machine.

"I knew she was in love with someone else," he said. "I'd water her plants sometimes when she went away to see him, and I overheard her on the phone one time, asking about his wife, but I never got his name. I tried to tell my lawyer, but without a name, it didn't do my case much good."

"Does the name George Parker Lennox sound familiar?"

He shook his head. "No—why do you want to know all this?"

Before I could answer, Bryce came back with the soda and Bronco took a grateful—if not staged—swig. I tried to give him a look that said, *I'll explain later.* All I got back was a glance that I translated as hopelessness.

Chapter 19

WHEN YOU WERE MINE

I took what was left of my paycheck to Trader Joe's and stocked my fridge with frozen meals and carton soups. I bought shampoo and toilet paper. I swallowed a sample cup of caramel corn and snuck a second when the sample girl wasn't looking. I stopped by Hartford and hid Philip's packet of dirty dainties in my Trader Joe's bag, and when I got off the subway there was a message from Sid. *Got behind on work,* he wrote. *I'll be by a little after six. Need me to bring anything?*

Just the usual, I wrote back.

A cheap bottle of wine and a corkscrew. One of these days, I'm just going to buy you one.

Then you won't have an excuse to come over anymore. I added a little smiley face so he'd know I was joking.

I'll always find an excuse, he wrote. *You have all my records.*

WHEN SID SHOWED up, he had two brown paper bags, one in his fist and the other under his arm. "Look what I found the other day," he said, setting the wine down on the table and holding out Cyndi Lauper's *She's So Unusual*. "Cyndi was my first crush. I haven't thought about this album in years, but it was right up front in a box of vinyl at the bookstore next to the liquor store. Thought we could listen to it tonight."

"You know how the turntable works," I said.

He went to the living room while I got our enchiladas out of the oven. I hadn't heard "Money Changes Everything" in years, but I still knew the tune enough to hum a little under my breath.

I came out of the kitchen and almost dropped the plates. There was something intimate and sexy about the way Sid was working to open the bottle of wine, his lean hand wriggling the cork with a soft squeak against the green glass. I had to remember to breathe, to set the plates down, to hold on to the glass he placed in my hand instead of letting it fall slack between my fingers.

"You have any luck finding the guy who made KitKat's tape?" he asked, ruining the moment he didn't know we were having.

"George Parker Lennox," I said. "A professor in Binghamton."

"Ooh, hot for teacher," he said. "How very Van Halen."

"Yeah, except I don't know what to do now," I said. "He's married, and I don't think he knows she's dead."

"You should return the tape to him," he said. "You should be the one to tell him. In person."

"How?" I asked. "I can't just call him up and say, 'Hey, your girlfriend is dead and I have your tape.' Besides"—I took a bite of my enchilada—"he lives in Binghamton, I don't have a car, and I'm sure as hell not taking the bus by myself to some strange city to tell a guy his mistress got murdered."

"You think he killed her?"

"I doubt it," I said. "Not with the songs he chose." I handed him the track list I'd typed up. "He broke up with her, sure, but he didn't kill her."

Sid chewed thoughtfully for a minute. "You're quite the Rockford," he said, grinning out of the left side of his mouth. "I wouldn't have put all that together." My heart did that little hollow flutter thing it does every so often when I'm about to fall in love, and he continued. "Look, if you want to go—and I think you should—I'll go with you. We might even be able to borrow Terry's car for a day. He's rarely in any shape to drive it."

My stomach dropped. I appreciated his offer, but that now meant I had to confront George and give him the news. And if his wife was the killer, that would put me on her hit list. I started to feel dizzy and flushed, like the wine had gone straight to my head even though I'd only taken two sips. "And if he's the killer?"

"Then you'll have me to protect you." He mopped up some sauce with a spare scrap of tortilla. "But let's not make any plans until I'm sure I can get the car." He took a sip of his wine and perused the track list like it was a menu at a fancy restaurant. "I don't know half of these," he confessed. "But the Smiths track is a nice touch. A classic in the pining genre, if I do say so myself. I think I put that on a mix tape I made the girl I sat behind in History."

"Did it work?"

"Nope," he said, blushing a little. "If I recall correctly, she threw the tape at me in the lunchroom, called me a loser, and walked away laughing with her girlfriends. Haven't thought about that sting in a while."

I poured a little more wine in his glass to balm the pain. "We've all been there," I said. "Dan DeRosier, like most seventh-grade boys, wasn't exactly thrilled by the mix tape I gave him before our field trip to Hersheypark. I found it stuck in a fence with all the tape unwound."

Now it was Sid's turn to refill my glass. "I'll drink to that," he said. "Cheers—to all the great music no one understood. Their loss."

"Eh, it wasn't so great," I admitted. "I think it had Sting's 'Fields of Gold' on there. I wasn't quite as sophisticated a listener as I am these days."

"I love 'Fields of Gold'!" Sid argued. "It's a romantic song!"

"Oh, Sid," I said. "Sid, it is so corny! Next you're going to tell me you like 'Have You Ever Really Loved a Woman.'"

"It's not my favorite, but it's not that bad."

By now I was laughing so hard I could barely speak. "It has a lyric about seeing a woman's unborn children *in her eyes*. That's *so* creepy."

"Oh, so when Peter Gabriel sings it and John Cusack's standing outside your window with a goddamn boombox, that's romantic, but when Bryan Adams says it, it's creepy."

"Yes." I gestured with my glass. "Because Bryan Adams sang 'Summer of '69' and he is gross." I was ignoring the fact that Catch had put "All for Love" on a mix for me. His memory was not going to darken this perfect moment.

Sid got up to turn over the record. "I guess I have to erase 'Heaven' from your mix tape," he said, rummaging through the crate. "Maybe you'd prefer something a little lyrically deeper, like 'This Is the Time.'" He held up *The Bridge* like evidence at a trial.

"That's not fair!" I shouted. "That record was forced on me!"

"Was it, Miss Bennett? Or are you just trying to cover for the fact that you lied to the good people of Barter Street about your tastes in music?"

I grabbed the lyrics to "Wither Without You" and held them up. "This song, Your Honor, should prove my innocence," I said. "Mac forced me to buy *that* record in exchange for finding out who wrote this song."

"A likely story."

I wanted to kiss him. The urge came on strong and sudden; we were laughing so hard and his grin was so perfect and genuine and beautiful that I just wanted to grab his face in my hands and kiss him hard.

But instead, fearing rejection, I snatched the record out of his hands. "And what's this? Cyndi Lauper cowrote and sang backing vocals on 'Code of Silence'? What do you have to say for *yourself*, Mr. McNeill?"

"I'd say we should finish our dinner," he said. "I think we're getting too silly."

He went back to the table and I went into the kitchen to cut and plate the lemon tart I'd picked up for dessert. When I came out, he was still standing, reading over the lyrics.

"It's beautiful, isn't it?" I said. "Like the kind of song you sit by the radio for, hoping your crush will dedicate it to you."

"What is it?"

"The last track on KitKat's mix," I said, taking a bite of my tart. It was still a little frozen in the middle. "I can't find it on iTunes or Pandora or anything. Makes me sad that she never got this. I think he really loved her."

"With a song like this, yeah," said Sid. "He deserves a chance to mourn for her." He took a bite of his own slice and reached over to squeeze my hand. "And you're the only person who can give that to him."

Chapter 20

ANOTHER SAD LOVE SONG

S id poured the last of the wine into his glass and pursed his thin, chapped lips like he was trying to figure out a math problem in the last ten seconds of class. "When was the last time," he began, his words paced and measured with wine, "you were really in love?" He picked up the tape off the coffee table and turned it over in his fingers. "Love like this," he said, waggling the tape. "Love that burrows into your gut, breaks your heart, and feels like salvation on Sunday all at once?"

I wasn't sure I'd ever been in love like that before. Love was always an ache to me, a slow, heavy burn, and I hadn't loved anyone since Catch had walked out of my kitchen. Even before that, I was never one of those girls who'd gotten giddy counting down the days until a one-month anniversary; I never drew hearts around a boy's name on the paper jacket of a chemistry textbook. Love always hit me upside the skull like a sock full of nickels in a prison riot, and too often, by the time I got to my feet, the stars that had been circling my eyes were all gone.

So whether it was the wine or "All Through the Night" or the way he was draping his other arm over the back of the couch like he'd forgotten it, like the spark of a lighter, the urge to kiss him returned, even stronger than before. I wanted to make out with him right here, take advantage of his pleasant inebriation to trick him into loving me, even for just the night, just long enough to fight back the sudden onset of loneliness.

"I don't remember," I breathed, my mouth dry. "You?"

His mouth split into a dizzy smile. "I'm in love right now," he said.

My heartbeat sped up. I ran my tongue across my lips. I waited for a confession that I knew wasn't coming, staring at him like we were separated by a TV screen. I could whisper *love* to Paul Rudd, and Ewan McGregor could serenade me alone with "Your Song," but, like Sid in this moment, I knew that whatever words he was about to whisper were never meant for me. Might as well get it over with.

"With who?" I asked.

"My beautiful Cinderella," he answered, gesturing grandly with his glass. "It's like high school again—we have these great talks when we're together, but I just haven't drummed up the courage to ask her out." He drank like it would give him that courage. "Soon," he said. "And I want you to be the first of my friends to meet her. I think you two will get along great."

My heart felt like broken glass in my chest. Where the wine made him sentimental, it turned me bitter. Bitter about KitKat and George, bitter about Catch, bitter about Sid and Cinderella.

"Here's what I don't get about love," I said, changing the subject. "If you love someone, why wouldn't you be with that person? There are all sorts of shitty songs, like Eagle-Eye Cherry's 'Save Tonight'—God, I hate that song—that are all about two people in love having to break apart. Why? Why can't people who love each other just be together?" I drained the last of my wine in one hard swallow. I wasn't posing the question to him—I was posing it to George and Catch and every other broken heart turning out a light in some lonely little apartment somewhere in the world.

Sid sighed and took another drink. "Circumstance," he said,

the glitter gone from his eyes. "I never understood it either until I had to leave Katy behind."

"Why didn't she come with you?" I asked. He'd mentioned his ex sparingly; if anything, it sounded like he missed Shayna, the dog he'd had to leave with his parents, more than he missed her. He still kept pictures of Shayna on his phone.

"It wasn't love enough, I guess," he said. "She had her life and I had mine and they just weren't going to mesh."

I stood, grabbing the empty wine bottle and taking it into the kitchen. Maybe my grandmother had an extra one stashed somewhere, a bottle left over from a party I'd forgotten I'd thrown, a housewarming present of Two-Buck Chuck or cheap champagne. "But love is supposed to be simple," I said, raising my voice so he could hear me from the kitchen. "It's math. You plus me equals us."

I found nothing and buried my face in my hands. After a deep breath I stood up and found Sid standing in the doorway with his coat draped over his arm, our bodies just inches apart.

"I'm sorry," I said, wiping tears I didn't know had formed out of my eyes. "It's just been a long time for me."

"I know," he said. "It's been a long time for me too." He cupped my chin in one hand and kissed my forehead. He smelled like cool water and red wine. "But it'll happen to you the same way it happened to me—when you least expect it."

I wanted to swat his hand away. I wanted to slap him across the face. I wanted to put my head on his chest and pound on him with balled fists while I howled with rage. Instead I just stood there with the empty bottle forgotten in my hand. "Don't go," I pleaded, lifting my free hand to his chest. "Stay the night. I'll sleep on the couch and make us breakfast."

He shook his head like it weighed a hundred pounds. "I can't," he said, closing his hand around mine. "I've got someplace I need to be. Some other night, maybe, when we've got tomorrow off. We'll watch *The Commish* and eat Trader Joe's baked brie. Promise."

She's So Unusual clicked off as I watched him close the door behind him. My heart felt like a Tom Waits song. My phone rang in my pocket and I had to set down the bottle to answer it.

"Want to come into Hartford tonight?" Susan asked.

Sid had left his corkscrew on the dining room table. I swallowed a rock in my throat. "Sure," I said. "I can be there in an hour."

Chapter 21

TEEN ANGST (WHAT THE WORLD NEEDS NOW)

had been asleep for about three hours when my phone rang. When I'd crawled home from Hartford at six A.M., I had been too exhausted to remember to turn it off. I fumbled to send the call to voice mail, but Natalie's voice came loud and clear over speakerphone. "You want to get some breakfast?" she said. "I'm hungover as shit and I'm, like, two blocks from your place."

"Your hangover and my three hours of sleep," I groaned. "We're perfectly matched misery."

"Put on a party dress and some heels and we can match better," she said.

She could get me out of bed, but she wasn't going to get me dressed. I put on some water to boil for coffee even though my stomach was hollow and jumpy from the three cups I'd had at Hartford. I eyed the two ring Danishes I'd picked up at Key Food because they were buy-one-get-one-free and, with a sigh, cracked open the plastic on the blueberry. She could have a piece of the free one.

I buzzed her up when she rang and left the door slightly ajar. She was wearing a striped hoodie over a short-sleeved dress that fit her like snakeskin, spike-heeled booties, and morning-after shadows of makeup. When we hugged, I could smell stale cigarettes and men's deodorant.

She smirked. "Guitar player," she said. "I know I keep saying I'll only sleep with bass players, but this guy was especially hot." Baldrick rubbed up against her legs. "Aww, is this KitKat's cat?" she asked, picking him up. "I was wondering what happened to him."

"I used to watch him a lot, so I figured he would be used to me," I said.

If she was listening, she wouldn't have been able to hear over the baby noises she was making at Baldrick, who looked at me with increasing distress. It wasn't until I said, "You want coffee?" that she finally put him down and paid attention to me.

"Obviously, but I'm not going to be seen with you dressed like that," she said, pointing to my Michael McDonald T-shirt and sushi pajama pants.

"Good, 'cause I'm not going out," I replied. "Today you dine at Café Jett." I put the Danish and our coffee cups on a tray, carrying it with one arm while I held the full French press with the other hand.

She rolled her eyes but poured a cup of coffee anyway. I added milk and sugar to mine and took a small sip. I wanted to be awake enough to talk to her, but not so wired that I wouldn't be able to get back to sleep when she left.

"Have you been out to see Bronco?" she asked.

I nodded and took a too-big bite of pastry. I had to chew for a minute before I answered. "Few days ago. You?"

"I'm heading up later today," she said. "Been busy planning the benefit—part of the money will go to his bail, the rest we're going to use to start a scholarship in KitKat's name. That's the tough part, all sorts of paperwork to fill out, shit like that." She ate her own piece of Danish and licked frosting off her thumb.

Scholarship. Maybe Natalie would have a line on our lovelorn professor Lennox. "Did KitKat ever mention dating someone in Binghamton? Someone besides Bronco?"

"Not that I know of," she said. "You know what? Check that.

We were out shopping one time and she took a phone call that she wouldn't let me hear. When I asked who it was, she wouldn't tell me. Said it was just a guy she knew, not to worry about it. But I know a fuck-ton of guys, and I don't sneak off into the dressing room to take their calls."

So it wasn't just me. I wondered what other life KitKat had kept hidden from all of us. A husband? A child? A whole week-end family parked in some cul-de-sac a hundred miles from here? It was outlandish, sure, but dating a married man was hardly the scandal of the century. She could have blabbed to anyone on Barter Street and the most she would have gotten was a disgusted look, maybe. Natalie probably would have let her guest-blog on the art of being a side piece. Between her and Bronco, they knew a thing or two about how to keep an affair a secret.

Natalie was over it. "What's your excuse?" she asked, gesturing again to my pajamas. "You kick Sid out when I called?"

"What do you mean?"

She took another piece of Danish and grinned. "You know what I mean," she said. "You and him, you're practically married. Does he have a big dick? He looks like he'd have a big dick."

"We're not sleeping together," I said. "That would screw up our—"

"Shut your girl mouth," she snapped. "Just shut it." She took out a cigarette and tapped it against her thigh. I pointed to the window and she parked herself on the radiator, lighting up and blowing a long, harsh trail of smoke through the screen. "You know you want to fuck him, so just fucking do it already."

"I'm not his type," I said. "He's got the hots for some stripper out in Queens."

She snorted. "You should fuck somebody," she said, pausing her smoking just long enough to drink some of her coffee. "I should get you my spreadsheet, find you a decent lay. Heaven knows you could use it."

I wasn't sure if Natalie's bluntness was normal or a side effect of her hangover, but whatever it was, she was probably right. "I think I can probably find my own date, thanks," I said.

"Do that," she said, opening the screen just enough to flick her cigarette butt out the window. "But when you do, leave your jammies at home."

Chapter 22

HOLD ON MY HEART

Maybe Natalie was onto something. Maybe a one-night stand would reset all this misplaced angst over Sid. But I wasn't about to pick up some guy at a bar, and after Natalie had left behind her half-finished coffee and a lonesome piece of blueberry Danish, I got out the Boyfriend Box. I closed my eyes and reached in, my hand wrapping around something plush. I pulled out a bear wearing a *Somebody at Rutgers Loves Me* T-shirt, a present from Gabe.

At nineteen, Gabe had gelled-back black hair like a G.I. Joe and pants that zipped off into shorts at the knee. He had silver eyes and a Han Solo smile; spoke fluent German, Russian, and Hungarian just for fun; paid for everything; and sent me a dozen roses on all three of our one-month anniversaries.

He'd been back from his freshman year at Rutgers and doing landscaping for his aunt in the next town over, and we'd dated the summer between my junior and senior years of high school—*dating* being a euphemism for making out in the red velour back-seat of his Buick Century. He was the first guy to get his hands down my panties and the first guy I made orgasm.

It was a brief and passionate romance, the only one I ever had that wasn't marked with a mix tape or CD. All he'd had in his glove compartment were U2 albums; "Where the Streets Have No Name" became our go-to song for dry humping. Even now when I hear it, I swear I can still smell the Calvin Klein Eternity he wore, hear the highway wind blowing past open windows on even the calmest day.

He went home to New Jersey for a week to visit his family and sent me three-page letters every day, each detailing the ache of his heart at the distances between us, the blue of the ocean that reminded him of my eyes. When he went back to college, he sent this bear as soon as he arrived on campus.

If we'd dated another month or so, I probably would have lost my virginity to him, but we broke up two weeks later and lost touch despite our pledge to stay friends. But unlike Ryan, whom I did lose my virginity to—as did my best friend, Amy—Gabe, like Jeremy, fell into the category of "good" exes.

Gabe's Facebook status listed him as single; his most recent pictures were from a family trip to Germany. He didn't look any different—like Tuck Everlasting, never aging, never changing. A private message didn't seem like the most romantic way for an old lover to reach out, but it was all I had. I kept it brief: *How are you, I'm in NYC, thinking about you, drop me a line.* I wasn't about to pour my heart out to someone who might just tell me to fuck off—if he wrote back at all.

I put the lid on the Boyfriend Box and shoved it into the closet. But I kept the bear out and took it with me when I got back into bed. I fell asleep holding it but dreamed instead of Sid.

I SLEPT UNTIL about one, waking only when Sid texted me about coming over that night. The Rutgers bear was on the floor; there was an empty mug on the bedside table and a message from Gabe in my inbox.

So good to hear from you!!!! Has it really been ten years!?!?! I still smile when I think of you. I still have those chili pepper boxers. Brooklyn, huh? I'm in Pittsburgh these days, translation work for top secret instruc-

tion manuals. *I'll probably have to kill you just for mentioning it. J/K. I'm actually in NYC until tomorrow, short notice, but can we get dinner?*

And a phone number. Not a bad way to restart the day.

I texted Sid and told him that I got called in for an evening shift. It was easier to lie over static characters than fumble for an explanation and a way to make it up to him later, but I still tasted ash in the back of my throat.

I called Gabe and got his voice mail. One P.M. on a Thursday; he was probably in a meeting. Meanwhile, I was sitting around an apartment I was all but squatting in, unshowered, in an oversized Michael McDonald tour T-shirt I'd permanently borrowed from my dad. I felt like a slacker.

The phone rang, but it wasn't my general ringtone. It was MetroReaders, and I snatched it up. "Can you go in to Hartford at three?" asked Susan.

It would be a tight squeeze, but if I didn't fully blow-dry my hair, I could make it. I gathered up Philip's lingerie as I agreed. "And there's a note for you here," she added. "'Bring the documents'—does that mean anything?"

I looked at the bra in my fist. "Just a little homework," I said. "Tell Hartford I'll be there at three."

PHILIP WASN'T IN, so I slipped the packet into his bottom desk drawer before returning to the temp lounge, where real work awaited. I drank a lot of coffee and marked a lot of sticky notes, and my heart beat so fast with caffeine and anticipation that I swore I was disturbing everyone else in the room. We weren't allowed to have our phones on, so every time I went to the bathroom, I checked for a message from Gabe. At four I resorted to the desperate girl's move of texting him despite having already called, just to let him know that I couldn't check my phone and texts were probably the best way to get in touch with me. I went to the bathroom twice more, just to see if he'd responded. He hadn't, and I was starting to regret canceling on Sid.

At four thirty, I texted Sid. He got back to me quickly and said he had plans. Just to make my day worse, I asked him what he was doing. He said he was going to see Cinderella. I fumed and didn't write back.

At five, when I was out of drafts to read, Susan let me go. I was about to get on the subway and call it all quits when my phone rang.

"I'm so sorry about not getting back to you," Gabe said. "I was in this insane meeting all day, and just as I was about to text you back, my boss called and yammered through the rest of my lunch break. I swear, every time I tried to pull out my phone, something distracted me. But I'm all yours now and I hope you haven't made plans for dinner."

I had, but they involved digging some half-forgotten TV dinner out of the back of the freezer and feeling sorry for myself in front of a rerun of *Parks and Recreation*. Whatever Gabe had planned, even if it was hot dogs at Gray's Papaya, sounded infinitely better.

"I'm free," I said. "What did you have in mind?"

"This probably doesn't sound ideal to you because you live here, but everyone and their brother has been telling me that I have to go to the Shake Shack, that they can't believe I've been coming to New York *without* going to the Shake Shack, that I should light a candle and confess to my priest that I haven't been to the Shake Shack. So I was thinking the Shake Shack. How does that sound?"

I laughed. "I've always thought Markburger on St. Mark's made a better burger, but if it keeps you in the good graces of your lord and savior, we can do Shake Shack." Early April still had a chill in the air, but I wasn't about to say no to anything Gabe suggested, even if it meant shivering in an outdoor line for half an hour.

"Oh thank God," he breathed in fake adulation. "Where are you?"

"I'm right on Union Square, so even six blocks away, I can just see the end of the line."

"Then why don't you hop on queue and I'll be over in a few."

"Will you recognize me?"

I could hear him grin through the phone. "Jett," he said. "I could never forget your beautiful face."

He hung up and I started the walk up Broadway, sweating with excitement. I wished I had time to change; my work clothes, bought on the quick and cheap, weren't exactly date-night fashion. Black pants, a red polo, and a black cardigan with polka-dot flats. Though in the right light, it had a chill, Amy Winehouse vibe to it. He was probably in a suit. But it didn't matter—if the dinner went really well, it wouldn't matter what we were wearing. Only what we weren't.

Chapter 23

LIKE A VIRGIN

saw Gabe before he saw me. He didn't look any different at twenty-nine than he had at nineteen, except the zip-off cargo pants had been replaced with khakis, and his preppy striped polo was now a crewneck sweater. When he spotted me, he rushed over and swept me up in a hug like he'd never put me down. He still wore Eternity, only slightly less than he used to.

"It's so good to see you!" he kept saying. "You look amazing!"

My face got warm and my knees got weak. The long line gave us time to make small talk. He asked what I did and I left out the part about trying to solve my friend's murder—at least on the first date, anyway. He was living in Pittsburgh, spending his days translating instruction manuals and his evenings watching Netflix with his dog. "My sister Trisha's watching Madmartigan while I'm gone," he said, holding up his phone to show me a picture of a bright-eyed schipperke.

"Of course you would name your dog after *Willow*," I said. "She's beautiful."

"She's the only girl in my life right now," he confessed. "What about you? You got anyone wondering where you are?"

"Not unless you count the cat," I said. I still felt bad about blowing off Sid. The worst part was that he was probably relieved—this way he could go see his Cinderella. I soured at the thought.

"That's a shame." He smiled that same dreamy smile I'd picked out of the audience during my show choir solo. "For guys, I mean," he said, correcting himself. "They're all missing out. They should be lined up outside your door."

We ordered: two ShackBurgers—mine without tomato—and fries. He got a beer and I got a glass of wine in a tulip-shaped plastic cup that could have passed for fancy glassware to a distant eye. He started to go for his wallet, but I got to mine faster. "You're a guest," I said. I was a liberated woman on payday; I could splurge for Shake Shack. "Besides, you paid for all our dates back in high school. Let me treat."

"One condition," he said with a wicked grin. "You let me get dessert."

WE DIDN'T GET dessert. He kissed me in a moment of soft silence, long after our burgers were crumbs and just as Manhattan was starting to turn neon against a deepening sky. We kissed in the cab back to his hotel in Midtown, and by the time we got into the elevator, it was all I could do not to tear his clothes off in the thirty-second ride to his floor.

His hotel room was a far cry from the backseat of his Buick Century—spacious, sleek, and white like heaven, with a bed the size of a cruise ship. My heart thumped in my chest like a rockabilly bass line. This was really happening. I was finally going to have sex with the beautiful, silver-eyed man who should have deflowered me a decade ago. If I had the ability to travel through time, I would have used it to go back to my seventeen-year-old self and give her a high five.

But I was still thinking about Sid. I wondered if he was banging Cinderella in the alley between dances. I wondered if he was thinking of me, lamenting the night we'd lost to my lie.

Of course he wasn't. He was up to his glitter-stung eyeballs in silicone and overpriced well whiskey.

I yanked Gabe's sweater up over his head. He mimicked the action with my polo shirt and pulled us both down onto the bed, me on his lap, him hard through his slacks. He kissed me, his mouth savory with beer and wanting. He lay back and I felt like a goddess. I wanted to run to my phone and tweet *I'm having a one-night stand with an ex! I am a liberated woman!*

Gabe rolled me onto my back and turned on his side, reaching into the nightstand and pulling out a three-pack of condoms he had next to the Bible. "Please don't think I'm presumptuous," he said, his expression sweet and soft and almost afraid. "Just hopeful. As soon as you messaged me, I went out and bought these, on the off chance that I might finally get to be with you."

I was surprised at how turned on I was by the gesture. In the back of my head, I'd always thought I should have given him my virginity in a fit of Eternity-scented passion.

In reality, it had been a very calculated affair; Ryan and I had decided on a time and place to mutually surrender, and there were ten minutes of well-rehearsed foreplay we'd been practicing in the backseat of his dad's Subaru, followed by another ten of awkward pumping. It wasn't the worst way to give it up, but it wasn't the most romantic or exciting either.

And it had been so long since I'd had sex that it was almost like I'd gotten my virginity back. That was at least one advantage to involuntary celibacy.

I kissed his shoulder while he tore one off the strip. He left it waiting on the bedside table as he pried open my zipper, guiding my pants down my legs. I wrangled open his pants. He was wearing chili pepper boxers. "Not the same ones," he admitted. "But I guess even these new ones are lucky."

I forgot about KitKat, about Baldrick, about Sid and Cinderella. For the moment, there was only Gabe, his chili pepper boxers, a condom on the bedside table, and my wanton, lonely lust.

I GOT DRESSED the minute he went to the bathroom. I was never into hanging out naked after sex; even if I was spending the night, I had to at least have panties on and, ideally, a T-shirt and maybe a pair of socks, because my feet get cold easily. I didn't see the point of remaining unclothed; the part that required you to be nude was over, anything else just felt like an awkward tease. After all, you don't wear your cheerleading uniform off the field or your tux at ten A.M. Nudity was the uniform of sex, and I was eager to get back to my work clothes.

"You want me to order room service?" he asked when he came out of the bathroom.

Gabe was beautiful and he was good in bed, but in the time between climax and comedown, I'd realized there wasn't much else to him than that. We'd only kissed because we'd run out of things to talk about. Already the conversation felt awkward as he stood there, clearly fine with post-sex nudity.

"I should go," I said, pulling on my socks.

"You can stay," he said. "My plane doesn't leave until tomorrow afternoon. We can have room-service brunch sent up."

I didn't want to stay, not even for room-service brunch. "I'd love to," I lied, "but the cat doesn't have any food." As a pet owner, I hoped he'd sympathize. If he didn't, well, I'd have to come up with some other excuse.

Disappointment registered on his face for a brief, fleeting moment. "I understand," he said. "Can I call you next time I'm in the city? After all, I still owe you dessert."

"Sure," I said. But I didn't expect him to, and even if he did, it might not be much more than a booty call. He wasn't the same teenage boy; he was a man, and a good one at that. But he wasn't a man I knew anymore, just a blind date, a sweet stranger, a decent lay. We couldn't reconstruct the sand-castle love affair we'd had with one night of sex; the tide had come in and washed away the foundation, leaving only pleasantries and half-hazy memories.

We took the elevator down in silence. He kissed me at the door, got me a cab, and waved until I turned the corner. My apartment seemed darker when I got home. Baldrick was asleep on the couch and my Rutgers bear was facedown on the floor. I put the teddy back in the box, put on the pajamas Philip had bought me, and went to bed.

Chapter 24

SING FOR ABSOLUTION

he low ceilings of the Brenner Gallery made Mac's band, Chicken Puppet, sound even louder than normal. The place was packed with Egg School regulars, record nerds from Ol' Vinylsides, SVA art students, and all the other wonderful Barter Street ilks. I was proud of myself—I'd finally had a flyer to leave at Hartford, and sure enough, Marty was there in his porkpie hat. I had worn KitKat's red dress even though I hadn't sewn the torn sleeve back on, hiding the damage under a gray cardigan.

"I brought this for the Irony Auction," I said to Natalie, holding out *The Bridge*.

She rolled her eyes and snorted. "You'd have to *pay* someone to take it."

I sighed and shoved it back into my lobster tote bag. Sid was already there and two drinks in, but he was clean shaven and bright eyed. He gave me a heavy, half-drunk hug and shoved a glass of boxed wine into my hand.

"Terry said we can borrow his car!" he shouted over Chicken Puppet's cover of Head East's "Never Been Any Reason." "He wants us to do him a favor first, but he won't tell me what. I'll let you know, though."

I wasn't sure I wanted to do any favor Terry would ask of me, but I had to get to Binghamton soon. "I still need to call George, but do you think we could go next weekend?" I asked.

"Hopefully," Sid said. "I'll try to get whatever he wants us to do out of the way."

Mac handed the microphone over to Natalie while Chicken Puppet started packing up their equipment behind her. "We've got a lot of good stuff tonight," she announced. "All the art on the wall's for sale and we're going to start the Irony Auction soon, but right now, we're opening up the stage for anyone who wants it." She held up a Barbie beach bucket. "Ten bucks gets you two minutes of mic time for your poetry, shitty stand-up—Sid, I know you've got that great joke about Panera Bread." Sid laughed and raised his glass in toast. "Fuck, read the dictionary if you want, but seriously, get up here and make an ass of yourself. All the proceeds go to the Save Bronco Fund and the KitKat Memorial Scholarship, so if you're not going to entertain us, at least buy something."

A guy with flippy girl hair and an ill-fitting T-shirt got up first to play a comatose love song on his guitar. Josie sang in German while her friend Elliot backed her up on the accordion, and Marty growled Leonard Cohen's "Famous Blue Raincoat." I took a deep breath and two fives out of my wallet.

"What have you got planned?" Sid asked.

I hadn't sung solo in front of an audience since that senior recital; even the few times I'd gone to karaoke, I'd stuck to group songs and hid in the back. When Catch and I split, I may have gotten Warren Zevon, but Catch had taken my voice like a hostage. But suddenly, I had to be back on that stage again. "You'll just have to see," I said, dropping my dead presidents in the beach bucket and signing my name on the list.

"Whatever it is," Sid said, reaching down and squeezing my hand, "you'll be great."

They called my name after a pretty bad stand-up act and bids for an *ET* cookie jar and an unopened case of Surge. I climbed onto the makeshift stage and took the microphone out of the stand.

"Th-this one's for KitKat," I stammered. "I know she would have loved it."

I closed my eyes, and then quickly remembered what my choir teacher Mrs. Whiteman told me about singing with my eyes closed: *It tells the audience you don't know what you're doing.* But I didn't know what I was doing. I was singing a song I'd only heard once and might have misheard the lyrics to. But I was up there and I'd already spent the only cash in my wallet—I had to at least try. I couldn't be any worse than the guy with flippy girl hair.

"I wither without you," I crooned. "I crumble before you . . ." I fixed my eyes on Sid but couldn't read his face. He was watching me like I was a stranger, like he might drop his glass, like my song was cutting straight into his heart. I muscled up on the second verse and put everything I had into it. "Stars fall flash and slash my heart . . ." I sang for KitKat, for George, for Catch, wherever they were. And I sang for Sid because he was right there in front of me, because he was all I had in the whole fucking world.

And I hit that last note so perfectly that it hung in the air like a crystal chandelier. I'd never hit a note with such clarity, such perfect roundness. I wished Mrs. Whiteman was there to hear it.

I smiled when I murmured my thank-you and the audience cheered with the same wine-drenched adoration they gave everyone. I wasn't special, I didn't blow anyone's mind, but I hadn't totally screwed up, and it was all worth it, just for that one note. Natalie hugged me. Marty grinned and shook my shoulder. Mac gave me a high five and Josie squeezed my hands with a squeal.

But when I tried to find Sid, he wasn't anywhere to be found.

Chapter 25

LETTERS FROM THE WASTELAND

My throat was a little sore when I woke up the next morning. I hadn't warmed up properly, probably hadn't had enough water to drink beforehand, but I was still glowing with post-performance warmth. I made tea instead of coffee and texted Sid.

Where'd you go last night? He didn't respond.

But Terry had promised us his car, which meant that I had one last piece of our itinerary to put together. I pulled up George's class page, his office phone number. I stared at his photo, wondering how the hell I was going to tell him.

I fed Baldrick, put a load of laundry in one of the basement washing machines, finished my tea, listened to the entire A-side of Warren Zevon's *Bad Luck Streak in Dancing School* and finally, finally got up enough nerve to call George Parker Lennox. Knowing he wouldn't be there on the weekend, I left a nervous message on his office phone. "Um . . . hi, my name is . . . Jett Bennett and I'm . . . uh . . . a friend of KitKat's. . . . I need to talk to you, so if you could, um, call me back, maybe we could meet. I have something for you. Thanks. Bye."

By the time I hung up the phone, I was sweating and shaking.

I had no idea how I was going to tell him, but I knew I didn't want to do it over the phone. I wanted to go to Binghamton, meet him in person, hand him the tape and tell him I was sorry. He loved KitKat. He deserved better than a disembodied voice on the other end of the line.

A FEW HOURS later I was making some pierogies and was surprised to see George Parker Lennox's office phone number ringing my line.

"This is George," a voice with a slight lisp said. "Who are you?"

"My name's Jett Bennett, I'm a friend of KitKat's," I said. "I need to talk to you."

"I have nothing to say," he said.

"Can we please meet?" I begged. "It's really important."

"When?" he demanded.

"Next Saturday?" I just hoped Sid didn't have plans he couldn't cancel.

George was silent for a minute, and I held my breath. "The Belmar," he finally said. "Nine o'clock Saturday night. And if you say anything to my wife, I'll tell her that it's a senior prank and call the cops." With that, he hung up.

My next call was to Sid. But before I explained the situation, he had explaining of his own to do. "Where did you go last night?" I asked. "You missed my set."

"I know, and I'm sorry," he said. "I just stepped outside for a minute; I wasn't feeling good. Something I ate, I'm sure, but what I heard was great."

I didn't believe him. I don't know if he really expected me too. "George says we can meet Saturday," I said. "Can you get the car?"

"Shouldn't be a problem," he said. "Cinderella's doing a show Friday night, but we could go up Saturday morning. I'll see what Terry wants in exchange and let you know later."

Fucking Cinderella. I was about to have the most awkward,

awful conversation of my life and all he could think about was a lap dance. "Fine," I said. "Meet me at my place at noon."

My phone buzzed the minute I hung up. I was popular today. A text from Natalie: *Benefit raised enough for bail, Bronco's out Friday!!!!* she wrote. *ES Sat. to CELEBRATE!!!*

I sure as hell couldn't drive to the worst day of GPL's life on an empty stomach. I texted her back and agreed. There was always time for brunch.

Chapter 26

GIMME THE GOODS

I didn't hear from Sid for another two days and when he did finally call, he had an ominous request.

"I need you to go to Chinatown with me," he said. "Terry wants us to score him some Oxy for a party he's throwing while we're away. It's his condition for letting me use the car."

"He can't get it himself?" I asked. I'd rather just give Terry the money. Hell, I'd rather blow him—at least if I got caught, I wouldn't have a felony possession charge fucking up my life.

"He doesn't trust anyone but this girl who won't return his calls."

"And how do we know this isn't some sort of setup?"

Sid sighed and I braced myself for whatever he had to say. "Gloria's one of the dancers from Fairy Tales," he said. "She knows me. She'll get the Oxy for us; all we have to do is pick it up and pay her. As long as she doesn't know it's for him, she'll play. Terry told me to tell her it's for you."

"Why me?"

"Because you don't have insurance," he said. "I've got health care, I could get my own damn pain pills. Terry said she cut him off when she figured out he was using it recreationally, but he insists that you haven't played *Mario Kart 64* until you've played while wasted on Oxy."

"He thought of everything," I snorted. "Are you sure she won't narc you out to your Cinderella?"

I could hear him roll his eyes through the phone. "Do you want to go to Binghamton or not?" he snapped.

"Fine," I said. "I'll meet you in an hour."

SID AND I went over our plan in vague whispers on the subway: I fell down some stairs, clinic only gave me Tylenol, just a few until the swelling comes down. I took his hand and he guided me past stalls where men whispered, *Gucci, gold watch, perfume,* and women pleaded, *Jewelry, Blu-ray, iPhone.* Three weeks ago, my friend Birdie from MetroReaders had her phone stolen, and some cheap dope probably purchased it from a booth like this, fully convinced that the low price and dimly lit stall made for a completely legitimate place of business, that the $200 paid for their latest-generation iPhone was proof of smart bargaining skills and not the culmination of material heartbreak. I double-checked to make sure my purse was zipped, not that my two-year-old brick of a phone would fetch a very high price, unless there was some irony black market I was unaware of.

Sid periodically checked his phone and followed Terry's directions toward a game store on Mott Street, up a dimly lit flight of stairs to apartment 2B. He knocked four times. "Try to limp a little," he whispered.

A chunky blonde with round tits and too-big sweatpants answered the door with neon eyes and a smile you could have sold toothpaste with. "Hi, Sid," she said with a Jersey honk. "I got the dumplings you asked for. You said ten, right?"

I had a momentary panic. Were we going to have to sit and eat takeout with this woman? I just wanted to get our drugs and get out. I was a proud DARE graduate; I had sewn the shirt into my

T-shirt quilt. I'd only tried pot once and hated it, yet here I was, about to purchase a fistful of illegal pain pills from a stripper. I'd never even seen Oxy.

"This your friend?" she asked, gesturing us inside.

"Yeah," he said. "This is Jett—she really screwed up her knee and the docs at the clinic won't give her anything more than ibuprofen."

I nodded. "Fell down some subway stairs."

"Been there," she said as we followed her into the kitchen. It didn't look like a drug den. It looked more like a funky apartment from a TV show: no doors but the front and the bathroom, with beaded curtains dividing the kitchen and the bedroom and bright green curtains in all the windows. The walls were that same beige of all cheap studios, but she'd garnished them with eighties movie posters: *Dirty Dancing, The Breakfast Club,* and, of course, *Flashdance.* She caught me looking and smirked. "I took a day off from my welding job to meet you guys," she joked.

She reached up into the cabinet, revealing the V of a lime-green G-string as she pulled down a bottle of pills. "You want some coffee or something?" she asked, doling ten out into her hand. "You might need it, these things will knock you flat—a little caffeine will even you out."

"I'm all right, thanks," I said. "I'll wait until I get home."

"Good plan," she said, lighting up a cigarette. "There's nothing quite as terrifying as being on painkillers on the subway." She held the pack out to me and I was strangely tempted to take one. I didn't smoke, but in the two minutes we'd been there, she'd already offered us two amenities. This wasn't just some anonymous drug buy, this was hospitality, a chance to sit and chat with strangers in the hopes that you might become friends. She would have fit in perfectly on Barter Street.

"You gotta be careful with that stuff," she said, gesturing with her smoke. "I busted up my knee playing softball in college. Slid into home, won the game, but I had to be carried off the field. I keep some around still, just in case I have a bad night at the club. Helps pay the bills when I get the early morning legs-and-eggs shift. Those guys don't pay shit."

"Where'd you go to college?" I asked, ashamed that I could hear surprise in my voice.

She pointed to the framed degree hanging over the sink. "Indiana University at Bloomington," she said.

"How'd you end up here?" I asked.

"America's Teachers," she said. "Oh, they promise you a nice master's from NYU, all expenses paid, then stick you in some shithole public school as an assistant, slash your hours until you quit, then demand the money back. It's indentured servitude." She stubbed the cigarette out in the ashtray. "I prefer stripping, actually. Or I did, until Cinderella showed up." She laughed another grim little laugh, all the sadness in the world flickering across her face. I didn't know what she was expecting—company, a friendly chat, maybe dim sum later—but I felt sudden sorrow for her. She seemed so fragile and alone as she lit another cigarette with shaking hands. "Now she gets all the good ones—like Sid here—and I get the creeps like Terry."

Sid shifted in his chair, and it took me a moment to remember that he was sitting right there. "Guess we'd better get going," he muttered.

She took a drag and exhaled like a deflating balloon. "Sure," she said. "Yeah, I've got to get ready for work. Hell, I'll probably see you there."

As if he didn't know what else to do, Sid took out his wallet and slowly counted out the bills. "Just put it on the table," she said, moving to the sink to tap out her ash. "Hope you feel better, Jett."

I almost didn't want to leave. I knew that sadness of hers all too well. It was a melancholy most people never feel, an understanding that this was not how the world was supposed to be. All the Girl Scout badges, the Very Special Episodes, and honor societies couldn't prepare you for the cold hard truth of life—that you get used up, you get kicked around, that sometimes it all just sucks and there's not a damn thing you can do but live through it. The only truth she seemed to have taken away was that, just like in high school, the pretty girl got all the good guys. Amen, sister.

Chapter 27

PEOPLE ARE PEOPLE

The entire crowd of Egg School went silent when Bronco and Bryce walked in Saturday morning. It was the first time I'd seen him since he'd gotten out on Friday and there was something different about him. It wasn't prison ink or west-yard muscles—not after only two weeks—or the drug-monitoring ankle bracelet bulging under his skinny jeans. It was the way he carried himself, as though he was holding a SWAT shield.

Mac gestured them over to our table and patted him on the back. "Good to have you home again."

"For now," he said. "I've still got the trial to get through."

"He'll be fine," Bryce said. "They'll find him not guilty."

I wondered if that meant that Bronco had finally given them his alibi, if this was his way of coming out. If so, he deserved a party with a rainbow cake, like my friend Chris had gotten when he'd made his big announcement our sophomore year of college. But if a courthouse admission was what would keep Bronco out of jail, we could have the cake another day.

"You've got better faith in the system than I do," Bronco muttered.

Natalie gave him a side-hug and smiled. "We'll worry about that when the time comes—how's the real world treating you?"

Before we could get an answer, an iced latte hit the back of Bronco's head and splattered all over our table, ruining the French toast plate I was treating myself to.

"Murderer!" came Brandi's unmistakable snarl.

Bronco whirled out of his seat like a cowboy called coward and faced his assailant, who was sitting at a back table with Jylle, who huffed her polka-dotted ass out of her chair. "I don't want to eat in a place that serves misogynistic murderers," she sneered, picking up a muffin and heaving it at him. "Take your order to go, asshole!"

"Leave him alone!" Bryce yelled.

"What, you think it's okay for a guy to beat a woman's head in?" said Jylle. "Take it back to Reddit, you men's rights activist!"

Bronco covered his face with a menu and shrank into his seat like he was trying to disappear. iPhones came out to record the whole thing, but no one else stood up to take sides. These were the same people who last week couldn't wait to put a ten-spot into Bronco's defense fund; now they were more willing to live-tweet the fight than stand up against it.

"Enough!" Lovelle shouted from the counter. To Bronco, she said, "I'm sorry, but I'm going to have to ask you to leave."

"What?" I asked. "They attack us and *we* have to leave?"

"We don't want any trouble," said Randy. "But if you're going to make people uncomfortable, we'll have to ask you to go someplace else."

"Fuck no!" Natalie said, grabbing Bronco's hand. "Those twats started this shit, they can pack it up in their snatch and scram."

"They've already got their food," Lovelle said.

"No," Bryce said, holding up a gluten-free, egg-free, casein-free muffin. "*We've* got their food."

I stood up. I was done watching people—the girl on the subway, Gloria, and now Bronco—get shat all over just for the sake of those who felt like shitting. I was sick of seeing people get kicked around—by jerks, by cops, by neighbors they trusted because rumors made better Facebook updates. I was tired, really fucking tired, of the you-vs.-us one-upping mentality of this bullshit neighborhood. But most of all, I was furious that these trust-fund bimbos had ruined the one nice meal I was going to have all week, the breakfast with my friends before I had to give a stranger the worst news of his life. Jylle and Brandi could snort cocaine off fifteen-dollar French toast any day. My last meal didn't matter to them. "We were here before them," I snarled. "Those bitches ruined my French toast!"

"Then why don't you go back to your kitchen and make more, you patriarchal whore!" Brandi snarled.

"Why don't you eat a bag of dicks?" Natalie shot back. "Oh wait, your daddy left, so much for that idea!"

Mac gave her a high five. It was a retort I wished I'd come up with, but before I could generate any follow-up, Bronco gestured to Bryce. "Come on," he said. "We'll go."

"I'll wrap up something, free of charge," Lovelle tried.

"Don't bother," he snapped over his shoulder. "Save your food for the customers you really value."

Mac, Natalie, and I gathered up our jackets. "I'm not paying for that," I said, pointing to my ruined French toast. "Tasted like ass anyways."

Chapter 28

COUNTING BACK TO 1

still hadn't eaten by the time Sid pulled up in front of my building in Terry's green Volkswagen. I huffed myself into the car and he passed me a cup of coffee.

"I heard all about it," he said. "Mac's already called a boycott on Egg School that's got about two hundred 'likes,' and Natalie Instagrammed a lovely photo of your ruined breakfast. Looks like a destroyed morning straight out of the seventies."

I was grateful for the coffee, but his chipperness about the whole awful mess made me want to strangle him. He reached into a brown bag in his lap and pulled out a maple-frosted doughnut. "I know it's not French toast, but I hope it'll do."

The doughnut made me forgive him. I took a bite and balanced it on my knee while I peeled back the tab on my coffee and took a grateful slurp.

"I went ahead and booked us a room at the Marriott on the Vestal Parkway," he continued. "I wish you'd let me go with you to meet him."

"I doubt he'll want an audience," I said, my mouth full of doughnut. "It's kind of a private thing."

Sid sighed. "So what do you think you'll say?" he asked.

I finished the doughnut and took a sip of coffee. "Not sure yet," I admitted. "My gut tells me it wasn't him or Bronco, but

I don't know anything about the wife. Still, I found that tape, I listened to it, and the least I can do is be the one to tell him that she's dead. If he can fill me in, that's great, but if not, well, he deserved to get the bad news in person."

I drank my coffee and stared out the window. The truth was that I wanted to give up, go home, forget the whole thing. Bronco had a good lawyer and cops on TV always got the bad guy in the end. I was not Detective Olivia Benson. I was not Vic Mackey. I was just a dumb girl with a mix tape and a dead friend who wanted to believe there was some justice in a world that seemed so utterly fucking devoid of it.

Sid reached over and put his hand on my knee. "You know, Binghamton has a bunch of carousels," he said. "They're free, all six of them. Maybe we can go ride a few before we leave."

"Maybe," I said. But it wasn't the promise of carousels that took my mind off what was yet to come. It was Sid's long fingers spread out over my knee, a gesture warm and delicate and tender. Sid and I had always had a generous friendship when it came to the physical, leaning against each other during a movie, him touching my waist to pass me in a narrow room, me reaching for his hand in a loud drunk crowd, but I found myself imagining his fingers moving up my thighs, between my legs, inside my panties. I sank into the seat and exhaled luxuriously.

"You all right?" he asked.

I snapped upright and suddenly remembered where I was, fumbling for an explanation. "Yeah, sorry, just got thinking about what I'm going to say."

He must have bought it, but he drifted from me anyway, reaching over to massage the screen of his phone. "I made us a couple of traveling mixes," he said. "They're not tapes, but it beats having to listen to Clear Channel play Rihanna once an hour."

He put on the Proclaimers' "I'm Gonna Be (500 Miles)," and within the first few notes, I was instantly transported back to my friend Amy's teenage bedroom, flannel pajamas and raccoon eyeliner, waiting half an hour to download and print grainy pinups of

Brendan Fraser off AOL, turning up the CD player to block out the sound of her sister, Emily, banging on the door, demanding we quit tying up the phone line.

"Haven't heard this one in a while," I said. "My ex–best friend always said she wanted this played at her wedding."

"Why is she your ex?"

"Because she slept with my boyfriend Ryan." After she'd given up her freshman-year dream of marrying Brendan Fraser, she began to join us on casual dates, and Ryan always laughed extra hard at her jokes, gave her the last slice of pizza, and joined her in ganging up against me in an argument. It wasn't until he offered to drive her home one night and didn't come back for an hour, and only then with his sweater on inside out, that I, not being completely stupid, figured out what they were up to. Call it the first case I ever solved—the Mystery of the Missing Boyfriend. I told her she could have him and never spoke to either of them again.

"Are they still together?" Sid asked.

"Who knows?" I replied. "It's not like we're pen pals." That was a lie. I'd Facebook stalked them one night last year when I couldn't sleep and Bob Dylan's "To Make You Feel My Love"— Ryan's song for me even though I'd never really liked it all that much—was used over the credits of some TV show I had fallen asleep in front of. My detective work showed that Ryan was engaged to a chubby Asian woman and Amy was dating a chinless guy who looked like the Johnny Depp puppet in *Corpse Bride,* and it was *not* a good look. "But it's not going to stop me from enjoying this song."

"And from now on, when you hear it, you can remember this trip," Sid said as the next song came on. "Do you know this one?" I shook my head. "The Clarks, 'Hell on Wheels.' Always makes me think of summer in Oklahoma, the endless miles of highway stretching out into nothingness. Oklahoma City's like that, patches of buildings and then nothingness for a few miles until you get to the next city street. It's strange and kind of beautiful. You ever been?"

"I haven't, but we did the musical in high school."

"And you'd better not start singin' it, because I've put up with that my whole time here," he said. "In between Terry incorrectly calling me a 'southern gentleman' and drunk girls demanding to know if I'm dating my cousin, I don't know if I can take one more deep-fried stereotype."

The Pet Shop Boys' "Suburbia" came on next and I froze. I'd avoided this song since Catch and I split up; it was one of our anthems for driving around when classes got out, drinking out of the same Dr. Pepper, and believing that as soon as we got our master's degrees, they would give us the keys to the city and we would be free to take over the world together. Even now, the song swelled up that same glorious feeling of freedom just beyond constraint, the youthful thrill of believing the world was ours to possess whenever we were willing to grasp it.

"Something wrong?" Sid asked. "I can skip to the next track."

"My friend Catch and I used to play this song all the time," I said. "It just makes me miss him, that's all."

He skipped ahead to Tom Cochrane's "Life Is a Highway," and the inherent cheesiness made me feel a little better.

"I hear that," he said. "I haven't listened to 'Just a Little Lovin'' by Dusty Springfield since Katy and I split up. I was saving that song for the perfect girl, and I thought I'd found her . . . now it just makes me feel foolish, like when you lose your phone on the subway. You know you should have held on to it better, but it's just . . . gone." He gripped the steering wheel and stared at the ribbon of highway stretching out before us.

"Maybe one day you'll have something better to associate it with," I said. "Like, you'll be out playing Frisbee in the park and you'll hear it on someone else's Spotify and you'll forever associate it with that new moment instead."

"Maybe," he said. "Except that I'm terrible at Frisbee. I always throw down."

"Me too," I said. "So we can play. Terribly. Together. Who

knows? We might actually learn how to throw a Frisbee like real fourth graders."

He put his hand on my knee again. I got that same nervous drumbeat in my heart as I had when I'd met up with Gabe. "I'd like that," he said. "As soon as it warms up."

I didn't want him to move his hand, but he drew back and took the wheel as Hall and Oates' "You Make My Dreams" came on. I hummed along with the chorus and he chuckled.

"You have to be Oates," he said. "You get to sing the 'hoo hoo' part."

"Why do I have to be Oates?" I asked.

"Driver always gets to be Hall," he replied. "Those are the rules of the road."

"I thought that was 'Gas, Grass, or Ass,'" I said.

"Different rulebook."

"Even if Oates is driving?"

"Absolutely." He wound through his playlist and put on "Portable Radio," grinning. "Now, let's try this again," he offered. "And this time, we'll do it right."

Chapter 29

I NEVER TALK TO STRANGERS

Sid dropped me off in front of the Belmar with a strict warning to call if I needed anything. "I'll just be at the hotel," he said. "I won't even go to the bathroom without my phone."

I was too nervous to do anything but nod and watch him drive away before sucking up a deep breath and going inside. From the look of the place, George had picked well. The bar was a Tom Waits song come to life: dimly lit and cramped with rickety tables, dirty mirrors, a pull-knob cigarette machine, and a jukebox with Elvis Costello and the Smiths. Perfect for an aging hipster to kill a few drinks while crying quietly in the back corner for the death of a girl he had clearly adored.

I was the only girl in the place except for the blond bartender, who didn't look old enough to get into an R-rated movie, let alone work the bottles and taps. Nobody seemed to notice that I had come in. I sat in the back and watched the door. I'd get a drink when George did.

A tall man with middle-aged weight and weekend stubble came in, glanced around, placed an order. If that was him, he didn't look like the aging punk I'd expected. He didn't even look like his photograph except for the Red Sox cap. No black jeans, no earring, just a guy in a blue scarf and a corduroy jacket. He'd taken punk all the way back to its blue-collar roots and left it there.

He finally spotted me and approached with the same caution one might use when nearing a skunk.

"You George?" I asked.

"That depends," he said, wetting his chapped lips with his drink. "Are you Jett?"

"I guess we're in agreement—you want to sit?"

He sat. "You want a G and T?" he asked, and gestured to the bartender without waiting for an answer. He waited until I had a glass in my hand to ask, "Did my wife send you?"

"Why would she do that?"

He drained his drink to the ice and wrapped his hands around the glass. The table shook as he tapped his foot against the table leg like a nervous rabbit. "I think she knows," he said. "About KitKat."

If I had been a private eye like Philip, I would have played this little Q and A all night long. Instead I steadied myself with a drink and gave him what he came to hear. "KitKat's dead."

I've never seen a man take a bullet to the chest, but the slow-motion look that crossed George's face was about what I'd imagine it would be like. I motioned to the bartender to fix him up a second.

"Jesus," he breathed, his fingers fumbling across the table as though he was trying to gather up marbles. "What happened?"

"Someone beat her to death," I answered. "I found her body."

But he hadn't come here to hear my sob story. He was shaking as though he'd fallen through ice. "Oh God," he hissed, rocking back and forth in his seat. "Oh God, no, not KitKat. Not KitKat."

If I'd had any doubt that he was innocent, it was all erased now. But I still wanted to know who he was to her, what that tape meant and why he'd sent it when he did. I put the cassette on the table between us. "Tell me everything."

He stood like I'd just put down a grenade. "I need a cigarette," he said. I worked on my drink while he wrestled a pack of Marlboros from the vending machine. I followed him outside and he bummed a lighter, pacing around the parking lot. I watched him like he was some kind of nature documentary: the habits of a man grieving for his mistress.

He lit a second smoke off the first. "No," he said. "This can't be real. This is blackmail." He pointed at me with the cigarette. "You're trying to get me to say I was sleeping with her so you can report back to my wife. I won't say anything. Not a goddamn thing."

"No one in our neighborhood has ever heard of you, and I don't think her boyfriend has either," I said. "So all I want to know is how long you two had been hitting the hot sheets." It was gaudy patter, sure, but I wanted to know how long this affair had been going on. The longer they were together, I rationalized, the more chances they had to slip up and reveal themselves to someone who might want KitKat dead.

He whirled on me. "Don't you dare!" he snapped. He was shaking so hard he could barely get the cigarette to his lips. "I wish it was that easy. I wish she was just another dumb grad student looking for a daddy figure and an internship. Those I can brush off. Those I can ignore." He stamped out his cigarette and shoved his hands into the pockets of his corduroy work coat. "But not her. Come on, let's go inside—our ice is melting."

"IT WASN'T ABOUT SEX," he repeated, just in case I hadn't heard him the first three times. "But Christ, I loved her. She brought color back into my life. I was living in black-and-white and she filled everything in like a paint-by-numbers kit. Did you know her?"

"She was my neighbor," I said, tapping the tape still between us. "I got this tape by accident and when I took it down to her, she was dead. Hope you don't mind, but I gave it a listen. Thought it might have a clue as to what happened." The gin was making me chatty; I took another sip to fill my mouth long enough to shut me up and let him plug the silence.

"Then you know how she was," he said. "She was here for a year before she moved to Brooklyn; we used to meet for coffee, go to the movies, make each other mix tapes. We kissed, but we only slept together once, when she came to visit. We'd been drinking, here, actually, and my wife was out of town. But it didn't feel right, like what we had was too *pure* and *perfect* to mess up with sex."

That much I understood. Maybe that's what Sid and I had, something beautiful and chivalric. And maybe that's where Catch and I had gone wrong, using sex to fill the silences between us. But if that was the case, why had he left me for someone who seemed like nothing *but* sex? It seemed like I'd never get the balance right.

But I hadn't come here to drink and overanalyze my relationships. I'd come here to drink and overanalyze *his* relationships. "How did you meet KitKat?" I asked.

"I had her in Punk Theory, a grad class I teach every few semesters. Her knowledge of punk was Green Day and the Offspring, neither of which she liked very much, but she took the class because she had this absolute hunger for knowledge. She wanted to know how music could make her feel the way it did, why the 6ths' "He Didn't" ate away to the marrow of her bones while Talking Heads' "(Nothing but) Flowers" made her blood sing. Music was an emotion she felt at her absolute core. It wasn't shit to dance or get drunk to. My love for her wasn't represented by music—music was represented by love."

I wish I had known the KitKat he knew. We'd never talked about music; it wasn't until I'd gotten her tape collection that I'd even known what she listened to. I thought of all the mix tapes and CDs I had buried, the music I could have shared with her, the playlists we could have made each other. I took another drink and tried not to cry for the friend I never got the chance to know.

"But my wife started getting suspicious," he continued. "She was threatening to check my phone and e-mails and she'd already scanned my Facebook looking for evidence." He held up the tape.

"This," he said, "is the elusive breakup mix, rarely made or given. It's all here: the Innocence Mission, the Sundays . . . I wanted her to know that I loved her and would always love her, even if we couldn't be together."

"What about that last song?" I asked. "The one that goes 'I wither without you'? I found all the others, but I couldn't find that one."

He drank. "That tape wasn't yours to listen to," he said, scowling.

"That's how I found you," I said. "That tape was in my mailbox and when I took it to her, she was dead. I used the tape to track you down, so now I've gotta ask—do you know anyone who could have done this? Any chance your wife could have . . . ?"

He took that better than I expected. "No," he said. "I don't think she loves me enough."

This was making less sense than before I'd come in, and it couldn't be blamed on the gin. "So why didn't you leave your wife for KitKat?" I asked.

He eyed me, half-squinting in the bar's darkness. "You're not married, are you?" I shook my head and he kept explaining. "Marriage isn't the same as love. It's just a legal contract, and I wasn't going to break the contract I made with my wife, my son, leave my job and my neighborhood and my life for something as fickle as love." He stared at the ice in his glass. "At least that's what I keep telling myself," he said. "Guess it doesn't matter now."

"For what it's worth," I said, "she never got the tape. She died knowing you still loved her."

He drained the last dregs of his drink. "Fuck-all that's worth," he said. Putting his hands on the table, he pushed himself to standing. "Guess there's nothing left to do now but go home to my wife."

It was the saddest fucking thing I'd ever heard a man say.

Chapter 30

ACCIDENTALLY LIKE A MARTYR

George smoked another cigarette while we waited for a cab, a beat-up station wagon with a chain-smoking driver who charged us six bucks each and didn't seem a whole lot more sober than George was. The heat and conservative talk radio were up full blast and the seats were patched with twisted strips of duct tape. At least this guy knew better than to try to talk to us. Some cabbies didn't know when to shut the hell up.

George leaned against the window and closed his eyes. I stared out at passing Laundromats, pawnshops, all-night convenience stores, and closing bars. There was a Kennedy Fried Chicken on the corner and I got a little homesick for Brooklyn. George hummed softly, like I wasn't there. In his mind, I guess I wasn't.

You don't have to see the sadness in New York. It's there if you want to look, behind neon signs and polished counters and girls dressed like they're waiting for *Glamour* to ask about their outfit. But this city wore its broken heart in pieces spilled down its sleeve. There was no hiding it, not behind the colleges, IBM money, or chic art galleries along the waterfront. It was a beautiful shithole, filled with bitter, broken men like George, drifting through lives soaked in booze and sorrow and absolute heartbreak.

Brooklyn fakes this kind of desolation. It deliberately dirties itself so people like me and Natalie and Mac and Marty can feel cool and sophisticated in our world-weariness. Sid was the only one who felt anything even remotely real. His love for Cinderella wasn't tethered to anything but his heart. What Sid felt, whatever it was, was true to the core of his being. I wondered if he was waiting in our hotel room, pining for her. I wondered if there was anyone out there in the world pining for me. And I wondered what it must be like to love someone to that unfathomable depth. I had liked all my boyfriends, I might have even loved some of them—but not the way Sid loved Cinderella. Not the way George loved KitKat. And ever since Catch left, I'd given up loving someone in a way that damaged anything but my pride when it ended. I was too scared to feel anything that deep, that terrifying, to risk that he might not love me back, that he might leave, that he might die without a chance to say good-bye.

But that fear also kept me from feeling the kind of love that came from someone whose heart was so heavy with it that even when we were together he missed me, because we could never be close enough to balm the absolute ache of his soul. And if someone loved me like that, whoever he was, I could love him with the perfect, giddy happiness of that couple I had seen on the train, and what we had would be pure and for all eternity.

The cab pulled up in front of George's dark house. I got out with him and signaled to the cabby to wait. "You gonna be all right?" I asked.

He nodded, stuffing his hands in his pockets. Then he shuffled up the walk, climbed the stairs, and turned back to me. "She's really gone, isn't she?"

"Yeah," I said, leaning against the hood of the cab. "She's really gone."

BACK AT OUR Marriott, I bypassed my bed and went straight for Sid's. The thought of sleeping alone in a hotel bed in this strange, dirty city terrified me. I didn't want to be alone the way George was—sure, he had his wife and his kid, but inside that beautiful house, inside the arrogant, fucked-up paradise of his mind, he was sleeping by himself.

Sid turned over and sat up, fumbling for the light. "Jett, what time is it?" he mumbled, shielding his eyes.

"Who cares?" I replied. "I'm exhausted."

He sat up, throwing off the covers. "You don't want to do this," he said. "Come on; let's get you over to your bed."

I resisted, burrowing down until the fake-feather pillow was flat. "Let me stay, Sid. Just let me stay here. I'm just so fucking sad. Let me stay."

He kissed my forehead and turned off the light. I put my head in the crook of his shoulder and tried not to cry.

"I broke a man's heart tonight," I said, not even sure if Sid was still awake or listening. "I had to tell him that KitKat was dead, and for a moment that was even worse than the one before, I had to wonder if he knew who killed her or if he did it himself. And whatever he had to tell her, everything that was on that tape, he didn't get the chance to say it."

"Oh, Jett," Sid murmured. "Jett, I'm so sorry."

Lying there in his arms and speaking it all out into the darkness exorcized the ghosts of the evening, the whole complex mess of emotions dissipating like the smoke rings Natalie blew when she was trying to impress a new hookup.

We didn't say anything more. I closed my eyes and Sid's breathing got soft. For a moment, the world seemed whole. For a moment, everything was all right.

Chapter 31

**BAD LIVER AND
A BROKEN HEART**

I wasn't drunk when I went to bed, but I woke up with a hangover of regret for the whole previous night. I hadn't heard Sid get up, but he was already showered and dressed.

"C'mon," he said. "There's an IHOP down the street—it's no Waffle House, but it'll fix you right up."

"I'm fine," I groaned, filling a tumbler with water and killing the whole thing in one gulp. It hit my stomach with the punch of a prizefighter, but it stayed down. I closed the door and showered with tiny shampoos that smelled like fairy puke. The towels were nicer than my bedsheets back home. I had fallen asleep in my clothes, so I re-dressed and embarked on a wet walk of shame across the room to my suitcase.

"You got a call while you were in the shower," Sid said, tossing my phone on the bed. "I didn't check to see who it was."

It was George's number. He'd left a message, but I didn't feel like hearing his voice right now. I gathered up my clothes, went back into the bathroom, and reemerged a cleaner, yet no less miserable, specimen of a human girl.

SID SNAPPED HIS menu closed and handed it to the waitress with a smile and a "Thank you, darlin'" that made her blush. I poured a little more of our endless pot of coffee into my cup and stirred in the last of our creamers. I felt a little better with the coffee, and my stomach had surprised me by perking up, rather than shriveling into a little ball, at the smell of bacon and syrup.

"He really got to you, didn't he?" Sid asked.

"Under my skin," I admitted. "Like Frank Sinatra. Like prison ink." I wasn't ever going to forget that look on George's face, the way he'd turned to me at the end of the night like I might be able to change it all back to how it should have been. It was that look—not the gin, not the bad news—that had made me need Sid as badly as I had.

I glanced up past Sid and there was George coming through the front door, holding the hand of a little boy in a Spider-Man sweatshirt. His wife, a plain woman in a cowl-neck sweater and blue jeans, was there next to him. He didn't look a whole lot better than I felt.

He looked away as soon as he recognized me and I heard her ask who I was. He said something about a student and ushered his brood to a table as far away from us as the walls of the restaurant would allow. His wife didn't look like a murderer. She didn't even look like a woman pissed at her husband for coming in drunk at one A.M. and putting on a happy family show for her son. She just looked like any ordinary suburban mom taking her kid for Sunday brunch at the IHOP on the Vestal Parkway.

I was now officially out of suspects. My detective skills had burned themselves out, and I had nowhere else left to look. Bronco was still the one in the metaphorical cuffs, and if I didn't find out who'd killed KitKat, the cops sure as hell weren't going to waste their time looking. My heart twisted up like a worm poked with a stick, and by the time the waitress put our plates in front of us, I had once again lost my appetite.

Out of the corner of my eye, I saw George get up and go to the bathroom, passing our booth without looking down at me. A minute later, my purse buzzed. *Sorry about last night,* he wrote.

Me too, I texted back.

I want to know who did this. Keep me posted.

Will do. I didn't know what he wanted me to do—send him updates, get him a ticket to the trial, break out the champagne when they convicted Bronco on a crime he couldn't have possibly committed? Maybe I could have the *Post* headline fucking framed for him. Frustrated with George, with the case, and mostly with myself, I hacked into my pancakes like a pirate with a rusty cutlass.

George crossed back to his family, and I tried not to look at them. Sid gave up trying to make conversation. When the waitress cleared away our plates, she smiled at Sid and ignored me. "Check's been paid," she said.

Sid eyed me and then slipped a sideways glance over to their table. "You think he . . . ?"

"Better be," I snorted, in no mood to be paid into silence. "I got the cab."

Chapter 32

WILLIAM, IT WAS REALLY NOTHING

Baldrick was howling like he hadn't been fed in months. He hadn't eaten more than half of the mixing bowl of food I'd left out for him, but I picked him up and carried him around like a baby until he stopped crying and started purring. It was nice to come home to someone who wanted to see me, something other than junk mail and the TV. There wasn't even a postcard from my grandmother to welcome me back.

I got Baldrick some fresh water and put him down in front of his food dish, where he started eating and purring with an enviable enthusiasm. I still felt like shit. The ride home had been long and silent except for Sid's recycled playlists; I dozed off around Liberty and woke up embarrassed a few minutes later. Sid had dropped me off in front of my apartment and I hadn't even invited him in. I wanted to be alone.

I put on some tea and changed into my pajamas even though it was barely four P.M. I was sick of thinking about George, about Bronco, about KitKat. But I listened to George's message. Just an apology for last night and a thanks for the cab. But he still hadn't answered my question about who wrote that song. Maybe I'd try him another day, when the wound wasn't quite so fresh.

I thought about what he'd said about his marriage. I knew

some people from my high school had gotten married, but none of my friends were even engaged, let alone hitched.

No one, I realized, except William.

I got out the Boyfriend Box and took it into the living room. I rooted around until I found a small velvet box underneath stacks of letters. Inside was a sterling silver ring with a pink enameled rose, the promise ring William had given me only two months before he met his so-called soul mate at the Dartmouth anime club meeting, proposed to her, and dumped me. It was my last big breakup before I met Catch, a hurt I'd hauled around out of pride for two years.

William had lived in the suite on my freshman-year dorm floor, which meant for the first two weeks of classes, he had no reason to come out other than in the morning for class and in the evening for dinner. But when I did finally catch sight of him during a two A.M. fire drill, with his wire-rimmed glasses and *Cowboy Bebop* T-shirt that was too big on his skinny frame, it was kind of like love.

He was majoring in math with dreams of being a statistician, planning to transfer to Dartmouth in the spring. We stayed up late watching fan dubs of *DNA^2* and *All Purpose Cultural Cat Girl Nuku Nuku* on VHS tapes he ordered from Japan. I paid for midnight Chinese takeout because all his money was eaten up on fandom. But I had gone to a couple of fair-pay, pro-choice rallies and figured that meant I was on the hook for paying for most of our dates. After all, I rationalized, that's what liberal, freethinking college women did instead of waiting around for a man to buy them French dinners and long-stemmed roses.

William's CD collection consisted almost entirely of imports: anime soundtracks and J-pop albums by cute girls in sailor uniforms. But the one album he'd played over and over and over was October Project's eponymous debut. Despite the fact that it was about mourning the death of a beloved, "Bury My Lovely" became our song for driving, making out, and post-sex staring into each other's eyes while he told me I was the only girl who'd ever loved him.

I'd taken that to mean he loved me too.

Right before he went home to Cleveland for Christmas break, he met me outside of class and we took a walk through the snow-covered nature preserve, holding hands through cheap gloves, blowing cold rings of winter breath like dragons. He'd gotten down on one knee and held up the ring, asking me to be his *kanojo,* his girlfriend, even after he went away. I said yes and although the ring was too big, he promised me we could get it resized when he came back to visit.

So when he dumped me for Kendra, I took it as though I'd been left at the altar, crying for days, listening to my burned copy of *October Project* over and over on my Discman, looking for clues in Mary Fahl's voice like a love spell I could cast to lure him back, cursing the sign I should have seen, that a song of mourning was probably not the best harbinger of a happy ending.

He e-mailed me only once about a year later, a bit of a casual chat, a *How are you?* and the mention of his wedding date, if I wanted to come. For a week I rehearsed the speech I would give when the minister asked if anyone had any reason why the couple should not be wed, holding this ring aloft as proof of our eternal love.

But then I'd met Catch and pretty much forgotten William existed.

I ran a quick search on Facebook and found him named in photos, but without his own account. He was still with Kendra and they had two kids: a toddler daughter, Meryl, and an infant son, Hunter. I rationalized that the cold knot twisting at the base of my spine was just leftover tension from my meeting with George. I found William's old e-mail and the phone number he'd left at the bottom *in case you ever want to chat,* an offer I'd never taken him up on, and dialed with apprehension and hope.

"You've reached William, please leave a message . . ."

Did anyone pick up their phone anymore? His still-familiar voice was so stiff and professional, it sounded like it was wearing khakis. I left a halfhearted voice mail, already regretting the call. What was I hoping to accomplish with all of this? Get him to cheat on his wife and marry me in Atlantic City with a cheap sterling silver ring? Brag about how much better off my life was without him? I felt like a jerk. I stuffed the ring back in the box, slammed the lid on it, and shoved the whole mess back in the closet.

WILLIAM CALLED BACK two hours later, and I almost didn't want to answer his call, wanted to just let him go to voice mail, delete him without ever listening to what he had to say.

"I can't talk long," he said when I finally picked up. "But when I heard your voice . . . I told Kendra I was going out for groceries and hightailed it out of there. She gets jealous of the women in my school; she'd flip if she knew I was calling you."

"I don't want to get you in trouble," I said, hoping it would be enough to end what I could already tell was going to be a very awkward conversation.

"I don't care," he said. "I just can't get over how good it is to hear your voice. I have these dreams sometimes that we're back together, and when I wake up, I go in the bathroom and just bawl my eyes out in the shower."

A decade of anger and hurt came rushing back like I'd swallowed an Atomic Fireball. "Then why didn't you ever call?" I demanded. "I've been here the whole fucking time."

"I was ashamed," he said. "I knew I fucked up. When you didn't answer my e-mail, I knew how badly I'd hurt you. I'm a coward, Jett, in case you haven't figured that out, and I've been kicking myself about it for seven years."

In my early college years, cowardice had been one of those traits I all-too-often mistook for sweetness, the same way I mistook fedoras for charm and arrogance for brilliance.

"It's okay," I said. "Guess it turned out for the best." I remembered what he'd looked like in a few worn photographs, but as he talked, all I could picture was George standing on his front steps, staring back at me. *She's really gone.* Maybe old loves have to stay gone, for everyone's sake.

"I saw your wife's Facebook page," I added. "Your kids are cute."

"Thanks," he said. "But the ends I've found myself in do not justify the way I left you. Especially since . . ." He trailed off, but I knew what he was trying to say and contemplated hanging up before he said it. "I love my wife, I really do," he said. "But I love her because I don't really have a whole lot of choice. She's the mother of my kids. It's not like I can leave her."

So it wasn't just George. Was this how all marriages were destined to end up, cold and stale, like leftovers forgotten in the back of the fridge? This was not what Disney movies had taught me about romance.

"No one's asking you to," I said, trying not to let anger creep into my voice. "I just called to say hi. I was thinking of you, and I wanted to know how you were doing." I was lying to him the way he was lying to me. The truth was that I didn't know why I'd called—to get back together? To prove my life had moved on without him? To make sure he wasn't dead, that I had nothing else to mourn?

"I know, I know," he said. "But if I so much as look at another woman, she gets so paranoid that I'm stepping out. She follows the *Huffington Post* divorce section like hippies after the Grateful Dead—she tells me it's so she can 'be prepared' for when I *do* leave her."

I hadn't intended to open his own personal Pandora's box. Up until now, my ex-boyfriend quest hadn't had any real consequences. Jeremy and I were sexually incompatible but already had plans to hang out again. Gabe and I had had a good time, parting on friendly enough terms.

But William had been doing just fine before I came in like a whirlwind, reminding him of his sin, boasting of what could have been without saying a word. For all the hurt he'd caused, he didn't deserve me as punishment. He'd fallen into the same lonesome trap as George, a prison of picket fences and PTA. And maybe one day he'd find his own Technicolor KitKat, but today wasn't that day and I wasn't that girl. Though it killed me to do so, the least I could offer was to end the pain quickly.

"I should probably get going," I said.

"I was just about to say the same thing," he said, sighing. "Kendra's already texting me, demanding to know where I am. God, I just want to throw this phone out the window and drive to wherever you are."

I heard him start the car's engine. "Don't do that," I joked, terrified it was exactly what he was doing. "Who will be there to teach your kids about *Trigun*?"

He chuckled. "Guess you're right," he said. "Jett, it was so good to hear from you. Can I call you again sometime?"

"Maybe it's better if you don't," I said, wincing. "I don't want to cause any problems."

"You're probably right," he said. "And that's my own damn fault. Hey, you still got that rose ring?"

"I do," I said. "Finding it inspired me to call you."

"Good," he said. "Wear it tonight. Just tonight, and then you can put it back wherever you had it before. I'm going to go back to my house, drink a bottle of sake in my game room, and pretend for a few hours that everything is the way it was. And, Jett?"

"Yes?"

He swallowed hard. "Don't take this the wrong way," he said, "but I love you."

Tears started to run silently down my cheeks. I was sorry I'd called, angry at myself for selfishly disrupting his routine because I needed to assert my own nostalgia. Now I had to be the one to put him through the awful heartbreak he'd run me through all those years ago. He could love me all he wanted, but it wasn't going to bring me back into his arms.

We hung up and I retrieved the ring. I slid it onto my left hand, wondering if I'd dodged a bullet or lost the love of my life a second time. I warmed up my tea, pulled up *October Project* on my iPod, played the whole album twice and had myself a good long cry.

Chapter 33

NOBODY'S BABY NOW

wo days later I was washing Philip's dainties and Mac's number came up on my phone. I dried my hands and picked up just before it went to voice mail.

"There isn't much, but I found something," Mac said by way of greeting. "It took me forever, finally managed to track down a copy of *Minnie Underground*, a University of Minnesota zine from 1993 that had an interview with the lead singer of a band called the Chauffeurs and a pretty shitty photocopy of the liner notes. Your mystery song is called 'Secret Girlfriend' from the band's only release."

Perfect title.

"It gets better," he continued. "The lead singer, Cassie Brennen, lives here in New York. She still plays gigs here and there; she's got a show tonight at the Bitter End. I'd go, but I'm at the store until ten. You should go, see if she'll sign your tape. Bet she'd love to hear that her old song is still floating around."

My heart did a weird fluttery thing and I couldn't discern if it was excitement or fear. "Mac, you're the best," I said. "Thanks so much."

"Anytime," he replied. "Still got three crates of *The Stranger*, if you need any more favors."

I CALLED SID and left him a message as I headed uptown. The show didn't start for another hour, which gave me time to drop off Philip's package and get back down to the Bitter End for Cassie's show. I told Sid to meet me there if he could and shot him a text message, just in case he didn't feel like checking his voice mail.

I loved the brick walls of the Bitter End. I loved that the bartender still ID'd me, and I loved sitting there imagining that I was seeing the next James Taylor or Lady Gaga, that one day I would be able to tell my kids that I saw such-and-such back before they hit the airwaves. I got myself an Original Sin cider and took a seat near the back because it felt like church in there. What I was hearing, what I was witnessing, was sacred and profound, and I didn't want to interrupt anyone else's worship.

Cassie wore burgundy Doc Martens with black tights and a flannel skirt; her dark-blond hair was crimped and pushed off to the side with a handful of clips. She was a relic of the last time music mattered, where a songwriter wasn't some Swedish computer geek plotting songs like math problems. Her silver nameplate bracelet and the necklace that matched were the only things about her that looked new and shiny. Everything else about her had the worn edges of a hard-won life.

She played an acoustic guitar, seated on a stool, her voice no longer the delicate, unsure alto of "Secret Girlfriend," now almost gravelly, but more confident, playful. She sang a whole set of originals, along with a cover of Billy Joel's "State of Grace" with such raw beauty that I began to rethink Billy Joel's entire catalog. With her talent, she could have even saved "Piano Man."

I closed my eyes and imagined myself on that stage, hearing her voice in my throat. This is what music was supposed to sound like—raw, tender, pure power held in check for the sheer safety of the audience. The sound coming from between her lips wasn't manufactured Auto-Tuned bullshit or soulless climbing between all the notes just to show off that you could hit them.

This was the kind of music I wanted to write about. I wanted to put words to the way the music must have felt to her as she warbled lyrics tinged with wisdom and melancholy. But nice as they were, none of them made me feel that desperate love I'd heard in "Secret Girlfriend." I found myself praying that she would sing it so that I would know I had truly found what I had been seeking.

She sang two more originals after that and announced she'd be taking a break. The bar filled with conversation, drowning out my own whispers as I tried to talk myself into approaching her. I crept up to the edge of the stage, feeling as though I was trying to steal the Mona Lisa.

"Your set was really great," I said.

She smiled as though she didn't quite believe me. "Thanks," she said. "Glad you came out." She set down her beer and shook my hand. "You a musician too?"

"Tried to break into music journalism, but I wish someone had told me print was dead," I joked.

"There's always the vast wasteland of the Internet," she said. "When I moved here, it seemed like all I did was temp and wait tables. Then one day, I just said, 'Fuck this shit,' picked up my guitar, and got back to it. Not full-time yet; I still have a day job, but the night is all mine."

"I've got the temping part right," I joked. "Now I just need to get back to the writing."

"You will," she said. "Hell, I spend my afternoons engraving 'Amber' and 'Tiffany' into plate necklaces for rich dudes' mistresses." She held up her necklace. "We do what we can to support our craft. Where are you temping?"

"MetroReaders," I said.

"That's hysterical," she said, cracking a grin. "I used to work there too. You'll make some good contacts, ton of good session guys." She took a sip of her drink. "You know, I'm going to be recording my new album soon, could use a press kit—maybe I could throw some work your way. Help us both out."

I couldn't believe what I'd just heard. Me, preview her newest album? My day couldn't have gotten better if Warren Zevon had risen from the dead. "I'd love to," I breathed.

She grinned and handed me a pen and a flyer. "Here, just write your name and number down. Might still be a while, but it's not like I've got *Rolling Stone* on speed-dial."

I obeyed, hands shaking. "You really capture exactly how it feels to fall in love," I said. "All the frustration and fear and excitement that gets mixed up inside you." It was all I could do not to smack my hand across my forehead right in front of her. Of all the dumb things to say . . .

"Wow," she said, sweeping a black-nailed hand through her crimped hair. "Can you put that in an Amazon review?"

"Sure," I said.

"So, this probably sounds completely arrogant, but can I ask what your favorite song is? I'll play it in my next set."

" 'Secret Girlfriend,' " I said. "I haven't heard a song like that in forever."

The smile dropped off her face like I'd slapped it off. "I don't play that song anymore," she said. "It was just some dumb song I wrote when I was a kid. You don't go to hear Patricia Smith's high school poetry, so you didn't come here to hear me play some shit I wrote on the back of a math quiz for some asshole who broke my heart."

I stammered an apology that didn't sound like words, and she went back to her sound equipment, pretending to fiddle with some knobs. I turned, fully aware that the six other people in the room were staring at me. I was just glad the room was dark enough that no one could see how red my cheeks were, the tears glittering in my eyes.

Chapter 34

BIGMOUTH STRIKES AGAIN

Everything inside me felt like it was being kicked out onto the pavement. I was humiliated and hurt. All I wanted was to hear one beautiful song, and it had been thrown back in my face.

I called George when I got out of the subway. I was surprised when he picked up until I heard how thickly his greeting came down the line. "Jett Bennett," he slurred. "Jett. Ben-nett. Any word?"

"None yet," I said. "But you never answered my question—who wrote 'Secret Girlfriend,' the last song you put on KitKat's mix tape?" I had to believe that this was just a coincidence, that he'd stumbled across that song in his research. I needed that much to hold on to, to believe that even though she hated that song, I could find something left in it to love amidst all the ugliness it was connected with.

I heard ice clatter into an empty glass and then the slosh of liquid—gin, I imagined. "Cassie Brennen," he said. "She was kind of a proto-KitKat." He chuckled and I heard him take a drink. "I was just this shy kid, listened to Jethro Tull, played *D&D*, wore black Wranglers. She used to wear these great vintage fur coats with these oxblood Doc Martens, and she was the first girl I knew who wore black nail polish."

"You knew her?" That much I hadn't been expecting. Was he the asshole she was talking about?

"She was my girlfriend," he said. "That song was about me."

"Yeah, well, I saw her tonight and she didn't want to play it," I said.

He choked. "You shouldn't have done that," he spat when he got his breath back. "You should have asked me first."

"How come?" I asked. I was getting that low feeling in my gut again, the same feeling I'd gotten the first time I'd heard that song. The details were starting to come into focus even if I wasn't sure what the whole picture was just yet. "You put that song on KitKat's tape."

"Why can't you just leave this alone?" he snapped. "I cheated on my wife, my girlfriend got *murdered,* and the last thing I need is you digging up some ex-girlfriend I haven't thought about in twenty-five years. I don't need this stress in my life right now."

"I am trying so goddamn hard to figure out who killed my friend," I hissed. "So I need you to explain why mentioning one stupid song got me snapped at in the Bitter End!" I was near tears with frustration.

He sighed and softened his tone with another rattle of his glass. "We had a falling-out," he said. "My senior year, she moved to New York to try and get a record deal. I was planning to join her, but she picked up a nasty heroin habit." He paused to swallow. "Such a cliché, I know, but that was the nineties. She'd call me in the middle of the night, smacked out of her mind, while I frantically tried to figure out a way to get out there and save her. Then she dumped me. Dumped me for some drummer." I heard the glass slam down hard. "I spent the next few weeks eating tranquilizers by the fistful and drinking myself to sleep. Maybe I forgot about her. Maybe I buried her. Either way, I met Linda, and we got married seven months later. And everything was *fucking fine* until I met KitKat. And then everything came to the surface."

He was getting drunker, and I was getting uncomfortable. I

wanted to hang up, block his number, figure out the connection on my own, but he kept talking. "I found her tape in the garage a few months back and I just knew KitKat would dig it. And that song, the one she wrote for me before it all fell apart, I could finally give it to someone else I loved. I could finally, *finally* let Cassie's ghost go."

"And then KitKat would have had to carry it around in her broken heart until she found someone else to unload it on," I snarled. "You're a selfish, rotten bastard."

He swallowed audibly. "That may be true," he said. "But none of that matters now."

I hung up on him and dialed Sid's number as I started up my apartment stairs. After it went to voice mail twice, he finally picked up. I heard dance music in the background, cars in the distance.

"Hey there, darlin'."

I burst into tears at the sound of his voice. "I need you to come over," I said. "Please. I'll make us dinner, I'll buy the wine. Please, Sid, I just need to see you." After Cassie, after George, I just needed someone who would be nice to me, not swear or snap at me for perceived infractions, someone who would hug me and pour me a drink and help me sort out this terrible feeling into something that made just a fragment of sense.

"I can't," he said. "I'm kinda busy."

Music. Cars. I could solve one mystery tonight. He was standing outside of Fairy Tales, choosing Cinderella over me.

"Sid, please," I begged. "I really need you to come over here. I've had an awful evening. I really need a friend right now."

"Jett, I'm sorry, but Cinderella's going on in, like, five minutes. I really can't be late. Can I call you tomorrow?"

"No," I spat. "No, you can't call me tomorrow. And you know what, Sid? She can have you. Let her listen to you ramble on about the Vapors. Let her keep your records at her place. Let her make you dinner, but I have a feeling you'll be eating the leftovers of a hundred other guys."

He was silent. I imagined he was impressed by my expertly crafted vulgarity. "You don't know her," he said coldly. "And clearly, you don't know me either."

"If this is who you are, I don't want to know you," I sneered. "If I wanted some sleazebag, I could go to one of Natalie's house parties and find one—but I thought you were better than that. Guess I was wrong."

The line went dead in my ear as I kicked open my door. Baldrick, as if sensing the storm, ran and hid under my bed. I fell onto the couch and pulled a throw pillow I'd made out of a vintage Boz Scaggs concert T-shirt over my face, sobbing so hard I was screaming. Everything was at a dead end—George, Cassie, my song, my case, and worst of all, Sid. My best friend, the only one who knew anything about what I was going through with KitKat's case, couldn't be bothered to come comfort me when I needed him more than ever.

I just let it all out, all my frustrations and anguish, until I was choking and trying to catch my breath. I felt a little better after my meltdown, but even if Catch had walked through my door with flowers and an apology, today would still have ranked up there as one of the worst days of my life.

Chapter 35

Except for brief periods of sleep and dumping food in Baldrick's bowl, I spent the next four days at work, trying to keep Sid off my mind. Every time the thought of him crept in or one of his songs came up on my playlist, I read harder, hit fast forward, did everything to try to keep him away. I crammed in six shifts and promised myself a treat when my paycheck came through. I even got Philip's laundry back in record time.

I was finishing up my Saturday afternoon shift at Hartford when Bronco came into the temp lounge with his courier bag slung over his shoulder and his bike helmet in his hands. He lit up a little when he saw me. "I didn't know you worked here."

"Just one of the many places that keep me gainfully employed," I said. "How are you doing?"

He ran his gloved hand across his scalp. "Pretty shitty," he admitted. "Bryce and I broke up. Last night." He tossed his helmet back and forth between his hands. "Kind of hoping work will take my mind off it. I sure as hell don't want to be home when he comes by to get the clothes he kept at my place."

The closest Bronco and I had ever been was the afternoon we'd spent together in the prison visiting room, but he looked like he could use a friend. And with no word from Sid, I knew I too could use some friendly commiseration. "Do you have anyplace else to deliver to?" I asked. "We could go get a cup of coffee, just hang out for a bit."

He looked like he was about to say no, but then he changed his mind. "I'm free," he said. "I could do coffee."

"Let me just double-check to make sure they don't have anything left for me to do," I said. "Why don't you go grab us a place so you don't have to walk your bike on the sidewalk, and text me so I know where you are?"

He nodded and put on his helmet. By the time I had checked in with Susan and gotten my time card filled out, I had a text that said he was standing in line at Bourbon Coffee and asking what I wanted.

And when I got there, he had a soy latte for himself and a hazelnut one for me, plus a seat at a dollhouse table in the back by the bathrooms. I started to get out my wallet, but he shook his head. "To thank you for coming to see me in jail," he said, taking a swig. "I know it probably wasn't easy, but it meant a lot."

"I know you didn't do it," I said. My coffee was still too hot to sip. "Do you want to talk about Bryce?"

"I do and I don't," he said, chuckling. "Isn't that the worst part of a breakup? You're just so pissed, and you want to tell everyone how badly you're hurting so they'll be extra nice to you, but you don't want anyone asking, *Oh, are you okay? How are you doing?* I've had enough of that bullshit in the past few weeks."

"I get it," I said. But more than anything, I wanted him to ask how I was doing, just so I could tell somebody what had happened with Sid in hopes that they might be able to solve it, coach me, figure it all out, and tell me how to say *I'm sorry.* "But how *are* you doing?"

"Holding up as best I can," he said. "My best friend's dead and the cops think I killed her. I just got out of the clink, and everybody hates me, then my boyfriend leaves? If this was happening on TV, we'd be waiting for a commercial so we could go get another beer." He fiddled with the knitted sleeve he'd fitted over his cup; I recognized it as one like KitKat had made me when I first moved to the neighborhood. "I told my lawyer where I was," he admitted. "I did that for Bryce. It took everything I had, and it still wasn't enough. He just doesn't get it, you know? He was all Pride Parades and *Drag Race* and the fabulous gay lifestyle; me, I just wanted a boyfriend.

"I'm not ashamed of being gay," he said, continuing. "Bryce always said KitKat was my cover story, but she really wasn't. I really loved her. The two of us could do everything together—everything but sex, obviously. But I think Bryce resented even that, and it just got to be too much for him. He kept yelling about how I needed to *show my true self* and *fuck all the haters* and that kind of bullshit. I think he was just mad because I hadn't officially proposed, like I was supposed to whip out a ring the minute New York legalized gay marriage." He smirked a little, sad and sardonic.

"My parents are being really supportive right now, and I don't want to burden them with one more surprise. Fuck, when I told them about dating KitKat, my dad patted me on the shoulder and smiled and said, 'I was starting to think you were a faggot.' Bryce just didn't understand that I needed to do things at my own pace. That pace was too slow for him." He folded his arms on the table and looked past me out into space. "Guess they're going to find out sooner or later," he said, "now that I've got an alibi."

"Shouldn't that be enough to get you off?" I asked, thinking back to all the alibis offered on Sid's cop shows. *Sid.* I swallowed a too-big gulp of my too-hot coffee, the burn in my throat distracting me momentarily from the knife in my heart.

"My lawyer can argue it in court, but it's not as easy as it looks on TV," he said. "He's got confidence, but I sure as hell don't. They've got my fingerprints, Jett, on the handle of that rolling pin. That's why I was at her apartment that morning. Bryce just couldn't wait to try out this vegan chicken pot pie recipe he got and the handle had come off my rolling pin. KitKat's marble one was good for pie crust, so she let me borrow it, and I was taking it back to her. Whoever killed her submerged one handle in the dishwater but not the other, and my fingerprints came up in the system from back when I was substitute teaching."

"But they didn't get the killer's prints?"

"I'm sure they were on there, and my lawyer will argue that," he said. "But I'm the one a witness can place at the scene on the day of the crime, with weed in my system from one stupid brownie two weeks previous. And I'm black, Jett. You know that's what this is really about. Drugs and color, that's all. That's enough evidence for a jury to believe that I'm the kind of man who would bash in his girlfriend's head. The prosecution will argue that I was high and she threatened to reveal that I was gay, so I shut her up. Hell, I'd probably watch that *SVU* episode if it wasn't my goddamn life."

I reached over and put my hand on his wrist. He put his hand over mine and squeezed a little, the skull on his left hand dancing just a little. "Thanks for letting me talk," he said. "You're a good friend. Seems like everyone else has dropped off the planet now that I'm not a cause anymore—those who don't see me as a straight-up pariah, that is. I've started having my groceries delivered so I don't have to risk running into Jylle or Brandi again. Fuck them. Shit, Lovelle tried to apologize by saying I was welcome back so long as I didn't cause a scene—like I'm supposed to just keep my head down and thank people for calling me a murderer. I still don't know why they all turned against me except that there isn't anybody else to blame. I have no clue who could have done this."

"No kidding," I said.

"So who was this George guy you were asking me about?" he said. "Were you able to find him?"

"You were right," I said. "He was her boyfriend. Her *married* boyfriend."

"No wonder she kept him quiet," he said. "Guess we had keeping secrets in common too. But I thought they broke up."

"What makes you say that?" George had told me he was going to use the tape to dump her, but if Bronco knew because KitKat had, perhaps, cried on his shoulder while the two of them pigged out on vegan ice cream, my dead ends were starting to look more like cliffs.

He tapped his left wrist. "Her bracelet," he said. "Chunky silver chain with a nameplate, etched with some song quote. I never saw her without it until . . ." He started to choke up, hand gripping his cup so hard I was surprised the top didn't pop right off.

"Until when?"

He gulped hard. "Until the medical examiner handed me her personal belongings at the morgue," he said. "The bracelet wasn't in with any of it. I thought I had seen her wearing it that morning, but when I asked the medical examiner if I could see the report, just to make sure some orderly didn't swipe it, it wasn't even listed. Guess I was mistaken about seeing it." He wiped his eyes with the back of his free hand. "I had no idea she'd had me as her emergency contact until they called me in. For whatever we had, for whatever lies we told everyone else, she really did love me. And I really loved her."

"I know you did," I said. "And I know you didn't do this."

He snorted. "Try telling that to everyone else."

Chapter 36

BUILDING A MYSTERY

I texted Hillary on the way to the subway. The answers I needed were too urgent to call her when I got home or to wait around for her to check Facebook. I didn't have a reply by the time I arrived though, so while I waited, I held Baldrick in my lap and scrolled through KitKat's photos. Sure enough, she was wearing the bracelet on her left wrist in every photo taken over the last six months. I tried to zoom in, but the light was never right to see what was written there.

Hillary called me an hour later and after our usual greetings, I asked, "Do you know of anyone who took an engraved silver bracelet from KitKat's memorial?"

"Not that I remember seeing," she said. "But that doesn't mean no one did. Why do you ask? Was it something you gave her?"

"Bronco was asking about it," I said. "He was just wondering who had it, since he wasn't there."

Her voice got ugly. "Bronco? Her boyfriend, the guy who probably killed her?"

"He didn't do this," I said. "And I need that bracelet to prove it."

"Can't help you," she said. "I remember seeing her wearing it, sure, but she wouldn't tell me who it was from. And even if she had, what makes you think I'd want to get him off?"

"Because your sister's real killer is still out there," I said. "You said you wanted her killer found, and I'm trying to do that. You have to believe me that it wasn't Bronco or you'll never trust that I've found the real murderer."

"Jett, that's cute and all, but leave this to the cops. . . ."

It wasn't cute. It wasn't a game or a foolish instinct. I was in this too deep, and I wasn't walking away when I was only a few answers away from figuring out this puzzle. "You asked me to help!" I told her. "And the cops have the wrong guy—now, are you going to help me or not?"

She sighed. "I guess," she said. "What do you need?"

I told her about GPL and our meeting, the tape, and the bracelet. I told her about Bronco and Bryce and a silence settled between us. I held my breath, waiting for her answer.

"Wow," she breathed. "You've really done a lot of work."

"I want her killer found," I said. "I don't want to see Bronco go down for this."

"I wish I could help more," she said. "If I find it, I'll give you a call. And let me know if there's anything else I can do to help."

I thanked her, hung up, and used all the willpower I had to dial George's cell phone.

"Hi, Jett," he said in an almost-whisper. "Can't say I was expecting to hear from you again."

I was on too much of a roll to waste time with apologies. "Did you ever give KitKat a silver bracelet?"

"For her thirtieth birthday," he said. "I had it etched with the lyrics to Joe Jackson's "Be My Number Two," *I'll do what I can do to make a dream or two come true*. It was playing on the radio in my car the first time I kissed her."

"That's very romantic," I said. My heart was pounding with caffeine and dread. "And she had no idea that you were breaking up with her?"

"You heard the tape," he said. "That's all there was. Jett, what's going on?"

"The bracelet," I said. "It wasn't found in her apartment and she wasn't wearing it when she died, but her friend and her sister both confirmed that she never went without it."

"So they took the bracelet when they killed her," he said. "Sounds like a robbery to me."

"Except that nothing else was taken. Her purse was still on the table. Whoever came in knew what they were looking for. Got any ideas?"

"Not one," he said. "Maybe whoever took it pawned it."

"I don't think so," I said. "I think they took it as a trophy, which tells me the killer knew it was from you. Did you have some other cute coed on the line? Maybe a student who saw KitKat getting special treatment?"

"Never," he said. "We didn't start seeing each other until after she was out of my class. I'm not stupid."

I wasn't about to argue that. "Your wife got a jewelry box?"

"I'm standing over it right now," he said. I heard shuffling, then a drawer opening, and I waited for him to speak again with my breath held like a kid in the throes of a tantrum. "But the bracelet isn't here."

I told him I'd call him later and hung up. I put on Warren Zevon's *Sentimental Hygiene* for background music and tried to put all the clues I had together, like assorted pieces from three different jigsaw puzzles. A secret boyfriend, a missing bracelet, a mix tape. I had the names, the locations, the pieces in play, I just didn't know what order they went in to make the tiny paper *Clue* checklist that would lead me from her dead body on the kitchen floor to her killer standing convicted in the courtroom.

But for all the evidence I had, I had overshot the solution somehow, missed one crucial word in a statement whispered when I was barely listening. But if the answer was that close, I also knew the key was hidden somewhere closer—and it was just a matter of finding what box I'd stashed it in.

My phone buzzed again and I rushed for it, hoping it was a truce from Sid. It was a message from Natalie asking if I wanted to go out with her later.

I was going crazy in my apartment, checking my phone too often and barely resisting the urge to get into the Boyfriend Box. After what happened with William, I'd sworn off the contents for a while. Not until Sid and I made things right. Not until I solved this case.

But I wasn't going to solve anything with my head cluttered up with my own personal brand of bullshit, and dancing, I'd found, was a good way to shake it all loose.

"The Heartache" played on the turntable. All I could do was text *Yes*.

Chapter 37

(LOOKING FOR) THE HEART OF SATURDAY NIGHT

Sid and I hadn't spoken, texted, or messaged in the four days since he hung up on me, so when Natalie invited me to join her and Josie at Axis in Greenwich Village for Homework, I went as some sort of private fuck-you. I could dance sexy and sweat out overpriced drinks under hot lights, too. I could make men want me as much as Sid wanted Cinderella. Maybe I'd even take someone home with me.

Homework was billed as a dark-eighties party for former Goth kids who kept their love of the Cure hidden except on Saturday night. It, like all good things, had been under siege by twenty-year-old skanks with fake IDs trying to be *totes retro,* but for the last few weeks, DJ MissTaken had combated the invasion by playing Wolfsheim's "Once in a Lifetime" any time some bimbo in a black tube top requested "Karma Chameleon," "Holiday," or "Vacation." One night, she played it eight times in a row, and the rest of us danced the whole time until they left and she switched it over to her signature song, Siouxsie and the Banshees, "Peek-a-Boo."

I didn't feel much like dancing. Normally I took great comfort in being out on the crammed dance floor with seventy-five other hipsters singing the Smiths' "Ask" at the top of our lungs, savoring the scent of broken glass and sweat and unbridled joy, but tonight I found myself thinking about KitKat. She used to love this party, and it didn't seem right that we were all dancing without her, as though she had never existed.

"Check out that guy," Natalie said, pointing at the bartender in the seventies purple paisley. "Sorry, I didn't realize we were in Studio 54."

"I think he's kind of cute," Josie said.

He had that second-rate hotness required of nightclub bartenders and acoustic guitar players in Washington Square Park—blond tips, leather pants, a wide, insincere smile. "He's all right," I said in agreement, just so I could have something to say.

Natalie examined him a second time. "You should fuck him," she concluded. "Either one of you. You could fight for him. Or take turns."

Not my type. Not my type because he wasn't Sid, and Sid was the only thing I wanted in the whole fucking world, if only because he couldn't be mine. MissTaken queued up Depeche Mode's "Just Can't Get Enough" and I drained what was left of my drink as though it was an antidote to poison. "He's all yours, Josie," I said. "His shirt's too ugly for me."

"*Life* is an ugly shirt," Natalie said dramatically, taking a long pull from her Red Stripe.

AROUND ONE A.M., Saturday night sadness set in—the realization that the night is almost over and I haven't had as much fun as I should have. I missed Sid with a longing I didn't know was possible. Natalie had gone outside for a smoke and Josie was flirting with Ugly Shirt. MissTaken began spinning New Order's "Bizarre Love Triangle," and two skanks in matching Victoria's Secret nighties were writhing against each other and looking around to see how many people were watching their little show. I couldn't help imagining Sid on some red velvet couch with Cinderella grinding her ass all over his hands, the secret smile he saved only for her. I wanted to throw my drink against the wall, put my head in my hands, and scream until he heard me.

I caught myself staring at a tall, skinny blond guy with combed-back shark-fin ridges and rimless cheaters. I imagined the tenor and pitch of his voice, the way he'd hold his drink with three fingers, the sad glance he'd give me across the dance floor. I imagined the brick cutting into my back as he pressed me against the alley wall of the bar, mouth wet and sweet with lime and vodka. I'd grope him through his jeans, he'd push up my skirt. We'd get a cab back to my place and suck face on the couch, fumble half-clothed on the floor, fuck for fifteen minutes on the bed. He'd slip out while I was sleeping, leaving no number behind.

Our eyes met and he gave me that bittersweet fuck-me smile I'd seen on a hundred other cads. His bow tie should have been my first clue. The Manic Panic pinup in the Forever 21 bustier next to him should have been my second. I rolled my eyes and glanced up at Natalie as she came back to our booth.

"I'm heading out," I said.

She pulled out her phone. "Already? It's early. We were going for diner gyros, now that Gray's Papaya has fucking closed. I mean, what's the point of even going out anymore if you can't get a decent late-night hot dog and some goddamn papaya juice?"

"I'm exhausted," I lied, sliding out past her. "I'll catch up with you guys later."

Josie waved from the bar; Natalie was suddenly too busy texting someone cooler to say a real good-bye. Outside I ducked my head and didn't look at anything but the sidewalk in front of me. There are only a few good hours in any Saturday night, when everyone's just drunk enough to share smokes and dance together and snap selfies with their new BFFs. But when that window closes all that's left is a bunch of drunk assholes, screaming girls, broken glass, and splatters of vomit. I hated all of it.

My phone rang with a number I didn't recognize. I answered it anyway and Sid's voice came from somewhere far away. "Jett . . . ," he said, his voice labored. "I need you to come get me."

Chapter 38

A SORTA FAIRYTALE

Sid was sharing the emergency room with a stab-wound victim and a drunk teenager getting her stomach pumped. His collar was bloody and his shirt was open to reveal a half-rack of bandages tied around his ribs. His face was purple, his left eye swollen shut, his fat lips the envy of every New Jersey housewife. He was shaking when I put my arms around him, but every time I tried to speak, the girl behind the curtain heaved so violently it sounded like she was being turned inside out.

"Shit, Sid, what happened?" I finally managed to get out.

He eased off the bed and wobbled in my arms. "I'll tell you later," he said, his voice hoarse and slurred. "I just want to go home."

SID SLEPT FROM the moment I got him in the cab until I got him up three flights of stairs into my apartment. He needed a better nursemaid than Terry, who would sell all his Vicodin before dawn broke—all that he didn't snort, anyway.

I hit the living room light switch with my elbow and kicked the door shut with my heel. Baldrick wove in between my feet, tripping me into the dining room. Sid was so out of it he didn't notice that I nearly dropped him on his face.

I set him down on my bed and he slumped forward, let his eyes flutter open, mumbled an apology, and was out again. I peeled off his vest, unbuttoned his mess of a shirt, and wondered if he always dressed this well for a lap dance. I took off his belt and shoes and stretched him out on the bed.

He opened his eyes and forced his swollen lips into a smile. "So much . . . ," he mumbled, ". . . for my Cinderella."

"She do this?" I demanded.

He lolled his head from side to side. "No," he drawled. "The bouncer. The big bad wolf." He was still grinning, sloppy with irony and painkillers, his teeth stained bloody. And with one last sad little laugh, he was out for the night.

I ran a sinkful of cold water with a squirt of Philip's laundry soap and left Sid's shirt to soak before I stashed Philip's half-dried underwear in the towel cabinet. I went back to the bedroom and fished through Sid's pockets. His wallet and his phone were both gone, but he still had his keys and a fresh bottle of Vicodin. My head throbbed, my feet hurt. I got a glass of water, dumped a pill down my throat, then pulled the covers up over both of us and waited for the room to start spinning.

Chapter 39

SOME GUYS HAVE ALL THE LUCK

I woke up to the sound of Sid retching in the bathroom. My head and my stomach were both swimming; my impulse Vicodin hadn't sat well with the drinks in my bloodstream. I waited until I heard him flush the toilet before I convinced myself to stand up, making my way slowly to the bathroom like it was a hundred miles away.

He was slumped against the tub, holding his head in his hands. There was blood on the tips of his fingers and his face looked like stew meat. He'd wound up a fistful of toilet paper and was holding it to a freshly opened cut. There were tears in his eyes. He sucked in a deep breath like it hurt and looked at me without words.

"I'll run you a bath," I murmured, cranking on the faucet. "Trust me, it'll help."

I got him a towel and a Smiths T-shirt that I'd been meaning to make into a dress for two years since I'd found it at the Salvation Army. His other shirt, still soaking in pink water, would need a few more washes before those bloodstains would come out. I dug a trial-sized bottle of mouthwash out of the junk drawer. After I closed the door and heard the water turn off, I toyed briefly with the idea of getting in the tub with him, just to hold him close, just so he didn't feel alone.

Around eleven he dragged himself into the living room and flopped on the couch. I got him a cup of coffee and made him some toast before he could ask. "Stretch out," I said. "I'll put on *Law and Order*. Jerry Orbach can cure any ailment."

"Just get me another couple of those Vicodins and forget the goddamn toast," he groaned.

The toast popped up in the kitchen and I buttered it for him anyway. I brought him a glass of water and held the pills hostage. "Eat first," I said. "You'll puke blood if you put these in empty."

He stretched out one arm and took a piece of toast in a shaking hand. Crumbs spilled all over his chin, his shirt, the couch. "Thanks for coming to get me," he said.

"What the hell happened to you?" I asked again.

"I don't really want to talk about it," he said with his mouth full.

"Was it Cinderella?" I asked, remembering what he'd said last night.

"Shit, Jett, I don't want to talk about it."

For the faintest moment I considered withholding meds until he confessed. But I found myself doling out the pills to him without asking any more questions. Some detective I was. Maybe he'd talk when his brain was swimming in opiates.

"You want to watch TV?" I asked.

"Sure," he said. "But I'll probably just sleep. I think I felt better while I was getting my ass kicked."

I got a pillow off my bed while he finished the second piece of toast. He drank a little more coffee and we started watching a marathon of *Burn Notice*. Michael Westen had barely uttered his first *When you're a spy . . .* before Sid was asleep sitting up, snoring through his swollen nose. I didn't bother tucking him in when I got up off the couch.

Whoever had jumped him had taken his phone. I hoped

Cinderella—or whoever had it by now—would be dumb enough to answer it. On the third ring, a woman with a voice like a concrete dance floor picked up. So much for his southern belle.

"Sid just wants his wallet back," I said.

"Who is this?" she demanded.

"A friend. We just want the wallet. Where can I meet you?"

"Are you a cop?"

"Why, you want me to get them involved? I just want the wallet—license, credit cards, gym membership, they've all been canceled. They're useless to you." That was a lie. Sid hadn't been in any shape to tell the cops what happened, let alone sort through the red tape of cancellation negotiations.

"And no cops?"

"They can't prove you spent the cash, right?"

She mulled that over for a hard minute. "South Third and Berry, little brunch place called Dolly's. Put your purse on the table so I know who you are."

I was about to suggest she just text this number right before she walked in, but she hung up. I wrote Sid a note, took his keys, and hoped I wasn't about to meet his same bloody fate.

Chapter 40

CINDERELLA UNDERCOVER

olly's was one of those tacky brunch places daddies take the daughters from their second families when they're trying to play like they live for having tea parties, as if that will somehow make up for ditching the starter kit they see every third weekend back in Brewster. It was all pink and lacy and it wasn't the Vicodin that made me want to retch when I walked in. I sat at a table near the back, away from the two women who looked over at their three sticky kids, only to tell them to stop interrupting their conversation about the latest pseudo-bondage novel they were both reading. I ordered a French lavender latte that took ten minutes to show up and came complete with a corgi face drawn in the foam. How fucking precious.

A girl in clear heels and a faux-vintage fur coat came in. She looked out of place even for Brooklyn, like Carrie Bradshaw on a five-dollar blow-job budget. She paused midstrut, as though she was waiting for every guy in the place to loll out his tongue like it was a red carpet. Except there were no guys to be had, and the women couldn't have cared less.

"What did you expect?" I asked when she dropped her black vinyl purse on the table. "Straight men don't brunch, but stick around; they'll all be in with family number two this afternoon. Where's the wallet?"

She smiled seductively. "What are you, his wife?" she teased. "You jealous? Wanted to see what he was getting on the side?" She stretched out one long, enviable leg and ran a well-manicured hand from her knee to her crotch. The women at the other table hissed in whispers. I couldn't make out what they were saying, but I'm sure it wasn't nice.

"Not his wife," I replied. "Not even his girlfriend. Just the kind of pal who picks a guy up from the emergency room after half his face has been busted—two cracked ribs, burst blood vessels in his left eye, mouth looks like hell. He's knocked out on Vicodin on my couch right now."

She rolled her lips into a nasty pout. "He got what he deserved," she said, all the honey drained out of her voice. "That's what he gets for objectifying women."

"That's pretty big talk coming from the girl in the G-string," I retorted.

"So you're saying I deserve to be treated like a sex object because of how I dress?"

I laughed for a good hard minute while she glared at me with kohl-rimmed eyes. "You are joking, right?" I asked, leaning in. "Sweetheart, you make a living taking your clothes off for money and you get mad when men look at you like a girl who's taking her clothes off for money? What, Daddy didn't love you enough to buy you ballet lessons?"

"I'm working on a PhD in womyn's studies." I could hear her pronounce the Y and tried not to roll my eyes.

"And stripping your way through college," I finished. "Got any other clichés you'd like to work out?"

She took out her tablet and I wondered which poor sap she'd ripped that off of. "Please, keep talking," she said. "I'd love to interview you on how you can pretend to be a feminist while justifying the patriarchy."

"No," I said, jamming my finger in her face. "You don't get to pretend you're a better feminist than me because you're up in some ivory grad-thesis tower. You're a stripper. That's fine. But your silicone tits and your waxed snatch sell a glossy version of sex no real woman could ever achieve, so you do *not* get to treat me like I'm some sort of baby-incubating housewife." Gloria sure as fuck didn't act like this. Where the hell did Cinderella get off?

"Men like your friend Sid think it's okay to treat women like a piece of meat," she said. "So I show men like him the power a real woman has. I make them pay and I make them pay *hard*."

"Well, aren't you just an angel of true fucking justice," I snapped, my face getting hot and papery. "What the hell were you expecting him to do? Slip you a twenty and tell you that you're better than this? Ever think that maybe, *just maybe,* he respected your choice to take your clothes off for cash?"

"Why are you defending him?" she asked, tapping her screen with a manicure that didn't have a single chip missing. I doubted she'd done any of the hard work last night.

"Because he loved you," I said, proud that the words didn't burn a chemical hole through my throat. "He didn't see you as an object. He saw you as a person, a person he fell in love with. He came in and saw you *where you worked* because that's what men in love do. And you rolled him because you're a hateful little bitch. You had some hulking hunk of steroids—that's the patriarchy, by the way—kick his ass because you're a sniveling coward. So give me his wallet—and his phone—right now, or I'll call the cops." I pulled out my own phone to show her I wasn't fucking around.

"I'll say he tried to rape me."

"Of course you would," I snarled. "And it's skanks like you who make those cockwad men's rights activists on Reddit drool." I poised my hand over the dial button, hoping she couldn't see how hard I was shaking. "Hand them over. Now."

She dug through her purse and slapped the phone on the table. A moment later came the wallet. I gathered both of them up and stood. "She'll take the tab whenever she's ready," I told the waitress. To Cinderella, I added, "Hope it doesn't cut into next semester's textbook fund."

THERE WERE FIVE missed calls from Gloria on Sid's phone. I dialed her as I walked back to the apartment, my stomach jumpy and hollow from adrenaline and rage. She sounded frantic when she picked up.

"Sid?" she asked. "Sid, are you all right?"

"It's Jett," I said, correcting her. "What's going on?"

"Is Sid okay?" she demanded. "I saw him go into the back room with Cinderella and Tommy followed. I know what happens back there, I know what Tommy does, but normally it's to guys who kinda have it coming. But Sid didn't deserve that. They hurt him really bad, Jett. I waited with him until the ambulance arrived and haven't been back to Fairy Tales since. Told my boss I twisted my ankle."

"You saved his life," I said. "I can't thank you enough."

The line went silent for a moment. "Look, I like Cinderella," she began slowly, "and sometimes I agree with her—some of the guys who come in are scum—but not Sid. Sid was a sweetheart." I heard the click of a cigarette lighter in the background. "That's the difference between me and her—I like my job. I like the guys like Sid." I pictured her at her kitchen table, smoking nervously, her own hands shaking as hard as mine. "And sure, you get guys like Terry in there, but most of them are pretty chill. I got a guy who comes in there and sketches us. Says it's cheaper than an art class. Who knows, maybe I'm hanging in a gallery somewhere. I'm art!" She giggled for a moment before her voice got hard again.

"Cinderella thinks this is a game," she continued. "She's got a trust fund; this is all research for her. This is a living for me. This is how I pay the rent on this shithole." She paused, presumably to take a drag. "She didn't have to do that to Sid. Some douche like Terry, sure, but not Sid. I hope her fucking tits fall off." She paused again and I could almost taste her cigarette smoke through the phone. "You know how she paid for her boob job? With a fucking university grant. For feminist studies. Some fucking feminist, right?"

I didn't want to get into a conversation on feminist theory when my bloody best friend was home alone. "I need you to do me a solid," I said. "For Sid."

"Name it, honey."

"I need you to turn her in," I said. "You said so yourself, she's bad for your business. Call the cops and rat her flat ass out."

"I don't know," she said. "I'm not a snitch. Besides, I'm scared as fuck of Tommy."

"So turn on him," I said. "Please, Gloria. Sid won't say a word against her. He told the cops he didn't know anything. But Tommy, he's good for it. Let's at least get him. I just don't want to see anyone else get hurt."

Gloria sighed. "She does have a pretty flat ass," she said. "Maybe she can get some big ol' butt implants with the next grant. Sure, I'll do it. Maybe they'll send in some cute under-cover and I can give him a freebie." I heard her take another drag. "Does Sid need anything? Or do you still have some leftovers?"

"Can I make a confession?" I asked. "The pills we bought from you, they weren't for us. I didn't fall down the subway stairs. We had to trade it to Terry so we could use his car."

"Figures—don't worry, I won't hold it against you if you don't make a habit out of it."

"No way," I said. "Fuck Terry."

"Exactly," she said. "Fuck that guy. But don't worry, Jett, I'll take care of what I can here, and you tell Sid to come up and see me sometime—in Chinatown. You can come too. I know a good dim sum place, the dirty kind where everything's cheap and deli-cious. My treat. I'll be making the good money when that twat is spreading her legs in some mobbed-up Russian nudie joint."

"Sounds like a good time," I said. "I'll pass the word along to Sid."

I HAD ONE final mission before I could go home to Sid. With his eyes as busted up as they were, he wouldn't be putting in his contacts any time soon, and without his glasses, he'd have a hell of a time finding his way back to his apartment to *get* his specs. Of course, this meant I had to face Terry at one P.M. on a Sunday afternoon. It might as well have been seven A.M. for the schedule Sid said he kept.

Terry's place was over in Park Slope—because of course it was. His dad had been a real estate tycoon and Terry had what seemed like a bottomless trust fund to snort, not to mention an apartment that Sid described as having more square footage than the house he'd grown up in. Why he'd taken in a roommate was beyond us; he certainly didn't need help making rent, but Sid said it was more than likely Terry was just looking for someone to bum drugs off of. By the time he'd realized Sid wasn't into his scene, he had already taken too much of a liking to him to kick him out. After all, the party girls Sid turned down needed to sleep with someone.

The doorman barely glanced at me, but the look he managed to give was filled with the contempt of a man who's spent his entire career mopping up the sick of all-hours guests. I let him. He'd earned it. On floor six I edged the key into the lock, hoping I could get in and get out without having to explain anything to Terry.

I've seen back alleys cleaner than Terry's living room. There were empty bottles and clothes everywhere. There was a broken mirror dangling off the coffee table, dusted with the remnants of last night's nose candy. I was glad I'd worn my Docs; the fear of stepping on a razor blade or a needle was very, very real.

A girl with makeup that Lady Gaga would have rejected as too outlandish stumbled out of the bathroom with one yellow shoe on. "Fucking cocksucker," she said, her face pointed toward me but her eyes a million miles elsewhere. "What, are you another one of Terry's fucking whores? Fuck that shit, I'm leaving. I'm not into whatever sick twisted shit he brought you here for. Where's my fucking shoe?"

I pointed to her other shoe on a cigarette-burned Anthropologie ottoman, tipped on its side like a derailed train. She picked it up and jammed it on while I slipped into Sid's room and grabbed his glasses off his dresser. I started to bag up some clothes, but before I could put together even a single outfit, the girl screamed, "Hey, Terry, your fucking girlfriend's here!"

I froze, pressing myself against a wall as though I could blend into the wallpaper. I heard a door open and heavy footsteps. "There's no one fucking here!" Terry bellowed.

"She's probably hiding under your fucking bed!" she shrieked.

The two of them exchanged another streak of hurt words that culminated in one door slamming, then another. I counted to ten, peered into the empty living room and, when I was sure it was safe to duck out, ran like the place was timed to blow.

Chapter 41

Sid was awake when I got back, staring slack-jawed at a rerun of *Let's Make a Deal* with Baldrick curled up next to him. "Where have you been?" he asked, eyes unable to focus, his words measured and paced.

I placed his glasses and his keys on the coffee table next to the still-folded note I'd left him. I tossed his wallet and his phone down on the couch. "Cards are all still in there—she didn't have time to use them. Cash is gone, but I suspect it's where it would have ended up anyways."

"Hope she bought something nice," he said sarcastically, clicking off the TV like the remote was made of lead. "How did you get this?"

"We met for brunch." I poured myself the last cup of coffee and sat down next to him. "She probably thought she could blackmail me, but I got the drop on her. Gloria called; she was worried about you. We talked for a bit. I kind of dig her."

"What did you two have to talk about?" he snarled.

"About what a sweetheart you are."

His eyes shifted to the side and his mouth pulled into a hard line. "About what a sucker I am," he repeated.

"Maybe," I said. I wanted to put my arms around him, hold

him tight against all the sordid ugliness of the world. "But you're my sucker."

He eyed me queerly, as though trying to smile. He lifted his hand to the back of my neck and pulled me in close, kissing me with swollen lips. He shifted back against the arm of the sofa and I braced myself, not wanting to land on his busted ribs. He arched his body into mine and put his arms around me, pulling me in close. If any of it pained him, he didn't let on.

My cheek was wet and I tasted copper. I looked down to see a smear of blood on Sid's mouth. "Shit," he said, sitting up and reaching for a tissue. "Sorry." He pressed it against his busted lip.

"It's all right," I said, disappointed. I hadn't been expecting the kiss, but I'd be kidding myself if I said I hadn't been hoping for it, a knight's reward for a completed quest. I was giddy and aching for more; I changed the subject before I attacked him again. "Want a grilled cheese?"

"That sounds great," he replied, his voice hoarse with what sounded like regret.

I'M SURE THE pills helped, but Sid couldn't stop laughing when I told him about my adventure in his apartment. I left out the part about my meeting with Cinderella and Gloria's scheme to catch her. He hadn't wanted to admit it was Cinderella last night, so all I could hope was that she had quietly been busted and everything would go back to normal.

We didn't talk much as we watched *The Commish* and ate potato-leek soup from the deli up the street, but I kept hoping he'd lean in for another kiss. I made up the couch for him, not wanting to make him feel awkward by inviting him into my bed. I didn't want to take the risk that he'd decline with the same forced politeness he used when turning down coke at Terry's parties.

But even after he popped another Vicodin and said good night, I lay awake in my own darkness, staring up into the night's abyss. I couldn't stop thinking about the bittersweet perfection of that kiss. Except for the blood, it wasn't too unlike my first kiss with Catch, the silent prelude, the electric distance between our mouths. We had been lying on the grass in the campus nature preserve, staring up at the cold stars as he prattled on about yet another girl who'd broken his heart. And then he turned to me, and I turned to him, and the next thing I knew, our bodies were tangled tight to each other. After that, we didn't kiss again for another three months, another girl for him, a short-lived relationship for me, and then the inevitable absence that led us back to each other. And then for a year it was just us, until Amanda came along and ruined everything.

After about an hour, I got up, turned on the light, and got out the Boyfriend Box. My eyes burned hot as I held Catch's letters, hands trembling as I opened one of the envelopes postmarked from Ireland, his senior semester abroad. He wrote in green ink about whiskey, about the beautiful countryside, and at last he wrote, *For all the fun I'm having here, part of me is counting down the days until I come home to you. The sheep are great, but they keep baaing over the TV, and my real best friend would know that I hate that.*

Those three months had been like a prison sentence and his letters were my only moments of release. I'd written to him every week, filling the envelopes with magazine clippings and photos, postcards with song lyrics written on the back. I wondered if he still had all of them in a box of his own, stashed in an attic or a basement or the bedroom at his parents' house.

The postmark on the letter was just two years before the final showdown, the fateful night when I watched him leave with her and never come back. In two years we'd go from being friends to confidants to something resembling lovers, and then, finally, to bitter adversaries, each mortally wounded by the other's inability to figure out what the fuck we were feeling.

And then suddenly Sid was there. I hadn't heard him get up. "What are you doing?" he asked, sitting down next to me.

I didn't want to tell him about Catch. I hadn't told anyone about him; even college friends like Reese only knew that we weren't friends anymore, with none of the details. If I told anyone, I rationalized, I could be blamed, or worse, they might side with him and I would lose one more friend to this terrible war of love. Even if I'd wanted to confess it all to Sid, Catch's name would have stuck in my throat like dry bread, choking me to death.

"Just thinking about old boyfriends," I lied, holding up a tape Ryan had made me. "George put so much love and thought into those mixes he made KitKat, and this one is just kind of standard. I mean, he put Third Eye Blind's "Jumper" on there. Who puts a suicide song on a mix CD?"

He shrugged. "The late nineties were a confusing time," he said, reaching over and taking the tape out of my hand. "But that's not who you're thinking about tonight, is it?"

He had me there. "How do you know?"

He picked up a postcard from where I'd let it fall by my side and for a terrifying moment I panicked, thinking he would read it aloud and demand an explanation. Instead, he handed it back to me, Guinness logo facing up. "Because no man who would have broken your heart like this would have made you a tape," he said. "CD, maybe, but no one outside of Williamsburg has made a mix tape since 1998 at the absolute latest."

"Except George Parker Lennox," I said, pointing to the tape on my dresser.

"Except George Parker Lennox," he said in agreement. "But my point is, as long as I've known you, Jett, you've carried around some kinda hurt that could only have happened recently. You're always looking over your shoulder like you're running from something, holding your heart in a lock box you don't seem to have the key to."

"You got me," I said. I put the postcard in the box and sucked in a long, slow breath. "This guy, Catch, my best friend through the end of college and into grad school. I can't get into it tonight; it's too complicated and I'd probably have to draw you a diagram.

But no matter how I tell it, the end is the same. He's gone because I didn't mean enough for him to stick around." It wasn't even that simple, it wasn't even that kind. Catch had the ability to love me better than any man I'd known and damage me just the same. The night he walked out, a coldness had settled into my soul, a chill I could never escape.

The chill was there until Sid put his arms around me. Sid understood everything as though by instinct, like our souls were such precise photocopies that we'd forgotten which one of us was the original. I began to feel warmth in the piece of my heart that I'd long given up for dead. And for a moment, I forgot about Catch.

Even with a face like a raw steak, Sid still had a proud beauty to him. His eyes got a glazed, feral distance as the pills kicked in. I remembered that look from the nights Catch would drink that last glass of wine and brush my mouth with his fingertips while I held my breath, resisting the urge to take one in my teeth, taste him on the tip of my tongue. Sometimes he'd tell me he adored me, stopping just short of saying *love* until one night the dreaded word spilled out of him. *A drunk man's words are a sober man's thoughts,* he'd said, breath fragrant with wine, mouth just inches from mine. It wasn't the first—or the last—time he'd said it, but that moment is frozen in time, crystalline, so easily shattered that I never dared to touch it, worried it would break and the two of us would just go back to being normal, terrified of how we made each other feel.

Sid took my chin between his fingers and my breath caught hard in my chest. He turned my face to his and kissed me. I could still taste the mint of his toothpaste.

"I have so much to tell you," he whispered, mouth against mine. "But you wouldn't believe me if I told you tonight."

Chapter 42

LEARNING THE HARD WAY

woke up to the faint sound of a kettle about to boil. Baldrick was sleeping in the space that Sid had been in the night before. How is it, I asked myself, that I couldn't feel 160 pounds of man rise just inches away from me but could hear a teakettle across the apartment and through a closed door? I looked at the clock. Six thirty A.M.

Sid was showered, dressed, and stirring coffee grounds in the French press. "Good mornin', darlin'," he said, pushing down on the plunger. "I didn't want to slip out without leaving you some coffee."

"Where are you going?" I asked.

"The office," he said. "Not all of us can take ourselves off the books."

His left eye socket was the color of a sliced-open plum. The swelling in his lips had gone down a little, but he still had a nasty cut on his cheek. "Sid," I said. "You cannot go in looking like that."

"I cannot afford to miss work," he said. "As it is, I'll be lucky if I'm only a half an hour late and no one asks how my weekend went."

"At least let me do something about that bruise," I said. "Make us some coffee and I'll see what I can dig up."

I found a sample of bareMinerals in Fairly Light and a cotton ball from the bottom of my grandmother's bathroom drawer, and while we sipped our coffee I smeared the powder on as much of his face as I could cover. "You're a little more olive," I remarked. "But it will at least take some of that color out. What are you going to say if someone asks?"

"The truth," he said, washing down another Vicodin with a sip of coffee. "That I got mugged."

"Maybe they'll send you home anyways," I said. "In which case, get some more clothes and come back here."

He looked up from under his lashes. He was so goddamn beautiful that I wanted to make him the wallpaper on my phone. "You mean that?"

"Of course," I said. "You think I'm going to let you go home to Terry like that?"

He let out a half breath, half laugh. "Okay," he said. "Okay, yeah. For a few days. I'll do that."

"And I'll go on a Trader Joe's run," I said. "We can hit the Redbox when you get back from work."

He stood up and kissed me on the cheek. Then he bent a little further and kissed me—quick—on the mouth. "It'll be like playing house," he said.

After he left, it was all I could do not to dance around the apartment. I didn't even know what this feeling was. Love? Joy? A grown-up version of the thrill you get when your mom says your best friend can stay the whole weekend? I was giddy in a way I had forgotten I could feel. I kissed Baldrick on the head, put on Sid's copy of the Psychedelic Furs' *Mirror Moves,* and spun around the living room. This was *heaven,* I mouthed along. This was *the whole of our hearts.* I didn't care that it was only seven A.M. If this was what early mornings looked like, I would get up with the sunrise for the rest of my life.

When I was finished dancing, I took a shower and used Sid's still-damp towel. Everything he'd touched suddenly seemed precious and holy and terrifying all at once. What if two days from now, when the drugs and the fear and Cinderella wore off, he realized that this was not meant to be, that the kisses and the two nights we'd slept beside each other were out of loneliness and need and nothing more? I couldn't stand the thought.

I filed away his record and put *Pretenders II* on in the background while I washed out our coffee cups. The phone rang. Philip wanted me to come in whenever I could get a minute. I didn't have any other plans for the morning, so I got dressed in jeans and a cardigan and my Doc Martens. Outside it was foggy and cool, but it would be summer by the afternoon. Maybe Sid and I would go out for a walk.

There was a newspaper stand on the corner and even from halfway down the block I recognized the face on the cover.

Cinderella. GLASS STRIPPER NABBED IN ROBBERY PLOT! the headline screamed.

Sid was going to kill me.

I HAD MEANT to tell Sid everything, but we'd gotten so wrapped up in that strange happiness that I hadn't wanted to disturb the moment by reminding him of the girl who'd rolled him. And I sure as hell didn't expect it to make the front page of the tabloids. It wasn't that big of a bust.

Maybe the next murder I got myself wrapped up in would be sexier, I thought as Lauren opened the door to Philip's office and showed me in.

Philip smiled, but it did nothing to settle my nerves. "You know," he began as I passed him the bag, "I have never had an assistant as good as you. I wish there was a way I could promote you, but this will have to do until I figure that out." He set a small lavender box between us. "Go on, open it."

I convinced my trembling hands to slip off the bow and it opened to reveal a slim silver cuff bracelet with my name etched in delicate script. "It's beautiful," I breathed. "Thank you."

"You're welcome," he said. "I figured that you deserved something pretty you could wear on the outside."

I slipped it onto my left wrist, admiring the way it caught the dim light of his office. But even though our jewelry looked nothing alike, all I could think of was KitKat, the bracelet she'd treasured, the one she'd been buried without. Before I could stop them, my eyes started to tear up.

"Jett?" Philip asked. "Is everything all right?"

I started bawling. I was at a dead end. Two days ago I had been so sure that it was all about to come together, but with Sid and Cinderella, I'd lost track of everything I'd had. And now I was going to lose Sid, and I had to confess to Philip that I hadn't followed his advice to leave this case alone. If I was lucky, I'd be able to keep the bracelet when he fired me.

He looked like he wasn't quite sure what to do, but he opened his drawer, got out a white handkerchief, and passed it to me. I wiped my eyes and he waited with his hands folded on his chest for me to get myself together. "I'm sorry," I said. "I really love the bracelet—it's just . . ."

I blurted out the whole story. I even told him about my search for her killer, despite his warning to me not to. He listened like I was telling him a fairy tale before bedtime. And when I'd gasped myself to the dead end, he leaned forward, hands still folded, face unreadable.

"I know I told you not to dig into this case," he began. "But I'm actually impressed with how you've handled it."

"How?" I sniffled. "I didn't solve it. I don't think it's going to be solved, and Bronco's going to go to prison."

"I wish I knew what to tell you," he said. "I really do. I wish I could impart some sort of PI wisdom to help you crack the case. But it's never as easy as it looks on TV. Most of the time, the bad guys get away. Hopefully they just don't send an innocent guy to jail in their place. Tell you what," he said, opening his drawer again. "I know a couple good lawyers, real sharks, but they get the job done. I'll put in some calls and see if one of them will take your friend's case. It's not much, but it's a start." He set down two business cards and a packet of his lingerie between us. "Just do me one more favor," he said.

"Anything," I said. And I meant it. A fair chance for Bronco was worth whatever he wanted from me.

He pointed to the bracelet. "Just keep it covered until you get out of here," he said with a wink. "Wouldn't want the other temps to get jealous."

Chapter 43

WHAT A FOOL BELIEVES

Waiting for Sid to get back was utter agony. I paced the apartment in silence, checking my phone every few minutes to see if he'd texted. I made rationalizations to myself: *The paper might be sold out by the time he gets home; he wouldn't have noticed it out of the corner of his eye if it was still almost swollen shut.* More than once, I had to lie down and take long, slow breaths like I'd learned in my college yoga class. I got a B in that class. Who gets a B in yoga? Someone who can't calm down, that's who.

The phone finally rang and I dove for it. "Did you see the paper this morning?" Gloria gushed. She was snapping gum that sounded like gunshots.

"I did," I replied. "You worked fast—how'd it go down?"

"Turns out Fairy Tales is a favorite spot for cops," she said. "And not just for the girls. They'd been looking at the owner for drugs, which he doesn't do because he's actually a pretty decent guy, and I'm not dumb enough to do my part-time gig at my full-time job. But when word came down from an anonymous source—let's just say she's mad cute and leave it at that—that guys were getting rolled, they shifted their priorities." She snapped her gum again. "Fun fact: you can't blow bubbles with nicotine gum," she said. "So Cinderella was working a couple other guys on the line when Sid wasn't around, and when she took that mark out back, someone other than Tommy followed—they caught her right in the act. Guy still ended up in the hospital, but only a couple of bruises."

"They got Tommy too?"

"Of course," she said. "And Cinderella will flip on him like a pancake breakfast. She'll probably skate on a misdemeanor, but she won't be back at Fairy Tales, that's for damn sure. And that's all I care about. But hey, one of the detectives slipped me a fifty on a twenty-dollar lap dance. I'll rat out the other dancers on parking tickets if it means he'll come back." She laughed.

I wanted to laugh with her, but I kept looking at the clock, wondering when—and if—Sid would walk back through my door. The buzzer rang, rattling both me and Baldrick nearly out of our skins. He skittered under the bed and I mumbled some kind of good-bye to Gloria. Now was the moment of truth.

At least he came back, I told myself as I waited the three anxious minutes for him to climb the stairs. And when Sid finally did arrive in my doorway, he had a copy of the paper under his arm. I stepped aside and he tossed it down on the table. Neither of us spoke.

"Not the most flattering photo of her," he finally said.

"Sid—"

He held up his hand. "Save it, Jett," he said. He crossed the room and sat on the radiator, staring out the window for a minute before he spoke again. "I thought I was special to her," he said. "I thought she felt for me the same way I felt for her. I'm not even so mad that she rolled me, but to find out she was doing this to other guys too? That I wasn't her first, or even her last, mark? I couldn't even be special enough to be the only guy she robbed in the alley." He ran his hand through his hair, took off his glasses, and rubbed his eyes. I stood there, hanging on his every word.

"I thought she was angry at me," he said. "I thought I'd done something wrong, disrespected her, like I deserved it somehow. That in itself was the fairy tale, some weird horrid hope that I could earn her forgiveness. But there wasn't any to be had. I was just a target. So not only has my heart been broken—I really did love her, Jett—but I feel like an idiot for falling in love in the first place."

I crept up behind him and put my arms around his shoulders. He leaned back into my hold. "One day I'll be grateful for this," he said, stroking my arm with a firm hand. "One day I'll thank Gloria for letting me bleed all over her fishnets. And one day I'll thank you for being right about Cinderella all along." He let out a long sigh. "But tonight, all I'm asking is that you please let me mourn. Go get us a bottle of cheap cabernet and let me play a bunch of depressing records and drink too much and maybe even cry. Just give me that, Jett, and tomorrow I'll be fine. I promise. I just need tonight."

I put on the Smiths' *Strangeways, Here We Come* and left him with the A-side while I went and bought wine. He drank two glasses in the living room and played "Last Night I Dreamt That Somebody Loved Me" three times while I made dinner. I joined him until all the records were played and the bottle was empty. And when we went to bed, I held him in the darkness as he let out a handful of soft sobs before surrendering to sleep.

Chapter 44

EVERYTHING FALLS APART

Aside from his preexisting injuries and a mild headache, Sid kept his promise about being better in the morning. He was almost cheerful as he made coffee, dressed in clothes I'd smuggled out of his apartment, let me smear more concealer on his fading bruises, and kissed me before heading into work.

I had just put shampoo in my hair when I heard the phone ringing. I dove out of the shower to grab it, hoping it was work. It had been almost a week since I'd been called in for anything other than laundry, and not only was my fridge nearly empty, my student loan was also coming due. As badly as I wanted the time to work on KitKat's case, I wasn't going to solve anything if I had to move back in with my parents.

Instead it was Reese, creator, in part, of the Boyfriend Box. I hadn't talked to him since Christmas, when he'd come to New Jersey for obligatory family gatherings. Whenever he was home, we made it a point to get together and catch up on everything we couldn't say over e-mail or Facebook.

"Didn't actually expect you to pick up," he said by way of hello. "What the hell are you doing up this early?"

I didn't want to tell him I was standing naked in my living room, dripping water and cheap shampoo all over the carpet.

"Could ask you the same thing," I said, taking the phone with me back to the bathroom to grab a towel.

"I'm not up," he said. "I haven't gone to bed yet. I've been playing *Gun Shy* all night. I got the fucking Uzi! It's insane, best game of the year."

"You say that about every game you play," I teased.

"That's because games keep getting better," he scoffed. "But I didn't call to talk about video games. I've got some bad news, and I hate to be the one to tell you this early in the morning. Really wish you'd just stayed in bed."

"If you'd had the man I had in my kitchen making coffee, you'd be up at the crack of dawn too," I said.

"If there was a man in my kitchen making coffee I'd be telling the fucking police that there was a lunatic in my house using up all my fucking coffee," Reese said. "But if that's the case, maybe this won't sting so badly. Is he still there?"

"He went to work," I said. "Reese, just spit it out."

"Catch's getting married," he said. "To Amanda. Saw it on Facebook this morning, thought I should be the one to break the news to you before you saw it someplace else. I'm sorry."

I could see Amanda as though she was standing in front of me, the impossibly beautiful curve of her bronzer-brown back marred with a Playboy bunny tramp stamp peeking out over the top of her low-rise jeans. Catch's lean, pale hand had covered the tattoo as he'd slid his tongue into her mouth, stealing a kiss in the stucco kitchen of my $350-a-month basement apartment like I wasn't standing there with dinner for two just out of the oven. It was the Killers' "Mr. Brightside" come to life right in front of me.

"Jett? Jett, stay with me."

"I'm here," I said, warping back to my ugly reality.

"You okay?"

"Not really," I said. "So please don't be offended when I hang up."

"No offense taken—"

I dropped the phone on the couch. I forgot I had a couch. The whole world went numb and empty, a white room with just a black rectangle for a door and somewhere, faintly, the sound of a record needle easing off the last groove.

Catch had left the door open and left me standing there in it, watching the two of them leave with their hands in each other's back pockets. She'd sneered when I tried to put *Excitable Boy* on the turntable and asked me if I had any Katy Perry because *records are for old people*. Catch had acted like he'd never heard of Warren Zevon, like he hadn't bought me that album for my birthday, the night he kissed cupcake frosting off my lips, tracing one smear on the inside of my knee before maneuvering his mouth further up my thighs. I should have just put the record on. Maybe it would have changed time like Marty McFly, stopping her from cuddling up to him and cooing, *I made him throw out all those hideous metal CDs,* like I would be impressed with the bone-china box she kept his balls in. Somewhere in the back of my mind I heard Huey Lewis, but he was wrong, so fucking wrong. The power of love was an ugly, unwieldy one.

Chapter 45

KING OF WISHFUL THINKING

By 8:20 A.M. I was on the Megabus to Baltimore, making a playlist for Catch and trying to rehearse what I was going to say to him. I wasn't going to get all John Cusack *Say Anything* on him with my phone held high and "Reconsider Me" blasting. Life is not a movie, I told myself, but I couldn't let him get married to the girl who'd come between us. I was going to have to do it calmly, rationally, and hopefully over lunch, because I was starving. There wasn't time for breakfast when I had to plead my case for true love. This terrible silence between us had gone on long enough.

I had been quietly compiling this playlist for years, songs that I heard at random times with his spirit still clinging: John Mellencamp's "Key West Intermezzo (I Saw You First)"; Donald Fagen's "The Nightfly"; the Cure, "Cut Here"; Sting's "Ghost Story"; the Smiths, "Bigmouth Strikes Again." It was a mix to say I was sorry, that I missed him. Songs strung together in hopes that maybe my tunes would carve deeper than my words could.

I downloaded Warren Zevon's final album, *The Wind*, recorded just months before he died. I had it back at home, buried at the bottom of the Boyfriend Box, but I hadn't listened to it since the day Zevon had died. Catch and I had skipped class and gone to buy the album, played it through once while we drank a bottle of wine, and kissed and cried. We vowed to only listen to it one more time in our lives: when the other was gone from this world. We hadn't used the word *death* because death does not exist when you're young and invincible. But if there was ever a moment that called for "Keep Me in Your Heart," it was this one.

My phone buzzed with a text from Sid. *I'll be late for dinner,* he wrote in his perfect grammar. *Have to get a few more things at the apartment.*

Any other day, I'd have been panicked that he was going back to Cinderella, but today, I was relieved. This gave me plenty of time to see Catch and still get back to Brooklyn in time to pop a frozen lasagna in the oven. *Don't forget to pick up wine,* I texted back.

I don't even have to bring a corkscrew, he wrote a minute later.

I stared at his message without words for a response. If everything went according to plan, if Catch remembered that I was the girl he loved, Sid would take back his corkscrew and his records and the shirts he'd hung in my closet. He might never tell me what he couldn't tell me two nights ago. In the back of my throat I tasted wine and blood, coffee and painkillers.

I ignored what I knew, the words unspoken between us, and turned all my concentration to the playlist in my hands. I could figure out what I would say to Sid later. He deserved more than a text message.

CATCH'S LINKEDIN PROFILE revealed that he worked for Traubert House Publishing, a music publishing company that specialized in jazz and blues. It was a short walk from the bus to his office building, which looked like a space station from those sci-fi paperbacks I'd always teased him about, chrome and wood painted the color of dried blood, floors polished to such a shine I worried people could see up my dress as I walked. The air was so eerily silent that the clicking of heels and the ringing of phones and the *ting* of arriving elevators all echoed with eardrum-shattering volume. Even the foyer had a futuristic elegance that made Hartford look like a one-room schoolhouse.

At the end of a corridor was a secretary behind a *Star Trek*–looking desk, her hair done up in a severe bun and her blouse all but sheer.

"I–I'm looking for Catcher McCarthy," I stammered.

She picked up a slim black phone and dialed with Pinterest-y nails more elaborately painted than the ceiling of the Sistine Chapel. "He's not answering," she said, gesturing with those same nails to a bank of sharp, low-slung chairs on the other end of the room. "You can wait, if you'd like."

I took a deep breath, as if that could reinflate my confidence, and picked up an old issue of *Rolling Stone,* staring at bylines on interviews with Adele and articles about Arcade Fire, wishing my name was there instead. Maybe then Catch would have noticed me sooner, seen that I wasn't content to just fade into his history. Maybe he would have found me instead, been haunted by my name, or maybe we would have found ourselves reaching for the last coconut-shrimp skewer at the same industry party. If only I'd tried a little harder, gotten a better internship, not been so scared to put myself out there in my career and in love . . . I ran through all the could-have-been scenarios, trying to figure out how to salvage the scene.

Then Catch stepped out of the elevator in a blue suit and pink shirt, mead-colored curls cropped close, and the whole damn world slowed to a freeze frame.

Chapter 46

KEEP ME IN YOUR HEART

His green eyes narrowed and my knees got buttery. The suit, the tie, the curls now shorn short—it was like staring at a stranger. Three years seemed like an eternity and a blink all at once, and I became acutely aware of how different I looked: the weight I'd put on, the hair I'd chopped off as though it might make me forget how his fingers had felt against my scalp.

He dismissed whoever he was riding with and approached me with a firm walk that wasn't his. Nothing about him was familiar, not even the way he put his arm around my shoulder and guided me into an empty hallway, out of sight of his coworkers.

"Reese told you, didn't he?" he said.

"I got on the first bus as soon as I heard," I said. "Catch, I had to see you. . . ."

"Why?" he demanded. "You think you're going to show up and talk me out of marrying the woman I've been with since you left me?"

"*I* left *you*?" I snarled. "Funny, that's not the way I remember it."

He held up his hands. "I'm not doing this here," he said. A girl in an emerald-green sweater set passed between us and he turned toward the wall. I didn't know what I'd been expecting. A kiss? Another slammed door? I wanted to reach for him across the void, apologize and beg. This was not how it was supposed to happen.

He took a visibly deep breath and faced me, a flicker of his old self passing across his face. "My first instinct is to just walk away from you," he said.

"And your second?"

He crossed the hallway, put his hands on the wall behind me, boxing me in. "To throw you in that elevator, pin you up against the wall, and fuck like we're back in the library during finals week," he murmured, his mouth all but brushing my ear.

All the breath I'd ever held escaped my body like someone had yanked opened a rubber plug in my side. "Good thing I wore a dress," I whispered.

He laughed—it was as velvety as I remembered—then stepped back and took my hands. "How about we just go to lunch?"

IN HIS SHARP suit, Catch looked a little out of place in a corner pub filled with tech hipsters and trust-fund freelancers. "You're worth a four-star steak," he said, taking the menu from the waitress. "But this seemed more appropriate."

We ordered burgers and a bottle of cheap pinot. The waitress returned a moment later with the wine and two glasses so clunky they might as well have been plastic. "Let's talk about music so I can write this off as a business lunch," he joked as she poured. He held up his glass for a toast. "To the late, great Warren Zevon."

We toasted. For a moment, everything seemed normal, familiar, and perfect. There was a jukebox in the corner. I briefly toyed with the idea of pumping in my last few bucks to make a soundtrack for this reunion, but that would mean leaving his side. The thought of doing that, even for just a minute, seemed unbearable.

"I heard you moved to New York," he said.

I didn't want to waste what little time we had on small talk, but we weren't going to be able to get to the heart of this matter until I'd had a drink. I nodded. "About a year ago."

"What do you do there?"

I couldn't exactly tell him I was trying to solve my neighbor's murder, at least not in here. "Temp work," I said. "Still trying to get the journalism thing off the ground."

"You still sing?"

"Not in public." I wasn't counting the night at the Brenner Gallery. I thought about the way Sid had looked at me, the way he'd disappeared. My heart felt like it weighed a hundred pounds. "You still play?"

He swirled the wine in his glass. "Amanda's not a fan," he said. "I think about it sometimes, maybe joining a little jazz trio to play at wedding receptions and gallery openings, but . . ." He stared at his glass for a moment before looking up at me. "My trumpet didn't sound right without you."

"I felt the same way," I said. "About my voice."

He leaned back in his chair and glanced around the bar. "I come here when I miss those days," he said. "I put a couple old songs on the jukebox—no Zevon, I already checked—and have a couple beers and a burger until I feel normal again. I've been here two years and I still don't feel like this is my normal life; it's like it's some sort of amnesia. Like the Talking Heads—not my beautiful house, not my beautiful wife." He took a drink and grinned. "But that's what you came here to talk about, isn't it?"

"You always could read my mind," I joked.

He reached across the table and put his hand on mine. "Is it wrong that I'm glad to see you?" he asked with a squeeze.

"Why would that be wrong?" I replied, the wine giving my heart small feathered wings that fluttered hard against my ribs.

"Because I've spent the last three years trying to forget you," he said. "I put away your letters, your pictures, all the CDs you made me. I'd be doing fine until the Pretenders' 'Night in My Veins' would start playing at the grocery store and I would just stand there, frozen in the middle of the cereal aisle, trying not to remember what you tasted like in the backseat of my car and trying not to cry."

I gripped my chair to keep from falling out of it. I couldn't tell if it was him or the wine that was making me suddenly dizzy.

"I did the same thing," I confessed. "But when Reese told me, I knew I couldn't hide from you anymore. I had to see you. I couldn't let it end the way it did, with you walking away like that." I took another drink, a momentary reprieve from the aching depth of our conversation. "You left me," I said. "You walked out my door and you never came back."

"Except that you're changing the story," he said. "Did you forget what you said to me that night? As I was leaving?"

Amanda had already been in the car. He'd pretended he'd forgotten something, come back downstairs, and knocked on my door. *What do you think?* he'd asked. *Isn't she great?* I'd known that eagerness in his eyes; it was the same look he got in the moments just before he would kiss me. But there were no kisses between us that night. He so desperately wanted his best friend's approval of his new girlfriend, and all I could offer him was *As long as you're fucking her, I guess you don't need me.*

Then I closed the door, and we never spoke again.

He was right. I had told myself the story wrong, recast myself as the victim for so long that I had forgotten what really happened. This silence had started with me, with the hurt I caused. I could have said anything else. I could have told him I was happy for him. I could have called him the next morning and apologized, talked it out, dealt with it. But in my head I made it so that he'd just thrown me aside when a new girl came along, just so that I didn't have to admit that I was the jerk who ruined everything.

I started to get up to go cry in the bathroom like the big girl that I was, but he wrapped his fingers around my wrist. "Stay," he said. "I haven't seen you in three years—I'm not letting you out of my sight now."

"I'm sorry," I blurted. "I never meant that to be a good-bye or a breakup. I was angry, I was hurt. . . ."

"I'm sorry too," he said. "I shouldn't have been making out with her in your kitchen. I should have called the next day, tried to smooth things over, but I was just so furious with you. But then those few days of silence turned into weeks, then months, and now years. Three years, Jett, and I still haven't figured out why you were trying to sabotage my happiness."

"Because *I* loved you," I said. "And I thought you loved me, so when you brought her over, it felt like you were flaunting that you *didn't* love me."

He put his glass down and dabbed at the edge of his gorgeous mouth with a napkin. "I never knew," he murmured.

That I wasn't buying, not for one damn second. Not after the CDs I'd made, the sex we'd had, all those nights where I'd held him so close in post-orgasm bliss that I swore our veins had intertwined and we were sharing the same blood. "You never knew? Catch, how could you have *not* known?"

"You never said anything," he said. "I must have told you a thousand times that I loved you and you never said it back."

How dense could a man get? "Do you think I put 'My Lucky Day' on a CD because I thought you'd like the Smoking Popes?" I demanded.

"That's just it," he said. "*You* never said it. You let everyone else do the talking for you. And believe me, I played those CDs over and over, trying to interpret, trying to rationalize that yes, yes, you did love me. And then I would blurt it out and you would ignore me, turn up the radio, go back to your dinner, and I would just sit there feeling like an idiot. At least when I had you half-naked in my bed, I could pretend you loved me."

I looked down at the piled-high plate the waitress set down in front of me, suddenly not hungry anymore. I grabbed my glass and drained it, hoping the wine would soften the awful truth— that I had broken his heart long before Amanda had even arrived on the scene.

"So maybe Amanda doesn't challenge me," he continued, pouring me another drink. "Maybe she's got terrible taste in movies and music, but *she loves me*. I need that. I need to be loved, Jett. It's a cold, lonely world out there."

"It was us against that cold, lonely world, remember?"

"It was, but too often, it just felt like there was you, and there was me, and we were operating in some sort of Venn diagram of music and school and making out on your couch."

"No," I said. "No, it wasn't like that. You were my first thought in the morning and my last thought before bed, even when you weren't there next to me. You were my everything: what I wore, what I ate, what I breathed. There wasn't a word for how I felt about you. *Love* wasn't strong enough to describe how my heart turned to stone when you had to go to a class we weren't in together. *Love* was a word for people who weren't capable of feeling what we felt."

"It would have done just fine," he said. "I would have known what you meant because I felt the same way. I understood, Jett, I was there, I knew what was between us, I just didn't think you did."

Suddenly, there was no Sid. There was no Bronco or George. There was no William or Gabe or Jeremy; there wasn't even Amanda. There was and had only ever been Catch and I. "Maybe we can repair this."

He reached across the table and took my hand again. "Life is not a love song, Jett," he said. "It's not a fairy tale or a John Hughes movie."

"Catch, give me another chance. . . ."

He shook his head. "It's too late," he said. "Even if we exchange numbers and friend each other on Facebook and have lunch every month, we're never going to be the same people we were. Even if I went outside and broke up with Amanda right now, we couldn't repair this."

"You don't know that—"

"I don't," he said. "But what are we going to talk about? Work? Our spouses? Jett, I don't want to remember you like that. I want to remember staring at the tops of your thighs during our jazz band rehearsals; you always wore those thigh-high stockings with the seams because you knew I could see the lace through the slit in the back of your dress."

"Is that why the director was always chewing you out for coming in late?"

"He should have been grateful I came in at all," he joked. "I want to remember lying on your dorm floor listening to *The Envoy* and complaining about how lame My Chemical Romance and Nickelback were. Not this. Not spreadsheets and conference calls and complaints about the kids we'll one day both have. I don't want grown-up Jett and I don't want to be grown-up Catch. It's ugly and it's unfair, but this is the way it has to be." He was breathing hard, and I thought I saw the faintest fringe of tears on his lashes. He dumped the rest of the wine in his glass and inhaled most of it, hands shaking. "For both our sakes."

I excused myself to the bathroom and he let me go this time. I put the lid down on the toilet and took out my phone and started to add one last song to his playlist, Simply Red's "Sunrise." *Maybe next time I'll be yours and maybe you'll be mine . . .* But as I looked at it there on the screen, all I could think about was Sid's corkscrew sitting on my counter at home, and I knew Catch was right. He always was. I didn't want this version of him any more than he wanted this version of me.

For as passionately as I'd always loved Catch, he and I ran along parallel tracks, reaching for each other but never quite touching. The unspoken knowledge that the fire between us couldn't burn forever was what had driven our hunger, like love during wartime. But the war was over, and all that was left were the lives we had rebuilt from the rubble. This was the life he had salvaged.

Back home, Sid would be waiting with a glass of wine and Oingo Boingo on the hi-fi. That was the life I had made, and that was the life I wanted. I deleted my selection, leaving the playlist as it had originally been.

When I got back Catch had paid the check. I held up my phone. "I made you a mix," I said.

He gave me a smile filled with sorrow but held out his phone. I tapped it against his in an odd sort of intimacy. "I don't know when I'll ever be able to listen to it," he confessed.

"But at least you know it's there," I said. "For when you're ready."

He escorted me to the bus stop, hugged me good-bye, and held on for the last extra second I would ever hold him. The expensive cologne he wore couldn't disguise the scent of him I knew so well. But there weren't words. No awkward good-bye, no last *I love you*. He just looked at me with a stern sadness and I looked at him through the stained glass of a broken heart.

He watched me get on the bus.

I watched him walk away.

I played Warren Zevon's "Accidentally Like a Martyr" six times in a row and cried silently the whole way back to Brooklyn.

Chapter 47

TURN THAT HEARTBEAT OVER AGAIN

had finally managed to stop sobbing by the time Sid got home, but the lack of Trader Joe's bags and my red, swollen eyes were probably a dead giveaway that our evening's plans had changed.

"He's getting married, Sid," I blubbered. "Catch. The one who broke my heart. He's still going to marry that *bimbo* and I never told him, Sid, I never told him how I felt and now it's *too late!*" I wasn't crying because he wasn't marrying me. I was crying out of pride, as though I could have saved him from that suit and his office and whatever cracker-box apartment he and Amanda had filled with IKEA furniture. And because Catch had given me the same speech that George had parceled out into sixty minutes of music. It was like watching his soul come out. KitKat never had to know this grief, but I felt hers along with mine.

I sank into a chair and buried my head in the nest of my arms. I watched under the table as Sid's worn brown oxfords carried him to the kitchen. I lifted my head and watched with blurry eyes as he uncorked the bottle of wine he'd come home with. But he didn't pour me any, didn't offer a few more ruby-colored hours away from my heartache. He sloshed a heavy measure into a dirty juice glass and killed half of it, then turned and carried it into the living room, his back to me.

I wiped away tears and mascara and rose to my feet, treading as delicately as a gazelle among sleeping lions. "Sid?" I ventured to ask. "Sid, are you all right?"

He dropped the empty glass on the carpet and took my face in his hands, kissing me deeper than any man had ever tried to before. It was a kiss to shut me up, to stop my sobbing, to save my soul. "I don't want to hear one more word," he whispered, his lips barely brushing against my cheek. "Not one goddamn word, not one more name. Not unless it's mine."

Those were terms I could agree with.

I AWOKE AROUND midnight to faint music and empty sheets. It took me a minute to place what it was: the Psychedelic Furs, "The Ghost in You." I put on my panties and Sid's yellow oxford shirt and found him stretched out on the couch in his gray undershirt and bike-printed boxers, the record player spinning and most of the bottle of wine gone.

The moment couldn't have been any more perfect if it had been set up on film. Everything I had at one time felt for Catch was magnified a hundred times as I watched Sid slumber. Nothing hurt. Nothing ached. I was just happy, an utter bliss like I had never felt.

I wasn't even afraid of what dawn would bring. If he wanted to walk out, chalk it up to a lonely mistake, I would be content treasuring these few hours.

He sat up and rubbed his eyes. "Didn't mean to wake you," he said. "I couldn't sleep."

I curled up on the other end of the couch, facing him. "It's a good album," I said. "I haven't played it in a while." I would play this song every day, I promised myself, if it would remind me of this perfect moment. It wasn't just the sex, as good as that was. I wanted to write his name just to see it spelled out. I wanted to get a locker just so I could hang his photo inside the door. And I never wanted to close my eyes, never wanted to fall asleep, just so that I could savor forever these first blossoms of love in my chest.

He leaned in and kissed me. "We never ate," he said. "You want to order some Chinese?"

I nodded and he pulled up the number for Hunan Fun, a twenty-four-hour dumpling joint that Barter Street had grown up around. Rumor had it that the secret to their longevity was that they'd dealt opium in the twenties, weed in the thirties, dope in the forties and fifties, acid in the sixties, and coke up through the eighties. If it didn't require getting dressed, I would have suggested we walk down there, sit in the red and gold vinyl booth next to the big ceramic dragon, drink tea under fringed dome lanterns, split blue and white willow dishes overflowing with sesame chicken and beef chow mein, slurp wonton soup from wide bowls with flat porcelain spoons.

While he placed our order, I went into the other room and made myself presentable. If there was a product that could make hair look as post-sex perfect every day as mine did in the big mirror on my grandmother's antique dresser right then, I would buy it by the shipping crate. There was a text from Natalie on my phone, asking if I wanted to get bubble tea six hours ago. I was almost compelled to text her and tell her that I finally slept with Sid and that it was amazing. I wanted her to be proud, but more than that, I just wanted to brag to anyone who would listen.

He switched the record to Duran Duran's *Rio* and held out his hand. "Let's dance," he said, eyes starry. "We've got twenty minutes before the food shows up."

I mimicked a shy *Me?* gesture and let him pull me in close. He slid his hand down to the small of my back, fusing our bodies as one. "This should be our next house party," he said as we grooved to "Lonely in Your Nightmare." "Late-night pajama dance party. No one can show up before midnight, music is entirely by request. And we'll just dance. No theme, no costume required, just bring food, bring booze, bring records, and dance until dawn."

"*Our* next party?" I teased. "Are you moving in?"

"I already have," he said, waltzing me in a circle. "While you were asleep. You can check the bathroom; my toothbrush is there on the sink. You can't get rid of me now."

"Not until after the food arrives, anyway," I said. "How did you get out of your rent at Terry's place?"

"Left him all my Vicodin," he said. "Figure that's worth at least a month, and if he gets caught, well, I'll just say he stole it."

"You've thought of everything."

"All I thought of was you."

We danced until the doorbell rang. I dove onto the couch, giggling, to hide my half-nakedness under a blanket while Sid exchanged money for food through a crack in the door. He returned with two I-heart-NY bags, and I poured us what was left of the wine.

"Cheers," I said. "To your toothbrush."

He grinned wider than I'd ever seen. "Cheers," he said. "To your sink."

Chapter 48

LOVE ME NOTS

Playing house with Sid was the only thing that kept my mind off KitKat's case. Every evening he arrived with a few more pieces of his apartment: a different shirt, a pair of jeans, the half-flat pillow from his bed, a yellow mug with a chicken on it. We didn't speak in official terms—*moving in, cohabitation, boyfriend, girlfriend.* We drank coffee in the morning and had sex at night. The sex had a strange spontaneity to it, as though every night was the first time we'd found ourselves naked, kissing as though we were discovering it for all of humanity. Even when he brought home a fresh pack of Trojans along with a bottle of wine, he didn't grin or slap my ass or do anything resembling seduction. Night after night, we found ourselves in bed, legs tangled, flesh pressed tight against eager flesh. And every morning, I woke up happy that he was there beside me.

Work picked up at MetroReaders. We'd walk to the subway together and kiss good-bye, meet back on the doorstep in the evening. I had money in my bank account and treated him to dinner. For a few days, I could convince myself that this was how normal people lived. Normal people who weren't trying to solve their friend's murder.

Bronco was going to trial in less than a month. One of Philip's friends had agreed to take his case, but Bronco still wasn't feeling like he was in the clear just yet. I called around to pawnshops, asking about the bracelet. No one had seen a chain plate with a Joe Jackson quote. I went back through her mix tape binder and stalked a few more of her ex-boyfriends on Facebook but found nothing that raised any suspicions. Calvin was living in France. David was now Diana. Neither Bronco or Hillary had any ideas either. I was failing him. I was failing Hillary. And worst of all, I was failing KitKat.

GARBAGE DAY ON Barter Street was like a neighborhood garage sale. There were two kinds of trash: the food scraps and coffee grounds and wads of paper you threw in white bags in the basement for the building super to take, and the boxes of perfectly good items you left on the front steps for people to browse through. I'd gotten an Express pencil skirt from the porch of the building on the corner and two Boz Scaggs records from a box two doors down from Egg School. The unspoken rule was if you found something, it was good karma to leave something on your own porch the following week.

MetroReaders hadn't called me in that day, so after Sid left for work, I gathered up the trash from the bathroom and the kitchen, dumped Baldrick's litter box, and briefly considered going for a browse. I was starting to like being up early, having coffee with Sid in the morning dream-haze. Baldrick liked it too; it meant he got fed earlier and didn't have to sit on my chest and howl until I appeased him.

On the way out the door, I grabbed *The Bridge.* For whatever reason, I couldn't stand the thought of having it in my house one minute longer. Billy Joel could still pack Madison Square Garden; someone on Barter Street had to like him, even ironically.

A 212 number I didn't recognize popped up on my phone. *This better not be Sid at the hospital again,* I thought. For a moment the fear of Tommy's retaliation was a real, concrete thing, until I answered and heard a woman's voice.

"Jett, hi, it's Cassie, from the Bitter End?"

The same Cassie who'd cursed me out for mentioning "Secret Girlfriend"? Before I could snap back with a snarky retort, she jumped in.

"I was a real bitch to you the other night," she admitted. "I don't blame you for not sticking around, and as soon as I noticed you'd left, I realized how hateful I sounded. I was kind of just hoping you'd gone to the bathroom, because I was trying to re-member the lyrics to 'Secret Girlfriend' so I could sing it to you by way of apology. But you left, which is exactly what I would have done. And then this guy called me up to have a bracelet en-graved for you—at least, I assume it was you, I don't think there are too many girls named Jett—and I took it as this cosmic sign that I should apologize."

I couldn't decide whether the feeling in the pit of my stomach was excitement or dread. I hadn't been expecting that kind of apology. I'd forgotten I'd even given her my number. "Yeah, the bracelet was for me," I said. "It looks great. Thanks for calling."

She let out a sigh that sounded like relief. "So now this is going to sound really weird," she continued. "But I'm going record shopping, and I got this idea that you might want to come along. You're so young, do you even know what records are?"

"I've got a turntable here in my apartment," I said. I hated when people asked me that, like I was born in a void with an iPhone in my hand, but I let it slide for her.

"I knew you were cool," she said. "You want to meet me at the cube on Astor? There's a couple good places near there, Salva-tion Armys and the like. You find the best stuff in the dollar bin."

Records *and* an apology? It wasn't going to get much better than that. I looked at the record in my hand. It was no longer destined for the junk pile or to become an ironic plant holder. It would have a home, as all records should.

Besides, it was a long shot, but I wanted to ask her about the bracelet. She said she did engraving, and George wouldn't have bought KitKat jewelry from some Chinatown stall. Maybe she could put word out to the other jewelers in case they had something useful for me.

Chapter 49

ONLY THE GOOD DIE YOUNG

t was easy to spot Cassie in the crowd, even with all the NYU posers taking selfies in front of the cube. She looked like she'd accidentally warped there from the nineties: 505s cuff-rolled over the same blood-red Docs, a tangle of long necklaces spilling down the front of a black tank top, her chunky chain bracelet dangling from her skinny wrist, a black-and-gray checked flannel dangling off her slim shoulders like it was in danger of falling to its death on the sidewalk. It took her half a second to recognize me and then she gave me a hug.

"I'm really sorry," she said again. "I've been staring at your number on my fridge for two weeks trying to get the courage to call you up and apologize."

"It's okay." I dug the record out of my bag and held it out to her. "You played 'State of Grace' at your show; I thought you might like this. Hope you don't have it already."

She took it with an enormous grin. "This is so cool!" she gushed. "God, when I was in high school, I used to play this album all the time. I thought 'Running on Ice' was, like, so deep. How did you know?"

I just smiled, not wanting to tell her its original destiny.

"I'm on this ongoing hunt for the Fontanelles' seven-inch EP," she said as we strolled through the crowd like we owned the crosswalk. "I saw them play out in L.A. when I was visiting my sister. I bought their EP that night—the guy manning their booth had a tattoo of Captain Crunch—but I've long since lost it. I keep hoping it'll turn up in one of these bins. I know I'll never find it but what's there to life if we don't have hope?"

"I've never heard of them," I admitted. "It's weird to think that in the age of iTunes and Spotify, there's a band that can't be found—then again, it took me weeks to track you down."

I jogged a little to keep up with her enormous pace as we started toward St. Marks. I don't get over to St. Marks very often; I don't have any need for Elmo hash pipes or T-shirts with the double bird where the Twin Towers used to be.

"I miss the old St. Marks," said Cassie. "Kim's Video, Love Saves the Day, Religious Sex . . . it all folded up overnight and now it's nothing but tourist T-shirt joints and places for drunk Westchester skanks to get belly-button piercings and hepatitis." She blew a stray curl out of her face. "I had this dream about New York when I moved out here from Minnesota; I saw this gritty, raw place and believed—like everybody does—that I could cut to the heart of it like a surgeon. Too many Lou Reed albums, I guess, but I got here, and I got dirty, and it wasn't at all like I planned."

We crossed Second Avenue and she continued. "But even now, a decade clean, I still miss the New York I bought drugs in, like old punks miss CBGB. So much of it is gone now; Times Square is just a huge Disneyland mall, and all the bright lights and manufactured shit is just fucking smack. You come here, you buy the sparkly M&M's World T-shirt, get your picture taken with some meth-addled homeless dude in a Shrek costume, sit through *Spider-Man: Turn Off the Dark*. Fuck, I'm so old I remember when Green Day was a punk band and not a Broadway show." She smirked and stopped in front of a rickety set of stairs and two card tables of milk crates filled with vinyl no one else wanted.

"Maybe I'm just nostalgic," she said, not looking at me as she began to paw through a crate of Toto records. "I get it, things change, but it seems like everything changes for the cheap and tawdry. People don't like to feel anything anymore; they don't like to take risks. They want what they know and they want it without questions, and that isn't any different than the reasons people take drugs. To hide. To escape. But why have some girl standing alone on a stage with a guitar, reminding you of all the sadness and ache of the world, when you can have Katy Perry shooting whipped cream out of her big plastic tits and telling you that you're just so fucking special?"

I picked through a crate of seventies singer-songwriter LPs and thought about Catch's girlfriend. His *fiancée*. At a time when all the other roads seemed unpaved and littered with potholes, she was smooth, straight highway. I couldn't fault him for choosing Amanda—Cassie and I may have had our pride, sure, but we were standing here flipping through records everyone else had forgotten, griping about a world we didn't understand. Were we really that much better off?

We didn't find anything in the dollar bin and descended into the darkness downstairs. This place looked nothing like Ol' Vinylsides; records were crammed in crates and piled in corners with no real order to them. The manager had tired eyes and a beard that would have put a pirate captain to shame; he barely looked up from an old issue of *Crawdaddy* to acknowledge us. There wasn't an ironic Bee Gees T-shirt or eight-track player to be found.

I picked a two-dollar bin at random while Cassie perused the stacks of seven-inch EPs. I could see what George had first loved in her, how she'd formed the foundations of his heart, which would later be turned toward KitKat. I wondered if he knew she was still here, if he ever looked her up, paused with one finger on the last digit of her phone number. It was a cause unknown to people my age, a fear of rejection, of loss, that we never had to experience. We never had to lose touch with anybody; our Facebooks were filled with people we hadn't spoken to in years, just in case we ever needed to find out how many kids our best friend from nursery school had or whether the guy who sat in front of us in Earth Science had ever come out as gay. We hoarded friends, memories, moments on camera we were too busy recording to actually enjoy. Nothing had the chance to become old, forgotten, or rediscovered by someone else.

I ran my fingers along the worn tops of the album covers, the cardboard fuzzy with years of use. Someone had let go of all of these. Someone had moved on, packed them up, said good-bye, and left them for someone else. There are no used-MP3 stores; you never have to delete an e-mail from someone you've all but forgotten. Everything we own is ours to keep locked up in our own private towers. Only rent receipts show that not everything is ours to possess.

I had almost psyched myself out of record shopping when a bit of blue caught my eye. I pushed a few Thompson Twins records aside and there it was: the Vapors, *New Clear Days*. The sleeve was pretty battered, but it was all there—"News at Ten," "Bunkers," and, of course, "Turning Japanese."

I plucked it from the crate like I was picking up the Holy Grail. "Nice." Cassie nodded her head. "I haven't thought about that album in decades. My girlfriends and I used to dance to 'Turning Japanese' all the time."

"It's my friend Sid's favorite," I said. "He's been looking for it for months. He's got it digitally, of course, but—"

"But vinyl is so much better," she agreed. "He'll love it."

We resumed flipping through bins until she pulled out Joe Jackson's *Body and Soul*. "This was my college boyfriend's favorite album," she said, clutching the record to her chest. "I bought it for him and we used to drink cheap red wine and play the whole thing by candlelight." She sighed, her eyes getting distant. "He was the only man I ever wrote a love song for," she said. "I almost didn't put 'Secret Girlfriend' on the album, but I wanted every-one in the world to know how I felt about him."

I knew she was talking about George, but I wasn't about to open that wound back up. "It's a beautiful song," I said. "It really captures what it feels like to be in love, those first early, uncertain pangs." I hadn't let myself think about that song after the incident at the Bitter End, but now, knowing that Sid would be coming home to me tonight, her lyrics took on a new gravitas.

"Thanks," she said. "There's nothing like being in love in your early twenties. Everything is so intense, so pure—it's just the two of you against the whole world. You must know what that's like." She dropped the record back into the crate. "But I guess he didn't feel that way—he got the house, the wife, the soul-sucking job. I doubt he's even picked up his drumsticks in years, just goes to work, teaches music theory without any of the heart, without having to *really* feel the music, the way he used to."

George hadn't even mentioned that he'd played drums. I thought about Catch's trumpet, stashed somewhere in the basement with the Christmas decorations, the case cracking with moisture and neglect.

"I would give *anything* just to see that ex one more time. Like maybe I could save him, we could run off and start over." She sighed. "It's a dream I've been having since I got out of rehab. But I guess he thinks he's happy, so I guess I wish him well. Makes me sad, though."

I imagined Catch going to work in his three-hundred-dollar suit, coming home and kissing Amanda on the cheek, listening to Top 40 radio in the car on his way to the mall during the weekend's excursion to Bed Bath & Beyond for holiday-themed dish towels. I wondered if he was happy, if he felt at peace, if he had some switch that I lacked that allowed him to just turn off all the frustration that he had poured into his music as a balm for the ugliness of the world. I felt sorry for him. And I envied him for a moment—until I remembered what I had waiting for me at home.

I half-listened as she told me her side of George's same story. She'd been married briefly to a guy who'd knocked her around and ended it when he got picked up for selling heroin. She'd gone to rehab for her own habit, then recorded her first album, opened for Joan Osborne, toured with Lilith Fair. Now she freelanced ad jingles and played small clubs.

"Look," she continued. "I may not be the most successful musician in the world, but at least I'm doing what I love. I still feel things, here, in my heart." She tapped her chest, then reached out and tapped mine, her fingers warm through my shirt. "You feel things too, I can tell. You won't ever sell out."

I wanted to clutch her hand to my breastbone. Was this what a kindred spirit felt like? Someone who read your thoughts before you had words to put to them? Was Cassie my Iona, like *Pretty in Pink*—the cool older sister I never had? We *were* in a record store together, even if neither of us worked there.

The light caught her bracelet and sent silver sparks scattering through the store. I made out just a few quick words on the plate, *a dream or two . . .*

"What's your bracelet engraved with?" I asked.

Her face went strange and she pulled her sleeve down over it. "Some bullshit love quote," she said. "I liked the chain; my boss let me have it cheap when the customer returned it. Guess his girlfriend thought it was lame. We get that a lot. That store keeps me decked out in more bling than any boyfriend ever did."

When I was a kid, I used to get this weird feeling in the pit of my stomach when my body knew I needed to escape before my brain did. It would start at the back of my gut and climb up my spine into my shoulders, and I would go to my room and get in my bed and play a tape until it went away. I had that same feeling now—the claustrophobic sense that there were too many people around me, hearing my thoughts and my heartbeat, even though it was just me and Cassie and a record store clerk who was ignoring us.

I couldn't let go of that feeling, even as we paid for our records. It got stronger, harder, like food poisoning.

"I'm going into the studio next month," she said once we were outside again. "And when my new album comes out, I want you to be the first person to listen to it. If you hate it, I won't hold it against you, but I really want you to do my press kit. I looked up some of your reviews and you do good work."

I hadn't heard that in months, but even her compliment couldn't ward off my discomfort. The walk back to Astor seemed to be a thousand miles. She hugged me good-bye, thanked me for the record, told me she'd call. But that brick at the bottom of my stomach didn't budge, and it wasn't until I was halfway back to Brooklyn that my idiot brain put all the pieces together.

I'd just given a Billy Joel record to KitKat's killer.

Chapter 50

MIKE POST THEME

id just stared at me with his big swollen bug eyes as I told him the story, the damaged parts of his face now a shade of yellow like hospital walls. "How can you be sure?" he asked. "You could walk outside right now and I guarantee you every other girl you see has something on her person with the word *dream* on it."

I was frantic when I got home from Astor Place. I was so close to closing KitKat's case that I couldn't think straight. I went out to buy groceries for dinner and had to go back twice because I forgot mozzarella and cat food. And now Sid was cooking dinner while I drank wine and sat on the counter and explained the whole case to him, stumbling over my evidence with excitement and nerves.

Cassie had the bracelet. Her story matched George's in everything but the names given.

"So why did she hide it?" I said, taking a drink. "I could see that it was part of a longer quote, and George told me he sent KitKat a bracelet with the lyric *I will do what I can do to make a dream or two come true.* It's her bracelet. I'm sure of it."

"That's a hell of a sick trophy to be wearing around," he said, turning from the stove to shred mozzarella into a bowl. "So what's your big plan now, Commish?"

"If I'm going to be a Michael Chiklis cop, can I at least be Vic Mackey?"

"I think you're more like Lem," he said. "Sweet, kind of goofy, good-hearted."

"And dead by grenade with my guts hanging out." I accepted the bowl of pasta he handed me and took a bite, talking with my mouth full. "Does that make you Shane Vendrell or Ronnie Gardocki?"

He put his hand to the stubble on his chin, pondering the ceiling tiles like he was giving the answer serious thought. "Shane," he said. "Accent and all."

I finished chewing, swallowed some wine to wash the taste of garlic out of my mouth, and kissed him, grinning. "Great," I teased. "This relationship is off to a doomed start."

"Either way it ends badly," he said, twirling linguine around his bowl in a gesture that reminded me of the way his tongue had wound pinwheels between my legs the night I'd found out about Catch's engagement. It was all I could do not to drop my pasta all over the floor and devour him instead. "But if you insist on being Mackey, does this mean you're planning to smash her face in with a phone book?"

"No," I said, my arousal cooled by implied violence. "I'm going to call George and ask him to meet with her. She might confess if he asks the right questions."

"And if she doesn't admit it?"

"Then I helped two long-lost lovers reunite," I said sarcastically. "And Bronco gets life in prison. Happy ending for all, right?"

"Now"—he gestured with his fork and a smirk—"you sound like Dutch Wagenbach."

I LET SID play through the A-side of Men at Work's *Business as Usual* while I waited for George to return my call. In the last minutes of "Underground," the phone rang with his 607 number and I removed myself into the bedroom, closing the door.

"I didn't expect to hear from you again," he said. "Has there been a break in the case?"

"Maybe," I said. "And I need your help."

"Anything."

"I was talking with Cassie Brennen today," I began. "I've got this bad feeling that she might have . . ." I swallowed the sick in my throat. "I think she was wearing KitKat's bracelet, the one you gave her. I think she might have killed KitKat."

The line went dead for a minute and I thought I'd lost him. "George? Are you still there?" I asked into silence.

"I'm here," he murmured. I heard the creak of a screen door and children shouting in the distance. Passing traffic hovered in the stillness between both our phones. "I should have said something," he said. "I didn't make the connection, didn't think it meant anything."

"What connection, what are you talking about?"

"The bracelet," he said. "When I called the jeweler to have it made, she answered. I could never forget that voice. When I gave her my name, she confirmed that it was her. We talked for half an hour, but she never asked me who the bracelet was for. She even friended me on Facebook, offered to come up and visit until she found out I was married. And when I posted on Facebook that I'd found her tape, she was so excited—until I mentioned that I'd passed it along to a friend. Hell, I even offered to introduce her to KitKat, told her that was who I'd had her engrave the bracelet for. She sent me a whole series of nasty messages—*I wrote that for you, how could you give it to some skank,* all that—before deleting her profile. I thought she was using again and didn't think anything of it, not even when you said KitKat had been killed. I just thought . . ."

It all fell into place for both of us. I rubbed my temples, imagined him doing the same.

"This is my fault," he murmured. "It's all my fault."

"You had no idea," I said. "How could you know she would track down KitKat and kill her over one lousy song?"

"People have killed for less," he said. "A lot less."

I didn't have time to play therapist, not when playing detective was a more important role. "I need you to get her to admit it," I said. "She still loves you; she'll tell you if she thinks it'll bring you back."

"How?" he said, his voice taking on that bitterness I'd come to recognize as his trademark. "Am I just supposed to show up at her apartment, pretend she didn't kill *the love of my life,* until she confesses, *Oh, by the way, I killed your girlfriend*?"

"However you have to do it," I snapped. "But figure it out. I need this favor, George. For an innocent man. For KitKat."

Another moment of silence. "I'll do it," he said. "For KitKat."

For the first time since I'd unlocked KitKat's front door a month ago, I let out a real sigh of relief. "Set it up," I said. "Just let me know when and where."

Chapter 51

ALL MY LITTLE WORDS

All the notes were falling into place. With George trying to set up a meeting with Cassie, it was my job to make sure we had the right people in place to arrest her. My own bracelet was heavy on my wrist when Philip called me out of the proofreaders' room and into his office. I was about to ask him for the biggest favor he could ever grant me and I gripped his bag of clean lingerie so tightly I was afraid my shaking hands would catapult them right onto the floor in front of him.

"Relax," his assistant said as she opened the door. "He won't bite."

That much I knew, but that didn't mean he would rubber-stamp an approval on anything I asked him, even if he did smile when I walked in. I pulled down my shirt cuff and held it in my fist, trying to gather up the confidence to speak. "I need your help," I blurted. "With my case."

He sat up straighter and folded his hands on the desk, like a father in a fifties sitcom. "I'm not sure what other help I can provide, but I'll do what I can," he said. "What's going on?"

"My friend KitKat," I said. "I think I might have found who killed her."

I told him about the bracelet Cassie wouldn't let me read, the engraving shop, her angry conversation with George. "I don't know if I can prove she did it," I said. "But I have to try. I can't let Bronco go to prison. I know he didn't do this."

Philip leaned back in his leather chair and I held my breath. "If she really is the killer, you've done some pretty impressive detective work," he said, cracking a grin like broken glass. "Let me make some calls and see if I can't pull a favor. I've got a few friends in New York's finest, might be able to get one of them to listen in on your setup, make it official."

"Thank you," I gushed. "You have no idea how much this means to me."

"Don't thank me yet," he said, sitting up. "We've still got a lot of work to do."

THE TRAIN HOME felt eerily silent; everyone was lost in their music or a game, reading a digital novel or watching tiny porn. For a few stops I was paranoid that Cassie might find me, get on the train in a sea of people, and know what I was up to. I cranked up my music a little louder, as though that could drown out my thoughts. It did nothing but make my ears ring.

Sid was making pork chops when I got home. He waved to me with an oversized red silicone oven mitt. "I picked us up a cast-iron skillet," he said. "Now that there's two of us, I thought we could share kitchen duties. I got some summer squash in the oven, if you want to set the table."

It was such a perfect "Our House" moment that I almost hated it. There's a reason they never show domestic scenes in crime shows or novels; when a case gets ahold of you, there's no time for dinner or setting the table or watching television. It's an all-consuming madness, I told myself as I laid out the placemats, the plates, the wineglasses, the knives. I was so close to finishing this that it was almost worse than when I didn't know anything at all. Now it was just waiting, anxiously ticking down hours until something got done, until the awful weight of KitKat's murder and Bronco's innocence could be lifted from my shoulders.

"What did Philip say?" Sid called over the popping sounds of frying pork fat.

"He said he'd make some calls, get us a surveillance team," I replied. "I just need to find out when they're meeting."

Sid abandoned dinner for a moment to see me in the dining room. "That's great news," he said, lacing his fingers with mine. "You must be so relieved."

"Not yet," I said. "Not until she confesses. Not until she's arrested. And not until Bronco's free to go."

He squeezed my hands and kissed my forehead. "You're at the forty-minute mark," he said. "You've just got a little ways to go before the credits roll. It's all down to the confession now."

"Except that now I have to wait for George to connect with her," I said to his back as he ducked into the kitchen. "Maybe she's onto me and she skipped town."

"That could be," he said. "But you won't know until you know. So do yourself a favor and focus your thoughts elsewhere for a minute—you got a postcard. I put it on the coffee table."

I set down the forks and got the postcard. My grandmother and Royale were in Prague; it was beautiful; they were nearing the end of their trip and would be home in the next month. I had no way of telling her that Sid had moved in, no way to ask how much longer I could stay. I couldn't tell if the world was unraveling at my feet or coming together like a tight-fitting corset.

We ate dinner. We put on *Go West*. And just before "Call Me," there came that low static hum that rattles off all electronics just before a text comes in.

Saturday, George wrote.

Chapter 52

POLICY OF TRUTH

I met George at Grand Central Terminal with a cup of coffee and a stomach that felt like Pop Rocks and Coke. He surprised me with a hug and I stood awkwardly in his embrace, one outstretched arm holding an Au Bon Pain cup that was burning me through the cardboard sleeve. A bum relieved me of the pain, snatching it out of my hand and hobbling down the stairs, spilling most of it on the rolling briefcase of a pissed-looking businessman coming off the train from Port Chester.

"Sorry," George said, releasing me. "I'll buy you another one."

"That was yours," I said sourly.

"That's all right," he said. "I've had about three cups already; I'm starting to get jittery."

Not what I needed to hear. "You think you can do this?" He nodded and I continued. "We're meeting up with Philip and his NYPD contact now; he'll wire you up and give you some tips on how to question her."

We made our way to the street and I flagged down a cab.

"Is it wrong that, despite what she might have done, I'm a little excited to see Cassie?" he said as we got in. "I'm excited, nervous, angry—it was a long drive from Binghamton; I told my wife I was visiting my sister in Beacon and took the train in from there. I mean, Cassie broke my heart. I should be overjoyed that we're getting back together, even just for lunch, even as I try to get her arrested for killing my girlfriend." He leaned his head against the window and exhaled, drawing a squiggle in the white circle left by his breath. "Life's so fucking complicated sometimes."

"You know you'll probably have to testify, right?" I said. "Are you prepared for your wife to know about all this?"

"I'm tired of lying," he said. "I'll tell her when this is all over, and if she wants to leave, well, that's her call. But I can't carry this any longer. I'm just . . . tired. Worn out. Too old." He turned back to me and smiled a little. "I quit drinking," he said. "Not doing meetings or anything, but I haven't had a drink in almost two weeks. I was teaching drunk. Office bottle, like an old detective. But one day, I was standing up in front of my class, trying to hide it all, and I swore I smelled KitKat's perfume—no, not her perfume, her *scent*. I sent my students all home early. I poured the gin and tonic I had stashed in a water bottle down the faculty bathroom sink. I want to be the man that KitKat loved—not the mess I was when she died."

"That's good," I said. "I'm happy for you."

"Thanks," he said. "For all of this."

We met Philip outside of Pete's Tavern, where he was standing with a man in a dark green overcoat that would not have looked out of place on Humphrey Bogart. He shook my hand and gestured to his partner. "Jett, George, this is Scott Parker, a friend of mine from the Ninetieth Precinct."

"Won this case in a poker game." Scott explained the favor with a pirate kind of grin. "But between us, Jett, I never thought the boyfriend did it. Detective Henley is going to be pissed when I crack his case for him. He and that worm of a DA were already flipping a coin to see who bought celebratory drinks." To George, he said, "You're our CI?"

George nodded and Scott cracked open the bag with the wire in it. "All you have to do is get her to confess," he said. "You can't get her drunk and you can't threaten her, but anything else is fair game."

"What if she doesn't say anything?"

"Then we've wasted an afternoon and you got a free lunch," said Scott. "C'mon, let me wire you up."

PHILIP, SCOTT, AND I holed up in Philip's unremarkable black sedan half a block down, watching George pace outside the restaurant. I didn't realize how much I was fidgeting until Scott offered me a piece from a pack of Beemans. Even the Brooklyn cops were hipsters.

"I go through two or three packs of this stuff when I'm on stakeout," he explained. "Smoking draws too much attention to the car."

"You should make a gum wrapper chain," Philip joked, slurping his coffee.

I crammed the gum into my mouth and pointed. "Here she comes."

Cassie was wearing a black dress, a too-long sweater, and her Docs when she ran up to him, embracing him like she'd never let go. When she kissed him, he didn't pull back. My stomach made balloon animals as I watched him lace his fingers with hers, and I wondered if she was wearing the bracelet under her oversized sleeves. George was either a master at this or he was going to blow the whole thing completely to hell. I swore I heard him sniffle back a sob.

We hunched around Philip's laptop. They sat down at a back booth, right where Philip had set up the camera earlier. George ordered a ginger ale; Cassie got a club soda. He was holding her hands across the table, leaning in.

"He's good," Scott muttered. "He's keeping the mic close. We should hire this guy."

"Yeah, his Gap sweater will really help him blend in with the drug cartels," Philip said, snapping his gum.

"I thought I'd never see you again," George said.

"I'm so sorry," Cassie said. "Losing you was all my fault. I haven't stopped thinking about you, not in all these years. I've wanted to call you, I've looked you up before, but you were married, I didn't want to intrude . . . and I was scared you'd hang up."

"Never," he said. "But there's nothing keeping us apart anymore. My marriage is all but over and my girlfriend, well, she's dead."

She buried her face in the menu. "I'm sorry to hear that."

The waiter appeared momentarily, blocking the shot. Scott swore under his breath and Philip held his earpiece in a little tighter. All I could hear was their order: a sandwich for him, soup for her.

"Do you remember that movie we saw at that little art theater?" he said when the waiter slipped away. "The one that started leaking in the middle of the show?"

"The Nelson Street Art House, yes," she said, grinning. "I don't even remember what movie it was—some kind of crime film, right? I think we were too busy making out."

He nodded. "The mistress murders her boyfriend's wife because she's convinced no one can love him like she does," he said. "And in the end, she's right. They run off together. And when I drove you home that night, when I watched you go inside, I thought, *I love her like that.* I loved you so deeply that watching you walk away from me felt like necrosis. Like dying. And I wanted to know somehow that you loved me with that same violent intensity. But how would I ever know? All I had were three stupid words to repeat to you over and over, but they were never enough."

I knew that feeling. It was the exact reason I'd never said those three words to Catch even though he said them to me. It was comforting, in a way, to know that other people could feel love to that sort of dangerous depth.

"He'd better be talking about a real fucking movie," muttered Scott. "I've only got one set of cuffs; this bastard better not have been in on it the whole time."

"And when you left me," George said, continuing, "I was convinced I was dying. I would dream about finding whatever new guy you were with, because he couldn't love you the way I loved you. I dreamed I would get him alone and . . ." He smiled. "But you really did love me like that, didn't you? And you proved it. With KitKat." She started to protest, but he brought her hands to his lips. "No secrets. Not now. Not if we're going to be together."

She paused for a moment, glanced down at the table, then back up at him. But she didn't speak. No one in the car dared to breathe.

"How did you find her?" George asked.

"I looked her up," she said. "When you gave me her name, you mentioned that she was a party planner in Brooklyn, so it didn't take me too long to find her. I called her up and made an appointment. But I just wanted the tape. I didn't want her to have that song. There are millions of other songs in the world, she didn't need the one I wrote for you. And when I got there, she invited me in for a cup of tea; she was baking pot brownies and the smell reminded me of that night at my drummer Cara's party."

George actually smiled. "I got way too stoned on edibles that night," he said, a grin cracking his face like a spring thaw. "I was convinced that all the stars were falling out of the sky and I would be sliced in half if I left Cara's apartment."

"It was the first night you spent at my place," she said. "I don't know how I convinced you to leave in that state, but somehow, I got you back to my apartment and I started writing 'Secret Girlfriend' while you slept." She glanced down at his hands and then back up into his eyes like she'd been rehearsing this moment for the last decade. "That was the moment I knew I loved you."

Stars fall flash and slash my heart . . . My favorite lyric, written about a paranoid, passed-out boyfriend. I thought about Sid asleep next to me the night I'd brought him home from the hospital, his body lax with painkillers and exhaustion, how sweet and sad and perfect he'd looked in that moment.

Cassie continued, drawing me out of my memory. "I asked

KitKat about you," she said. "And her face just lit up. She wouldn't stop talking about how much she loved you, how much of a relief it was to finally be able to tell someone about her *soul mate*." Her voice began to rise to a frustrated, panicked pitch; she pulled one hand out of his to gesture with tense, calculated moves. "And I just wanted her to *shut up*. I asked her about the tape, but she tried to tell me she didn't have it, but I knew she was lying. I grabbed the rolling pin and . . . and I just lost it."

"We got it," said Philip. "We can go in."

"Wait," I pleaded, holding up my hand. "I want to hear the rest of what she has to say."

"This isn't a bedtime story," Scott said. "Let me spoil the ending—fifteen to twenty-five on murder two, up for parole after seventeen."

"I just want to hear if she gives up any more."

"She's right," Philip said. " 'Lost it' isn't exactly a detailed confession."

We turned back to the feed. "She wasn't lying," George said. "The tape went to the wrong mailbox. Her neighbor got it instead."

Cassie's eyes went wide and she sank back against the leather bench. "She never heard my song?" she said. "But this girl at my show, she requested it, where else would she have gotten it . . . ?"

"Go now!" Philip cried. "She's putting it all together; get her before she makes a run for it!"

It was almost too late—Cassie sprang up from the booth and made a dash for the door. Scott kicked open the passenger-side door and met her under the awning with Philip flanking her on the other side. George followed her out of the restaurant. She looked to her right, to her left, and then back at George with eyes like a cornered dog. She took two quick strides back toward George and pulled his face to hers, kissing him hard.

He didn't resist.

"I love you," she murmured, holding him tight. "I've always loved you."

Scott pulled her away, twisting her arms behind her back with his handcuffs ready. George just stood there dumbly, her lipstick still dark on his mouth. She struggled in Scott's hold.

"George, please," she said. "Please don't let them do this. I love you. I love you!"

Scott pushed up her sleeves to get the cuffs on, revealing Kit-Kat's bracelet. "Bag it," said Philip. To George, he added, "This look familiar?"

George swallowed so hard his eyes bugged out. "Yes," he muttered, staring at the scuffs on his shoes. "It's the one I bought KitKat—Katie. For her birthday last January."

Scott pulled out a plastic evidence bag and dropped it in.

Cassie looked at me, standing next to the car where I'd frozen in place, watching this all go down. She smiled sadly. "I thought you, of all people, would understand," she said.

"You killed someone over a song," I replied, my throat dry.

"I killed someone for love," she said as Scott ducked her head into the backseat of his unmarked car. "Isn't that how all great stories go?"

For a moment, it made sense. For a moment, she was beautiful, a tragic lover, a wronged woman. If this was a movie, she would still be the heroine even as they led her to the hangman. But this wasn't a movie, and when that moment was up, she was just a bat-shit lunatic who'd beaten my friend to death over a song she'd never gotten to hear.

I thought about the music I had hoarded, my fear that if I heard the songs in the wrong place and time it might mean they no longer belonged to the moments I clung to. If Catch had grown up to mirror George's suburban malady, was I then fated to follow Cassie's, grow bitter and mean because I could not let go of all my junkyard yesterdays?

No, I decided. It had to end. Now Jeremy and I could have something new. Gabe and I could have happy memories. But William and Catch had to stay firmly in my past. Because I was not like Cassie. Not anymore.

George stood in the doorway with that same empty gaze he'd had when I'd told him that KitKat was dead. We watched the car pull away. Cassie never once looked back, never made one last plea, seemed to simply accept the fate she must have always known was coming. And then it was just George and I, standing on the sidewalk, watching her go. He was as blank as a Munny figure. I couldn't stand the silence.

"What now?"

"I'm going to go home," he said. "And tell my wife everything."

"Probably a good idea," I said. "You want me to go back to Grand Central with you?"

He shook his head. "No offense, but I'd rather be alone."

"Then take this," I said, reaching into my coat pocket and pulling out the tape. "It's your secret. KitKat died believing you still loved her."

Tears filled his eyes. "I really did love her," he said, turning his face from me and staring into the wide window of the restaurant. The gawkers had already grown tired of the scene playing out before them and had gone back to their lunches. "Both of them. I meant every goddamn word I said to Cassie in there."

"I never doubted that," I said. "I don't think they did either."

I had a momentary instinct to get us a cab back to Grand Central for a proper good-bye, follow him on Twitter, friend him on Facebook, to make sure we stayed in touch. But with all we had in common, I realized it was probably best if we parted ways now.

"Guess I'll see you at the trial," I said.

"Guess so," he replied.

And then we didn't have anything else to talk about.

Chapter 53

THROWING IT ALL AWAY

The L train was filled with people chattering about Cassie's arrest, and I thought of how fucking *nice* it must have been to live in an era where the newspaper only arrived once a month, maybe, if the postmaster's horse didn't die. By the time I reached my stop, I'd heard so many armchair lawyers spout their TV court cases that part of me hoped Cassie was acquitted, just to prove them all wrong.

At home, I tore the Boyfriend Box out of the closet. Fuck nostalgia. Fuck all of it. Cassie murdered KitKat because she couldn't let go of the past. I pulled out love letters, mix tapes, and burned CDs with decoupaged liner notes, stuffed animals, college T-shirts, broken necklaces, guitar picks, the black bowling shirt Catch used to let me fall asleep in . . .

Into the bathtub it went. Everything but the stuffed animals; Gabe's bear and the rest of them went into a Trader Joe's bag destined for the Salvation Army. I lit a match and tossed it onto the pile in the bathtub. A stack of bad poetry went up first. Then William's Sailor Moon stationery, the last love letter he'd sent me before getting engaged. All the track lists, the notes passed in math class, postcards from halfway around the goddamn world. And when the smoke detector began shrieking, I smashed it open with a broom and ripped out the battery. Baldrick dove under the bed.

I sat on the toilet and cracked open the cassettes. I gripped handfuls of tape, pulling it out like it was a cheap weave in a reality-TV catfight. I tore up *Rent,* the Smiths, Devin Townsend, the Shins. I smashed CDs into shivs on the edge of the bathtub. *Hardcore Pining, The Portable Saturday Night, The Wind.* It wasn't until I tasted the acrid black smoke in my lungs that I even noticed I was sobbing.

But there was one piece I hadn't torched, one item left dangling off the edge of the sink. Sid's blue toothbrush, the bristles worn and almost dry from when he'd brushed his teeth before leaving for work. I threw that in too. Everything must go.

Then finally, I cranked on the shower and extinguished the blaze. I gathered everything up into a garbage bag and dumped it in the basement of the building. I scrubbed the black out of the bathtub. I washed the tears off my face. And when I went to the drugstore, I left the windows open to air out the place and release all the memories lingering in the smoke above my head.

Sid didn't ask about the remaining burned smell. He didn't ask about the busted smoke detector. He didn't ask why Baldrick wouldn't come out from under the bed.

"Where's my toothbrush?" he asked, emerging from the bathroom with the toothpaste in one hand.

I got up and rummaged through my purse to retrieve the new one.

"What, did you clean the toilet with mine?" he joked, cracking open the package.

"Just thought you should have a new one," I said, trying to sound nonchalant, as though hours before, I hadn't almost burned my apartment to ashes, his toothbrush included. "New apartment, new girlfriend, new life, new toothbrush. Leave what's past in the past."

"New girlfriend, huh?" he asked, his mouth full of toothpaste. "Who might that be?"

I swatted him on the arm. He ducked back into the bathroom to rinse and spit and wash his face. "This is real, right?" he asked after, holding my face with two long, delicate fingers. "Us?"

"It's as real as you want it to be," I said. "You and I are both coming off a lot of weirdness and if you want to take things slow, I get it."

"Why, Miss Bennett, are you trying to appeal to my chivalrous cowboy nature?" he teased.

"Perhaps I am, Mr. McNeill," I replied in a honeysuckle drawl.

"Well, don't," he murmured, kissing down my neck. "Not tonight."

Chapter 54

HERE'S WHERE THE STORY ENDS

Things went back to normal pretty quickly. The charges were dropped against Bronco, and Cassie pled guilty to KitKat's murder, sparing us all the stress of a trial. I wondered if George had really told his wife all about his affair with KitKat, if she left him, if he was okay. But I knew better than to call him. He, like Gabe and William and Catch, was a man better left in my past.

Three weeks went by. Sid and I formally announced ourselves as a couple at a party Natalie threw to celebrate the launch of the KitKat Memorial Scholarship. No one was surprised. But the morning after the party, I woke up after Sid had gone to work and found a box of Swiss Colony petit fours and a mix tape stuck in my coffee cup on the kitchen counter. Except it wasn't a mix tape; it was just a rubber case that looked like a cassette, slipped onto my phone, with a hot-pink sticky note attached that read "Play Me."

I smiled and cued up the *New Toothbrush* playlist to track one, the Vapors' "Waiting for the Weekend."

There are bands that are so precious to the listener that their songs aren't given away lightly. These songs are held close, the listener waiting until he or she finds the perfect person to deliver them to. When you assign a track to a lover, that track will remain attached to that person forever. I was never going to exorcise Bon Jovi's "I Am" from Catch, and Sid was risking forever entangling his precious Vapors with me, the way all the grand lovers before him wound their hearts in ninety-minute bursts of magnetic and digital hope.

I spent the rest of the morning on the couch, listening to his mix and eating the tiny cakes. I didn't even get coffee. I just sat there in love, with Baldrick at my side, as everything Sid had never said played: Depeche Mode, "World in My Eyes"; Tenpole Tudor, "Love and Food"; Huey Lewis and the News, "Stuck with You"; Cyndi Lauper, "I Drove All Night"; Sting, "Fields of Gold." He even put on Hall and Oates' "You Make My Dreams," and I laughed, singing along with the "hoo hoo" parts like the Oates that I was.

My phone rang. "Hello, dear," came my grandmother's melodic lilt. "We got home late last night and I'm just getting settled. How are you?"

"It's been a crazy few months," I said. That didn't even begin to cover it. "How was Prague?"

"Prague was beautiful, Paris was beautiful, Dubai was beautiful," she gushed. "I have so many photos to show you. Can we get together for lunch?"

WHEN I WAS eight, our homework was to write a paragraph on what we wanted to be when we grew up. I'd written that I wanted to be like my grandmother, and, sitting across the café table from her as she scrolled through photo after photo on her tablet, I still felt the same way. She somehow seemed younger than when she'd left. She joked that she'd gotten a facelift in France, but I knew better—that radiance was the result of a life lived with joy. She'd never let the fact that her husband died young and suddenly sink her spirits. She'd surrounded herself with friends and art, took risks, and savored her days. You can't bottle that, although someone had tried—among the many gifts she brought me, silk scarves and perfume and a hand-painted T-shirt from Tokyo, she'd filled a bag with French creams and cosmetics.

"Not that you need them," she said. "But I thought you deserved a little pampering for that pretty skin of yours. Now, tell me, how are you enjoying the apartment?"

"I love it," I said. "It's a great neighborhood; I've made a lot of friends."

"I'm delighted to hear that," she said. "You are welcome to stay as long as you'd like. We'll work something out with the landlord to get you on the lease, but I don't want you to worry about that right now. That's Royale's bailiwick."

I got out of my chair and hugged her. "Thank you," I breathed. "Thank you!" There weren't other words. I couldn't wait to tell Sid.

She squeezed me tight. "You are very welcome, my dear," she said with a warm smile. "Just assure me you won't change the locks before I've had a chance to gather up my things!"

I LISTENED TO Sid's mix again on the subway, smiling like I'd eaten a fistful of Molly. And when he got home, I had fajitas cooking in our cast-iron skillet and the Vapors record propped up on his plate. It didn't matter that I had bought it while out with Cassie. It wasn't a memento of my cracking KitKat's case. It was a gift, one I knew he would adore.

He grinned and kissed me and put it on the stereo. "It does sound better on vinyl," he agreed.

"Sounded pretty good this morning," I said, holding up my phone.

There isn't a better feeling in the world—not an orgasm, not a first kiss, not even that glorious soaring sensation you get when those first few notes of a new song pierce your chest and fill your whole body with absolute bliss—than acknowledgment that your mix tape was not only received and played, but enjoyed. It's a dance of sorts, balancing songs you think the listener will love while trying to say everything that otherwise dries up in your throat before you can get out the words. The way Sid smiled at me, his fresh-peach lips parting in a grin and a breath held in his chest, I knew that he must have been feeling that wonderful relief.

"I've been carrying that mix around for a month," he began. "That night at Natalie's gallery party, when you got up on that stage, I couldn't stand the fact that you weren't singing exclusively for me. I'd had a couple drinks on an empty stomach and when you started singing, all that cheer turned to this, this irrational *thing* in the pit of my soul. I just . . . left. The whole way home I just wanted to kick trash cans, and when I got back to the apartment I poured another drink, sat on the edge of my bed, and bawled my damn eyes out. I made that mix the next morning on the subway."

I traced my fingers down his cheek and he held my palm against his face. "Why didn't you ever say anything?" I murmured.

"Because I thought I was in love with a stripper," he said. "Because what I felt for you wasn't giddy or jittery, the way love feels when you're a teenager. What I felt when you started singing was something so much deeper, something that hurt. And the only thing I could think to do was start putting together this playlist in hopes that maybe one day I'd get enough courage to give it to you. It didn't even have a title until this morning."

For a moment I thought about telling him that I *had* been singing for him, that there had only ever been him. William and Jeremy and Catch had all been vapor. Instead, I just kissed him. There were words, sure, maybe even songs. In my head, I began composing a response, a way to tell him that I felt the same way. Tom Waits, "Little Trip to Heaven (On the Wings of Your Love)"; Ryan Adams, "My Winding Wheel"; Duran Duran, "Last Chance on the Stairway"; Warren Zevon, "Searching for a Heart."

And then I stopped. "There isn't a song in the world that can tell you that I love you," I said, taking his hands. "I'll just have to say it myself."

ACKNOWLEDGMENTS

To my beloved husband, Ian, who has cherished and supported me from the moment we met, filling my life with art and happiness.

To my sisters, Hilary, Laura, Shaun, and Beth, the first and most loyal of my champions. And to my nieces, Lucy, Melody, Rachel, and Josie, and my nephews, Max and Jacob, the next generation of storytellers.

To Matthew, my writing partner and BFF, whom I trust more than anyone.

To my dearest friends and fellow writers. I could write a whole other book just explaining why and how much I love each of you. And many thanks to my agent, Jim McCarthy, and to my editor, Chelsey Emmelhainz, who have been two of the most brilliant and nurturing people I have ever had the honor of working with.

And lastly, to Jason. He knows why.

ABOUT THE AUTHOR

Libby Cudmore worked at video stores, bookstores, and temp agencies before settling down in upstate New York to write. Her short stories have appeared in *PANK, The Stoneslide Corrective, The Big Click,* and *Big Lucks. The Big Rewind* is her first novel.